Strange Is A Hazard Here

STRANGE IS A HAZARD HERE

Jim Hughes

PRECOCITY PRESS

Editors: Deborah Steinberg and Brenda Lange
Creative Director: Susan Shankin
Cover Designer and Illustrator: Tim Kummerow
Book Design and Layout: Susan Shankin
Precocity Press, Los Angeles, CA

ISBN: 978-1-972561-06-5 (Trade Paperback)
ISBN: 978-1-972561-07-2 (eBook)
Library of Congress Control Number: 2026912502
First edition printed in the United States of America

For Linda

CONTENTS

PROLOGUE

No one had died that day in the Grim Reaper's region. He wondered if it was the same in the regions of other Reapers, or if it was only his misfortune. He should have enjoyed this rare breathing spell, but he felt at loose ends; he liked to keep busy.

A lass, Mabyn, had come close to drowning in a river that morning. But her mother had kneaded her chest until she spewed the water out. Her mother now feared Mabyn would die from the chill she couldn't shake. Reaper thought she'd pull through, but he'd keep an eye on her. As for the very old and those who were fatally sick or injured, they were holding on for dear life, though he couldn't imagine how they could consider life *dear*.

As midnight approached, Reaper remembered that it was Jocelyn's eleventh birthday eve, which meant she was in danger of dying before this day was out, and it cheered him. Not that he took pleasure in people's deaths; rather, he appreciated the sense of purpose his vocation gave him, which was to detach spirits from dead bodies with his scythe and lead them to the afterlife. He made straight for Jocelyn's home.

The modest country house, not large and lavish like those of the aristocracy, was dark, except for a single candle that blazed in the upstairs bedroom of Jocelyn's mother, Idris. There, she was donning her witch's garb. It resembled Reaper's own hooded cloak, except hers was pristine and made of velvet.

In truth, Reaper was ashamed of his tattered outfit and had been meaning to replace it. Most spirits of the dead didn't comment on his attire; they had other things on their minds. But he liked to look neat. Besides, shreds of the hood would fly off in even a middling wind and flutter about his head, some blowing into his face. He stood now behind the house, cleaning the bits of black cloth from between his teeth with the tip of his scythe.

As he'd expected, the witch was soon on the move, the light from the candle she held illuminating her way as she strode to the attic stairs and marched up to her daughter's room. There, while Jocelyn slept, Idris took a rustic musical reed and a pig bladder—what Idris called a *balloon*—from her satchel.

Reaper paused in cleaning his teeth, not because of apprehension over Jocelyn's fate (he had none, which was not to say he hadn't developed a fondness for the girl over the years), but because old Nye, in the town of Brynmor, had just now shrieked in his bed, tumbled out of it, and cracked his skull. The bleeding was profuse.

Nye's need for me is more certain than Jocelyn's, thought Reaper. *And Mabyn has taken a turn for the worse, becoming feverish.*

Still, Reaper lingered outside Jocelyn's house, as Idris cast a spell, filling the pig bladder with her daughter's sadness. It wasn't long before Jocelyn, short of breath, wheezed and had a coughing fit. Idris, in a rage, shouted at the sleeping child, "Stubborn girl! You will tempt death once too often!" and stormed out.

How odd, thought Reaper, *that Idris blames the girl for her illness and possible death, when it is clear . . . No, it is not clear. Why would taking sadness from the child sicken her?* He shook his head. *I shall not bother myself with such questions. It is not my job to solve puzzles.*

Reaper checked the grains of sand in his hourglass and saw that Nye was taking his last breaths. Mabyn's fate, however, was inconclusive: though gravely sick, she had the care and love of her mother to sustain her. As for Jocelyn, there would be no help from Idris. Even so, it appeared from the hourglass that the girl would not die on this birthday eve.

Two Years Later

CHAPTER 1

BIRTHDAY INCITEMENT

"AM I IN YOUR WAY?" asked Jocelyn, who lay on her bed reading in her attic room, as Maag stood astride her on tiptoes, reaching up for cobwebs with the duster.

"You aren't ever in my way, chickadee," replied the housekeeper. "Asides, I'm almost done for."

"Do you want to change the bed?"

"You'd like a new one?"

Jocelyn laughed. Maag's humor made life so much more bearable, though she wasn't sure if the housekeeper always understood her own jokes. "I meant the bedclothes," said Jocelyn.

Maag sniffed. "I'll wait till they're more ripe, unless your nose is dilating. But the dust, my duckling, does it annoy your inspiration?"

"No, my lungs aren't bothered by dust," said Jocelyn. "Or pollen. It's something else. I don't know what."

Maag hopped to the floor, tossed the duster down, and stretched out on the bed alongside Jocelyn, who scooted over to give room. "Those balloons are hard to spruce," said Maag.

Jocelyn glanced up. As usual, the balloons were drifting about the room, most of them near the ceiling. "Don't worry about them," she said. "They keep their luster just fine."

"Except the blue one," said Maag, "but it never had any. What're you reading?"

"What a Girl Ought to Know," replied Jocelyn. "Mother assigned it." She turned to the cover. "It's by Lady Addfwyn Pugh." Turning back to where she'd left off, Jocelyn said, "It's ridiculous. Listen: Mother is a girl's best friend."

"That's Feeno," said Maag.

"The gnome, yes. But you, too," insisted Jocelyn.

"No, Feeno's your nanny. Makes me malicious, it does, he gets to play more with you. I'm too suppressed by housekeeping and crookery. But I'm off the tack. What else does Lady Pugh say?"

"Your mother is also your most sympathetic confidant," read Jocelyn.

"Methinks the Lady's never collided with your mother."

"She couldn't have," agreed Jocelyn. "Mother found this book in a chest full of my great-grandmother's things. Listen: To her mother, a girl may speak freely of herself."

"That's a risk. What does it say about the father?" asked Maag.

"That chapter's ripped out," said Jocelyn. "And look, pages from other chapters are missing and lines are inked out."

"Her Judgmental's severe with the syllables she allows."

Jocelyn put the book down and rolled in the housekeeper's direction. "Tell me about my father, Maag."

Maag snapped her head toward the girl. "You've never afore asked me to expound on him."

"Mother says he was a swine."

Maag hesitated. "It's not pragmatical for me to depose your mother, but . . . he equivocally wasn't a pig or wild boar."

"What was he like?" Jocelyn asked.

"I'm not supposed to discuss him, in case I give a warm indentation of him."

"You felt good about him, did you?" coaxed Jocelyn.

Maag leaned her head closer to the girl. "I did," she whispered. "But if I say more, my gosling, and your mother gets wind, she'll deduce me to a tangle of knots. Asides, I knew him just a brief while, when you were but a babe in alarms."

Warm, Maag had said. That was what Jocelyn had been feeling the last several months after her father began appearing in her dreams. *Snug* and *safe.* They described the feeling he gave her, too. It was almost as if he were actually there, and she could hear his heart beating in a soothing rhythm, unlike her own which all too often—

"Oh, my heart!" cried Jocelyn. "It's starting up."

"Has it been in a stall?" asked Maag.

"No, but now it's fluttering."

"That's from birthday incitement," asserted Maag.

No, thought Jocelyn. *If I'm not having a heart attack, my rapid, irregular heartbeat is from fear.* Her thirteenth birthday was tomorrow. Odd-year birthdays made her frightfully anxious, because during the night before them, her lungs always acted up. Her breath felt as if it were being stolen from her, and she desperately sought to retrieve it. *Spells,* Mother called these events.

What if this time I do die? Jocelyn wanted to scream. Mother did not approve of screaming, and Jocelyn was trying to contain such outbursts (though Maag wouldn't have minded), even if a good, loud shout would have made Jocelyn feel better.

"Follow me to the gazing glass, my puffin," said Maag, rising from the bed. "You know how my refining your hair pacifies you."

Jocelyn sat on a stool in front of the mirror that hung above her washbasin as Maag gently brushed her hair, which did soothe her some. Her hair was bright red, which made it look as if it were on fire, whereas Mother's was auburn and curlier.

I'll never be as pretty as Mother, reflected Jocelyn. *My green eyes have turned grayish, and my cheeks are too round.*

Then there were the freckles, the big ears, and her button nose. She'd overtaken Feeno's height when she was seven, and she'd had a spurt of growth recently, surpassing Maag's height and approaching her mother's. But the spurt had made her ungainly.

Maag, in contrast, flitted about nimbly on thin legs in spite of her stout body. She was no beauty, her face narrow and jutting, but she had lovely brown eyes, and her long hair, which she combed straight back so that it hung halfway down her back, was black with a dark-purple sheen.

"I have to make supper," said Maag. "Has your heart sat down?"

"It has," Jocelyn replied, though it was a lie. Her heart still trembled, but she didn't want Maag to be late with supper, because it would make Mother mad—no, angry. Mother was strict about language and demanded she not use *mad* for *angry,* because *mad,* Mother said, was *vulgar* and *imprecise* (it could be mistaken for *crazy).*

Maag circled Jocelyn with her arms from behind and rested her cheek against the girl's ear. "Put those heart assaults out of your mind," she said. "It's jitteriness, Jocie."

After the housekeeper left, Jocelyn's heartbeat became more erratic. *I'll do something useful,* she thought, lying again on her bed and resuming her required reading. But *What a Girl Ought to Know* didn't settle her. She couldn't help wondering about the health of her heart, and the more she tried not to think about it, the more it filled her mind. In response, her heart beat even more wildly. Surely Feeno, who had seen her through many a crisis, would know what to do. Tossing the book aside, she reached behind her bed and rang for her nanny.

CHAPTER 2

PIG BLADDERS

My heart's calming, observed Jocelyn, her hand pressed against her chest. Likely it was because of the fresh air. Too restless to remain on the bed until her nanny came, she'd crawled through the dormer to her favorite spot, the sill of her attic window. She had to be careful. As Maag often warned, "A fall from this height'd be terminal." But here she could sit, her legs resting against the steep roof, and gaze at the woods that lay beyond the neat and tidy grounds of this country house.

What adventures I could have in those woods! imagined Jocelyn. But her mother wouldn't allow her to even set foot in them. Yes, they were dangerous, as Mother said. But wasn't she turning thirteen? She was old enough to look after herself.

Hearing Feeno clambering up the attic stairs, Jocelyn crawled back into her room, pulling the window closed behind her, because Mother didn't like open windows. "Something unacceptable might get in," she'd said, though she hadn't told her daughter what it might be. A big, bad wolf, Jocelyn imagined. Or a wicked stepmother.

Feeno's not being careful! she thought, a moment before the gnome burst in, tripped on the throw rug, and fell flat on his face.

"Oh, Feeno!" she cried, hurrying to him. "Have you hurt yourself again?"

"No, no, I'm the one who's supposed to ask after you," he said, rolling onto his back.

"But I'm better now," Jocelyn said, feeling guilty over having called for him. "You're the one who . . ."

He sat up, cupping his nose.

Jocelyn frowned. "It's bloody, I imagine."

Peering into his palm, Feeno shook his head.

Jocelyn knelt beside him, gently took his head into her hands, and turned and tilted it, surveying his face. "Your nose looks fine," she observed.

"It doesn't hurt like that time I broke it," he said, struggling to his feet and hobbling to the mirror. He swatted at the flies that circled his head. "You've had the window open. Not that I mind," he added. "I like it that way, in spite of the flies." For some reason flies pestered Feeno but no one else, and they did so only in this room. It was as if they didn't dare venture into the rest of the house.

Staring into the mirror on tiptoes, Feeno observed, "At least the fall hasn't made my nose more deformed."

"That wouldn't be so bad," said Jocelyn. "Mother says deformity suits you; it's what a gnome is—a crooked dwarf."

"I don't think Lady Idris has ever seen any gnome but me," said Feeno. Using the base of his palms, he flattened his short-whiskered double chin into a single one, stretching the skin up his cheeks until it bunched at his large, pointed ears. "The fact is, I'm the only one *I've* seen. For all I know," he mused, smoothing his thick hair, "I'm the only gnome who's ever been."

Jocelyn could easily imagine how lonely Feeno must feel, because she'd never had a friend or even an acquaintance who was a girl or boy. How she yearned for a friend her own age, having as yet only experienced such a relationship in books! *Maybe, now that I'm turning thirteen, Mother will let me play with girls my age,* thought Jocelyn. It was children, Mother insisted, who were horrid, not adolescents, and in a few hours she would no longer be a child.

"You can't be the only gnome who's ever been," said Jocelyn, as she rose from the floor. "Your mother and father must have been gnomes, don't you think?"

"I haven't any memory of them," said Feeno. He clapped at a fly but missed it. "I don't recall a time before I was your nanny."

"You couldn't have been born full grown!" protested Jocelyn.

"I fall so often, maybe I broke my head, and my childhood memories fell out," Feeno suggested.

"I don't think . . ."

"But if so," Feeno cut in, pressing his palms against the sides of his head, as if he might still be leaking memories, "why haven't I come across them? His eyes darted around the room. "I should do a search of—"

"Your memories aren't as important as your life," interrupted Jocelyn. "You'll lose *that* if you aren't more cautious."

"But when you rang for me . . ."

"Your leg is lame, Feeno. You should never rush."

"But your heart . . ." protested Feeno.

"Haven't you told me my so-called *heart attacks* are false?"

"But I knew, *particularly tonight,*" he said, emphasizing the occasion, "you'd show the symptoms and be afraid, no matter how often I've reassured you."

"It's not that I don't want to believe you," said Jocelyn. "I do." Tears trickled down her face.

Crossing to where Jocelyn stood, Feeno gave her a comforting hug. She was a couple of heads taller than he in spite of his being an adult, and she leaned down and laid her cheek on his head, nuzzling in his soft, chestnut-colored hair speckled with white. She loved the earthy smell of him. Today, it was especially strong.

"Were you in the garden just now?" she asked.

"You must smell cress," he said, laughing. "I had a couple of mouthfuls in the garden before I went to my room for a nap."

"Oh, I woke you!" Jocelyn exclaimed, backing away.

"No, I was only half-asleep—more than half, to be honest, but less than sound asleep."

"I shouldn't have rung!" Jocelyn declared.

"Yes, you should have," he insisted.

She shook her head. "I trouble everyone."

"You're being Miss Glum."

She sighed. "Does it make you *sick and tired* like Mother says it does her? Try as I do, I can't keep gloom from coming over me. Mother's right, of course, but I wish she hadn't named me Miss Glum. I haven't always been sad, have I?"

"Off and on," he replied. "But you were mainly sad only after you turned nine."

"Miss Sorrowful, my mother started calling me then. What's the difference between *sorrowful* and *glum?*"

"Both are sad." Feeno thought for a moment. "Glum, I think, is darker than sorrowful. Anger is mixed in. And remorse. Look at how you take the blame for everything, like me falling on my face. It's not your fault I'm clumsy."

"But you wouldn't have fallen if I hadn't rung," she reasoned. "Just because my heart trembled, I shouldn't have panicked."

"You can't help that."

"Mother says I can. But she doesn't tell me how. Panic makes my heart shiver even more. Can you die of fright?" she asked.

"I haven't," he answered. "And you know how your mother scares me to death. But it must be half to death, or else . . ."

Tears again filled Jocelyn's eyes. "I don't know what I'd do if I lost you."

"You'd be brave and strong," affirmed Feeno. "But I doubt your mother will kill me, though I do fear that one day I'll so displease her that she'll turn me out, like those servants who were here before Maag and I arrived."

"She hasn't killed Maag or let her go," pointed out Jocelyn, thinking how often her mother threatened to wring the housekeeper's neck or shouted at her to get out of sight.

"She tolerates more from Maag than from me," retorted Feeno, "maybe because Maag tends house and I tend you."

"You're my nanny," said Jocelyn affectionately.

"Which is why I have to be careful," said Feeno. "I mustn't interfere with your mother's rearing of you, like your grandmother did. Lady Idris makes me feel that I'm only here—indeed, I only exist—at her pleasure."

She is a danger to Feeno, thought Jocelyn. How often her mother complained that she had to waste time hunting for the gnome, because he did not reliably respond when she rang for him. "I am not playing a game of hide and hunt!" she would bellow.

Is there anything I can do to protect him? Jocelyn wondered. *Oh, but I mustn't think that Mother would kill the gnome or send him away—at least, not so long as I'm alive.*

"As I think about it," said Jocelyn, "you're more likely to lose me first. I don't believe I'll survive the night."

"You always have," asserted Feeno.

"That doesn't prove I always will."

"It improves your chances, doesn't it?"

"I don't think so," said Jocelyn. "Mother says it depends on proper breathing. This afternoon she lectured me on it. She made me memorize what she called the *essence* of it."

"Let me hear this *essence,*" said Feeno, tossing his hands in the air to ward off flies.

Jocelyn straightened her arms at her sides and repeated the words Mother had taught her. "I may inhale without worry, as I have done my entire life, because Mother created for me a virtuous atmosphere."

"A what?"

"Atmosphere. It means *air."*

Feeno scratched his head. "She made the air?"

"No, no. She must have put something in it to make it good. Or taken something out. Listen: It does not have—"

"It?" he inquired.

"Feeno, please don't interrupt. I'm having a hard time as it is. I must say the words without halting, or Mother will be angry." Jocelyn took a deep breath. "It . . . Oh, that's the it you were asking about. The good air—that's what it is. Now, hush. It does not have the wicked impurities that cause . . . that would cause me to have wrong ideas and behave badly. All I must do is inhale this wholesome air, and it will fill me with good health, fine manners, and a spirit of devotion and obedience to Mother."

"Why hasn't this air affected me and Maag?" asked Feeno. "Your mother says we're impossible, but we live in the same . . . Oh, I'm sorry for interrupting," he said, clapping his hand over his mouth.

Jocelyn relaxed her lips, which had been pursed in disapproval, and carried on with the recitation. "I am cursed by a poisonous spirit that is all my own, but proper breathing out will rid me of it. I must just let the poison go." She pressed her lips together again, this time puzzled. "How am I supposed to let go of something I don't know I'm holding? Oh, Feeno, I fear this poison will kill me."

"Your mother won't permit you to die."

"I'm not so sure," said Jocelyn. "Sometimes . . ." *No, I mustn't think that my mother means to harm me,* she thought. *Mother always acts for my good, doesn't she?* "Maybe even she can't prevent it," suggested Jocelyn.

"Oh, I'm certain she can!"

"Then why won't she stop the attacks on my breathing? It's not as if everyone has them. You and Maag and Mother don't get sick on your birthdays, do you?"

"How should I know?" said Feeno. "I don't know when mine is. I don't think Maag knows when hers is either. And Lady Idris won't admit to hers."

Jocelyn's eyes widened. "Let's pretend I don't have a birthday!" she cried. "Or at the least, that I'm not turning thirteen. I don't have sick spells on even-year birthdays."

"You used to," said Feeno. "You got sick every year until you turned five. Then it only happened every other year. I don't know why. Your mother doesn't even mention the even ones, much less celebrate them."

"Which is my point," argued Jocelyn. "If we don't celebrate, maybe I won't have a sick spell."

"We can ask your mother," said Feeno, "but I think the tradition of the birthday pig bladder—"

"You know Mother doesn't want us to call it that," interrupted Jocelyn. "She's decided *balloon* sounds more festive."

"Yes, yes," acknowledged Feeno. "It's important to her, that tradition of the birthday *balloon;* it's a measure, not just of years. She was heartened by the last pig . . . the last balloon." He pointed at the pale-blue one. "She said it shows progress."

Jocelyn looked up at the eight balloons, hovering here and there. Often, they'd float down to her, as if they wished to be close. She, too, felt drawn to them. They'd bump her, and she'd gently bat them about. She'd come to think of them as playmates. Each morning when she woke up, they were resting on her bedcovers.

But the pale-blue one wasn't festive at all. She could hardly bear to look at it. From the beginning it had drooped, not having the capacity to rise to the ceiling or move quickly about like the other seven. Though less than full, it acted heavy, as if at any moment it might sink to the floor. Tomorrow there would be a new balloon. The first, the green, was as big and full, Feeno said, as when it had appeared twelve years before. The blue wasn't nearly its size, not to mention that of the orange, which was the largest and looked as if it might burst. In fact, the blue balloon was the smallest and least buoyant.

"Blue makes me feel sad," Jocelyn said. "How is that a sign of progress?"

"I guess we have to trust your mother," Feeno replied, clapping his hands and at last squishing a fly between them.

CHAPTER 3

THE PUNGENCY OF NATURE

SUPPER WAS SERVED in the dining room. Its table was longer and its chairs more numerous than such a small household required, particularly because Mother didn't give parties or entertain guests and almost always dined in her chambers. Maag, having shut the drapes to keep out the natural light of the spring evening (Mother insisted on it), had lit the candles of the chandelier that hung above the table and the candelabrum that stood on the sideboard. For years, the candelabrum's three candles had illuminated Grandmother's hand-decorated pottery until, one by one, the pieces had vanished. On the stone walls were two landscapes that had been painted by Jocelyn's father, Angwyn.

Jocelyn hadn't much appetite. Maag hovered over her, trying to give comfort. Feeno, attempting to cheer her, stood on his head only to topple over, which *did* make Jocelyn smile. The distractions, while well intended, caused her to let time slip by, and now she was late for her nightly visit with Mother.

She hurried up the main staircase to the first floor, then through the arched entry into the sitting room that adjoined Mother's bedroom. The clock showed nearly 7:30.

"Thank you," she whispered, giving the grandfather clock a pat, which caused it to hum. She'd been taught that mechanical things weren't conscious, but how else could the clock give her time when she was late or take it away when she was early? She had been instructed to knock at her mother's door precisely at half past the hour, when the clock chimed once. If Mother didn't respond, she was told to wait by the door until *Old Grandfather,* as her mother called it, struck eight times, then go directly up the attic stairs to her room.

Sometimes, when Mother didn't answer, Jocelyn heard noises in the bedroom, such as the clearing of a throat or the setting down of a cup on a saucer or the heeltaps of someone's pacing. Often, she heard her mother talking to herself—a habit she had acquired, Mother said, because there was no one of her intelligence with whom to speak. In any case, Jocelyn supposed her mother was too preoccupied to receive her. Still, she had to stay in the sitting room in case her mother changed her mind.

On this birthday eve, as the clock chimed, Mother called for Jocelyn to come in even before she knocked. An overpowering stench struck Jocelyn full force as she was closing the door behind her. Gagging, she covered her nose and mouth with her hands. *What has she done now?* she wondered.

"Marvelously disgusting, is it not?" Mother asked with a smile. She lounged on her thick-cushioned bed, propped up by pillows. She wore her favorite nightdress—the violet one. "It is the distillation of a mole. When you boil a thing down to its essence, it exudes a most sumptuous stink. I like how I worded that. I must write it down." She picked up a notebook and quill.

"Are you saying," Jocelyn ventured, wiping her stinging eyes, "that you killed a mole to see how it smelled?"

"That was not well said," observed Mother. She paused, her pen poised over the page. "I changed its consistency to reveal its nature. Now, does that not sound better? I do not destroy animals in my workshop; I transform them. Solids, in my hands, become fluids or vapors with their own peculiar tastes and scents. Anything, reduced to its most base (its essential) nature, shares in what I have termed the *universal pungency*. In short, all of creation needs a bath. As the proverb says, 'Cleanliness is next to godliness.'" Applying her pen to the page, she said, "Sit down, child."

Jocelyn went to the straight-backed chair in the corner. Whenever her mother wrote in her presence, Jocelyn had no idea how long she would be occupied. Sometimes, it seemed as if she forgot that her daughter was there—until the clock struck eight and her mother would point at the door for her to go.

Jocelyn's nose slowly adjusted to the smell. It came from what had once been the nursery but was now Mother's workshop—her *proving ground,* she called it. The door to it from the bedroom was slightly ajar. The workshop could also be entered from the hall, though that door was always locked.

Mother often boasted about her *unnatural gifts* and *extraordinary feats,* but Jocelyn had seldom witnessed them. Indeed, she'd never been invited into her mother's workshop, though in times past, when she'd been bored while waiting in the sitting room for Mother to receive her, she'd bravely tiptoed back into the hall to the locked entrance to the workshop and peeked through the keyhole. Inside, it usually was dark, either because of the season or the close-woven drapes her mother had drawn.

Once, though, she'd spied Mother there, pouring liquids from vial to vial, her tall figure framed by a low fire of burning wood on the hearthstone behind her. A tabletop candle had dimly lit her V-shaped face and the auburn ringlets that tumbled around it. All of a sudden, Mother had raised her eyes—now glowing—and glared at the keyhole. Shrieking, Jocelyn had fallen back, her eye feeling as if it had been pierced.

Feeno, hearing her cries and finding her on hands and knees midway down the cellar stairs, had carried her to his room and held her all through the night and most of the next day until the pain subsided.

That evening, without mentioning the event, Mother had warned her of the unpleasant consequences that resulted when her daughter did not mind her own business. From that day on, Jocelyn had not peered into her mother's workshop or through any other keyhole. She'd avoided, too, looking directly into Mother's eyes.

"Child," her mother now said with a laugh, having put down her quill and picked up her nail file, "you always choose to sit so far away. But do not get up! You know the distance pleases me."

Jocelyn settled back into the chair, as Mother commenced sharpening her nails.

CHAPTER 4

THE VIOLENCE OF APOSTROPHES

"WELL?" MOTHER ASKED, having set the nail file onto her side table. Jocelyn had been fidgeting and now tried to steady herself.

"Get on with it!" demanded Mother. "What have you accomplished today?"

"I've been too scared to accomplish much of anything," answered Jocelyn.

"No contractions!" shouted Mother. "Have I not told you they signify laziness? Say it correctly."

"Yes, Mother." Jocelyn straightened her posture. *"I have* been too scared—"

"Whatever for?"

"My sick spell, Mother! You spoke of it today. I'm . . . *I am* due for another."

"My explanation of proper breathing was sufficient for you to overcome it," declared Mother.

Jocelyn slumped forward. "But you did not tell me how to rid myself of—"

"Really, Miss Glum, you are so tiring!" interrupted Mother. "Must I do everything for you? I told you enough. Put your mind to what puzzles you. I have more important work to do."

"Such as the mole?" asked Jocelyn, creasing her brow.

"Of course, the mole! You think it is a trifle compared to my mothering of you? Oh, child, you must get over your unwholesome preoccupation with yourself. It is most unbecoming. You are not the center of the universe."

"But aren't . . ." Mother had recently introduced the rule of not using contractions, and Jocelyn was struggling with the challenge. *"Are not* you frightened for me?" asked Jocelyn.

Her mother appeared perplexed by the question. "It is your birthday," she said. "I am excited for you."

"But the sickness may kill me!"

"Ah, but it may not!" retorted Mother. "I refuse to succumb to your gloom, Miss Glum. I prefer to look on the bright side."

That the attack on her lungs might not kill her did not strike Jocelyn as much of a show of optimism. "I have come up with a *bright* idea," she ventured.

Her mother looked at her suspiciously.

"Really, Mother! I am not being disrespectful. Haven't you . . . *Have not you* . . . Mother, that sounds so awkward. I can hardly finish the sentence, much less keep the thought. May I use *some* contractions?"

"There is no need," said Mother. "If you change the word order, you will speak properly with ease. Instead of *Have not you?* say *Have you not?* Does that not sound melodious? Now continue. You were talking about your insolence."

"Have not . . . " Jocelyn's sigh was one of frustration. *"Have you not* told me I am over being . . . "

"The word is insolent," said Mother. "You know the meaning: insulting, contemptuous. Thank goodness that period of your life was temporary; it seemed as if it would go on forever."

"There is nothing glum about my idea either," went on Jocelyn, "though I suppose it will not succeed."

"Did the gnome give you this *bright idea?"*

"No, it is mine. I was thinking, Mother, that I didn't . . . *did not* have a sick spell when I turned twelve, ten, eight, and six—the even years."

"You have forgotten how ill you were on your second and fourth birthdays," corrected Mother.

"But we celebrated those two birthdays, Feeno told me, just as we always have the odd ones. So, I was thinking maybe it is the celebration that causes the sick spells, and if we did not—"

"Nonsense!" interrupted Mother. "We have never *had* a birthday party, either because your birthday came on an even year—as you know, even numbers are unlucky—or because you have taken ill."

"But on my odd-year birthdays, someone decorates," said Jocelyn.

"The new balloon? That is not a party! It but continues our tradition of preparing for one. Perhaps this year it will come to pass. Oh, poor child," Mother said.

Jocelyn was unsure if she was expressing sympathy or reproaching her.

"It must seem that you will never overcome your odious malady. I often feel, too, that you will not. But that is why I am optimistic. You know that old tale of the wives I like to recite: It is darkest before the dawn. The science, of course, is dubious. I have meant to investigate it, but it would require rising early, and you know how much I detest that. I wonder . . . "

As was her habit when she became lost in thought, Mother fingered the small, white crystal—that *potent bit of quartz,* she often called it—which hung from a silver chain around her neck. She seemed oblivious to Jocelyn's presence, until she suddenly remarked, "When you were turning eleven, you suffered horribly, Feeno told me. I imagine you felt as if the Grim Reaper had come and you were in the grip of death."

"How would I know if it were he?" asked Jocelyn.

"Reaper?" questioned Mother. "Why do you ask?"

"In a dream the other night—"

"He appeared?" exclaimed Mother. "I am jealous!"

"Mother, if it was he, it may mean that this year I *will* die!"

"Oh, Miss Glum!" said Mother, shaking her head. "Reaper does not intend any harm. The harm either has already been done or it has not; he just comes to check your pulse. He is, I agree, hard to be around. He is not much for small talk. Such gravity he bears! Also, he has a knack for making skin crawl. His is gray and very taut, as if it might peel off the bone. Do you really think it was he? Sunken eyes. Hooded robe. Carries a scythe. I ridicule him for it. It makes him look as if he is a common—"

"He was not like that at all," interrupted Jocelyn.

"Really?" Mother leaned forward. "What was he like?"

Before speaking, Jocelyn paused a moment, disturbed by her mother's rare interest in what she had to say. She had no clear picture of the person in her dream and worried that Mother would punish her if she didn't at least appear to be exact. "There was no hooded robe, no scythe," she said, certain of those features. "He called me Kettle."

Mother sat bolt upright. "How dare he show his face!"

"Who?" asked Jocelyn.

"Angwyn has no business interfering."

"Father?" exclaimed Jocelyn.

"Who else would call you Kettle?" asked Mother.

"But why would he call me that?"

"I agree," said Mother. "It is imbecilic. My little Kettle is boiling over, he would quip, as if your red-faced bawling were endearing. I forbade Maag and Feeno to ever call you by that name. Did either of them disobey me?"

"They never said the name," Jocelyn assured her.

"Then it must have been Angwyn," muttered Mother to herself. "But how?" She cocked her head toward Jocelyn. "What else did he say?"

"That he had come to take me away."

"The nerve!" snarled Mother. "He has done nothing to raise you. Now, he wants to claim the spoils."

"He said, 'Kettle, you needn't come if you desire to stay.'"

"That *sounds* like your father," said Mother with disgust. "How he would torment me with contractions! Worse perhaps, he was weak-willed. Look at how he did not even pretend he knew what was good for you. Had he a reddish wart here?" she asked, pointing at her own left cheek.

Jocelyn thought quickly. "I only saw the right side of his—"

"He didn't have a good side," cut in Mother. "True, he was sharp-featured when I met him, even handsome, but his face softened quickly, until there was nothing noteworthy about it." She shifted in her bed, clearly agitated. "When next he bothers your sleep, tell him I demand that he come to *me* in a dream. He will not, of course; he has not the backbone." Suddenly, Mother shot a look at Jocelyn. "But are you certain . . . Look at me when I speak to you!" she snapped. "Are you certain it was a dream?"

"What else could it have been?" asked Jocelyn, as she gazed at the space between her mother's eyes. "Father could not very well rise from the dead, could he?"

"You are right; he has not the spirit. It surprises me he had enough to insinuate himself into your dream." Fingering the small, white crystal, Mother muttered, "Where could Husband have had in mind to take the girl? Surely not to the world of the dead. But if it were to a place in our world, how could he take her there? Is it possible that he escaped the Grim Reaper's scythe?"

Jocelyn was shocked. "Are you saying Father may not have died?"

Mother started, as if surprised that anyone was there, and let go of the crystal. "After you woke up from this dream," she said, "did you sense a man had been there?"

"How could I possibly know?" asked Jocelyn.

"They leave a strong odor," explained Mother. "Not earthy, like that of Feeno, but penetrating and rancid. The smell would not be familiar to you, although there are places in this house where it faintly lingers."

"Mother, you didn't . . . *did not* answer my question!" Jocelyn's breath was quickening with excitement, and her heart was racing. "Is Father alive?"

Mother studied her. "Does it worry you, dear? You need not fear. I will not let him steal you away and corrupt you."

Jocelyn wasn't afraid; she was confused. Her entire life she'd thought ill of her father, because he'd abandoned her when she was a baby—at least, that was what Mother said. She also said he'd been killed, which caused Jocelyn to give him little thought, because even if he'd intended on returning, he couldn't have. But if he were alive, he had no excuse, and Jocelyn was surprised she didn't feel angry at him. Instead, she felt excited, perhaps because in the past few months, out of the blue, he'd begun appearing in her dreams as comforting and kind.

"For his sake," went on Mother, "he would be safer dead. But child, I have upset you for no reason. I give your father too much credit. If he lives, he has not the nerve to face us after running off. If he is dead, he only pretends to be alive. In either case, he is of no consequence."

"Mother, couldn't . . . *could I not* have had a dream that was my own?"

"Your corrections please me, although I find it disappointing that you still have to make them. But what were you talking about? A dream that was called up by yourself? Of course, you could have. But if that were so, how could you know that your father called you *Kettle*? And how could your description of him have been so accurate? Within only a short time after you were born, he was nowhere to be seen."

"But I could not describe Father's appearance. I could only—"

"Father's? Another apostrophe! I loathe apostrophes. They riddle our language with nicks. Can you not feel them in the spoken word—like little darts thrown at the listener? Tomorrow, I plan to begin the process of weaning you from possessives. They, like contractions, show a laziness of language. Instead of saying *Mother's crystal,* you will say *the crystal that belongs to Mother."*

Jocelyn's jaw had dropped. "Mother," she said with dismay, "it's . . . *it is* very hard to talk to you."

"But instructive. As a pupil, unfortunately, you take after your father. He could not—or would not—imitate my elegance of speech. I will not allow you to follow his miserable example."

There was a light knock at the door. "It's Maag, Lady Iduress. I have cups and pots of tea."

CHAPTER 5

A POOR EXECUTIONER

MOTHER REACHED FOR THE DISH of feverfew on her bedside table. The bitter leaves were a protection against headaches, which Maag's presence often induced in her. Why she kept the housekeeper on was anyone's guess. Having munched (what Mother would call *masticated*) a handful of leaves, she motioned for Jocelyn to open the door.

In tiptoed Maag, which was how she usually walked. She wore a simple shift, its bodice low necked, and held the tray by balancing it from beneath on her long fingers. She stopped. "My," she said, wrinkling her nose, "it smells like a thing even a buzzard would never catch itself dead with."

"Mother likes it," warned Jocelyn. "She says the stink is sumptuous."

"She's right," said Maag. "It does impose."

"The tea, Maag, the tea!" Mother called impatiently. "Has the pot for Miss Glum the birthday blend?"

"Yes, my Ladyboat."

"My Lady*ship,*" corrected Mother.

"Oh, my Head Mischief," said Maag, reddening, "I don't demerit such an epitaph. I hunt after no title. I know my place in the spitting order."

Mother frowned, and Jocelyn cringed, though her mother had mostly given up taking Maag to task over her peculiarities of language.

No matter how often Mother corrected her, Maag's words rarely came out right. Mother didn't even bother about contractions.

"Her tea embraces lungwort for in-and-out haling," Maag recited, "a tinch of lemon balm to press down regrettable spirits, and thyme to . . ." She scrunched her face and cocked her head. "I don't recoil what that's for."

"It purges," said Mother. "Did you increase the thyme?"

The housekeeper nodded. "Double up, like you computed. My, isn't Jocie pretty as a magpie this birthday eve?"

"Jocelyn," corrected Mother. "Or *Gothelyn*. You know I prefer the latter."

"The Latter? It's not *Gothelyn* you favor? But no matter: Jocelyn by any other name is still Jocie. And each year she looks more like you, Malady."

"My Lady!" barked Mother. "You have the pronunciation wrong."

"Yes, Malady. But doesn't Jocie's red hair beat all?"

"It is much too bright!" snorted Mother.

"You're right," conceded Maag quickly. "You know how I'm a fool for the blight and shiny." She skittered across the room and put the tray on the small table next to the bed.

"I have told you not to bring spoons from the kitchen for evening tea," scolded Mother. "I desire that Gothelyn develop a taste for the exquisite. These two polished spoons," she said, holding them out beneath Maag's chin, "I took from the family silver."

"I only begot the lackluster ones, just in case," explained Maag.

"I do not follow," confessed Mother, a rare admission. "In case of what?"

"You know how you torment me when I steal something or other, saying my moral turpitude isn't competent, even when that something or other is pretty as a goldfinch. So I escorted the everyday spoons here in case you have a moral alteration and give back the shiny ones—not likely, I admit, but you might in a weak moment of conniption."

"Contrition," corrected Mother. "But I am not contrite. I did not steal them, Maag. I am family. The silver spoons are mine, as are the pots and teacups."

And everything else, thought Jocelyn.

"Which teapot contains the blend you made for Gothelyn?" asked Mother.

"Birthday's in the blue pot," answered Maag.

"Are you certain you have not mixed them up?"

"I never thought of that," replied Maag, as if it were an idea worth entertaining.

"Put it from your mind," warned Mother.

"I don't hold onto much there," Maag assured her.

"Unfortunately, you forget your tasks, too," said Mother. "Do you not remember that the gowns Miss Glum has been wearing have become too short? She requires longer dresses. See if any of the ones Mother-in-Law made for her daughter will do."

"This frock she's wearing," observed Maag, "is one of her daughter's most prolonged. The sister of your decreased husband was but a wisp when she passed out."

"How inconsiderate of Lynette to be sickly and die without reaching her full size!" chided Mother. "What will Miss Glum wear?"

"One of Old Lady's?" suggested Maag.

"The gowns of Mother-in-Law are mine!" snapped Mother, deliberately fingering the white crystal. Maag stepped back, as if fearing that she was about to be punished. "On second thought," said Mother, "perhaps I could share."

"That's . . . *That is* wonderful!" cried Jocelyn.

"Do not lose your composure," cautioned Mother. "I have in mind the ugly dresses I would never wear, such as the ones I have loaned Maag. But you are right, Maag."

"I am?" exclaimed the housekeeper, astonished.

"Gothelyn has nearly attained the stature of Mother-in-Law, which is, of course, still beneath me. But we must not be wasteful, Maag. Let down the dress Miss Glum is wearing and others that are suitable."

The housekeeper turned to Jocelyn. "Once you shed that frock, Jocie, drop it down the servants' steps, if you please, and the day afore the day after tomorrow, I'll pounce on it. Any other dresses that are legible for you, I'll stretch down and out in the hereafter." Suddenly, Maag's eyes watered. "Oh, my polliwog, it was only yesterday you were skinny as a snake in the grass." Crossing to Jocelyn, she wrapped her arms around her, then uncurled them, stood back, and said admiringly, "You're turning into a young lady afore our airy eyes."

"That is not so!" Mother retorted sharply.

Maag quickly begged pardon. "I repent, my Overseer. My eyes aren't as sensible as yours. They've diverted me to my common place of being in the wrong. But . . . isn't she filling up?"

"Are you providing cucumbers to cool her down and the exercises I prescribed to keep her lean?" questioned Mother.

"I have . . . when I remember," admitted the housekeeper. "I'm a poor executioner."

"I insist that you improve," said Mother. "You, too, Gothelyn," she added, turning toward the girl. "Maag should not have to remind you of your diet and exercises. That she must shows that you do not yet possess the attributes of a young woman. Exhaustive exercise, especially, will keep you from maturing before you are ready."

"But isn't maturing a naturality?" inquired Maag.

"It is, which makes it suspect," said Mother. "Gothelyn will not be ready to take on the burden of being a woman until she stops her childish ways and achieves perfection."

"But first," noted Maag, "she has to make it through the night. Pardon, Lady Iduress, for the danger, like you say, of me and Feelo thinking—"

"Feeno," corrected Mother.

"That's the one, my Wordsmith. As I was saying, me and Feelo were wondering, in spite of the overdose of thyme, maybe he ought to spy on Jocie tonight on account the tea hasn't ever protected her from the eruption of her lungs."

"His service is unnecessary," replied Mother. "She will not suffer unless she chooses."

"Chooses?" exclaimed Jocelyn.

"If she does," said Mother, "she will have to fend for herself. Now, tend to your duties, Maag, so Miss Glum and I can have a heart-to-heart. Oh, one thing new: leave sprigs of rosemary on the attic stairs for her to put under her pillow to keep away dreams."

"Poor lassie!" cried Maag. "Do you have the dark dream of being in a cage?"

Jocelyn shook her head.

"That's why her Ladyboat subscribes them to me," said Maag. "Pardon, my Sage, but methinks it's more infective at scaring off nightmares if Jocie splatters those spouts on, not 'neath, her pillow. Make a nest of them, I do. I like them in my hair and round my face. Near implausible to be haunted by demons with maryrose up your nose and sticking out your ears."

"Do as I said, Miss Glum," Mother declared. "It is more sanitary. Maag, you presume upon my goodwill. You overstep."

"Oh, Malady, I don't expect you to do me good, and I have no aim to step on your foot. My crack I was thinking was wise, but I forgot my place, which is to be gone."

As Maag high-stepped quickly toward the door, Mother rubbed the crystal and spoke in a mumbling voice.

"Aaaahhh!" screamed the housekeeper, clutching her stomach and dropping to one knee.

"Maag!" cried Jocelyn in dismay. "Not again!"

"Check her bosom," said Mother.

Jocelyn stood up and circled to the front of Maag, who was now moaning, and removed from between her breasts a small, silver box. "Mother, free her! She is helpless."

"Ah, but then how is it she can *help herself* to my things?" said Mother. "I am making a point, child. For one with her brain, it requires many repetitions. The painful state allows her to experience the consequences of stealing from me. Her nature is no excuse. But why are you so concerned for her? Where is your concern for me? You know how casting spells tires me. I do it not for me, but for the good of the household." Stroking the crystal and mumbling, Mother released the housekeeper from the pain.

Maag nearly collapsed.

Regaining her footing, the housekeeper turned around to face Mother. "Pardon, my Mercy," she apologized. "You know it's not palpable for me to swear off when the thing's sparkly. Seems like it leaps into my bubbies. I'm shamed and bumbled that . . . Ai!" cried the housekeeper, as she dropped to both knees. "Peas, Lady Id . . ."

"Must you give her cramps?" cried Jocelyn.

The housekeeper doubled over, her head striking the floor.

"She brings them upon herself," retorted Mother. "I cast that spell years ago. Maag knows she cannot lie to me without suffering for it."

Jocelyn fought the urge to again intercede, because she knew Mother would only punish the housekeeper more severely and perhaps punish Jocelyn with cramps as well.

"I'm *not* shamed and bumbled," Maag confessed in a strangled voice. "*Irked* I am that I didn't get away with it." The truth produced in her an abrupt intake of air; she shot to her feet. "I'd least be scarce," she said.

Mother waved her away, and the housekeeper tiptoed backwards. Bowing her head, Maag drew the door closed behind her.

CHAPTER 6

POISONOUS SPIRITS

JOCELYN CONTINUED FACING in the direction Maag had exited. Her back to her mother, she stared at the floor and bit at her thumbnail, trying to contain herself. *It'll end badly if I show I'm mad,* she thought. Her reasoning, however, was to no avail.

Whirling about, Jocelyn strode to the bedside table and slapped down the silver box, then leaned over her mother and, breathing heavily, said in a trembling voice, "You say I won't be sick unless I want. Why would I want that? I may be glum, but I'd never . . . No, I won't choose to become ill. I won't!"

Her mother had raised her hands, using them as a shield. "Cease contracting!" she commanded, violently pushing against the air. "*Will not! Will not! I'd* is bad enough, but *won't* has a horrid sound! Also, it distorts your mouth, disfiguring your face; you look like a fish. I cannot think. You are too close. Stand at the end of the bed while I expound upon your obstinacy."

Jocelyn did as she was told, though she continued to fume inside. *I'll stand here, as Mother commands,* she thought, *but I won't listen to what she says.*

Mother poured herself a cup of tea from her own pot. Only after breathing in its aroma and tasting it with the tip of her tongue did she freely sip. "You are contrary, child—intentionally so. How else to explain the persistence of your poisonous spirits in spite of my charms? After spoiling your first four birthdays, you have ruined every odd-year birthday since. I am always so disappointed when Feeno or Maag finds you nearly dead. Even worse, once you begin to recover, you are more unruly than you were before—until I put my foot down."

Jocelyn's eyes welled with tears. She had not been able to not listen to her mother and had taken her words to heart. "I'm . . . *I am* sorry, Mother. I should have known I was at fault for my sick spells."

"Who else would you blame?" questioned Mother. "But quit sniveling! You are reaching an age when you must face up to your responsibilities. You were born a natural child. That is unacceptable. Nature must succumb to nurture. I have provided you with the wherewithal. It is time for you to take matters into your own hands if you are to stop the spells and rise to perfection."

"But how?" asked Jocelyn.

"I have already told you," scolded Mother. "Let go of the poison that afflicts you."

Jocelyn felt at a loss. "I have put my mind to it. I really have. Still," she said, sniffling, "I do not know how."

Mother put her hands over her ears. "Those sniffles, too, produce a horrid sound. Must you persist with vulgar habits? Even mucus you do not know how to properly discharge. Blow your nose if you must."

Jocelyn looked about helplessly.

"I shall not lend you a cloth of *mine,*" said Mother in a tone that indicated the very thought was an abomination. "Quit crying, as I told you, and you will soon dry up."

Swallowing her sniffles, Jocelyn said sadly, "I fear I will never be the daughter you desire."

"I demand it!" declared Mother. "All you need do, child, is mind me."

Jocelyn's mouth fell open. "Minding you is taking matters into my own hands?" she asked, astonished.

"Bravo!" congratulated Mother. "You grasp the idea."

"But . . ."

"A paradox? Yes," acknowledged Mother, "but one that is true. Instead of minding me, you have yielded to nature—to that within you that is base. It does not become you as it does the mole. You have no business being part of the universal pungency."

"Are you saying I stink?" protested Jocelyn.

"You do offend," affirmed Mother. "Nature has brought you low, Miss Glum. It has made you grim, not cheerful, as I would have you. Mind me, and you will be filled with the *spirit of the household,* as I like to call it, which is enthusiasm for what is pleasant and opposition to evil Mother Nature."

"Evil?"

"She corrupts, filling you with poisonous spirits, one after another," explained Mother. "But do not fear. They are contained, and soon we will destroy them as well as Mother Nature."

"But . . ."

"All will become clear in good time," Mother assured her. From the sleeve of her nightdress, Mother pulled a jar. "Herein is ash of an ash." She paused. "That is a pleasantry, is it not? I imagine you are puzzled by my play on words. The jar contains the thoroughly burned wood of an ash—the tree, of course. It augments the lemon balm, exorcizing any evil spirit that has claimed you." She lifted the cap and sprinkled ash into Jocelyn's pot of tea. She thought for a moment, then poured in the entire contents. "You cannot imbibe too much of this," she said. "You may even enjoy the sooty flavor."

Next, she removed a jar from her other sleeve. "Before you take this sleeping powder," she said, "recite for me. As the old wives say: 'Practice makes perfect,' although I expect you to be perfect at the outset."

I just have to recite the speech, thought Jocelyn. *Then, she'll send me to my room, and I'll be free of her.* Jocelyn took a deep breath and said, "I may inhale without worry—"

"Breathe in," corrected Mother.

"Pardon?"

"You said inhale; *breathe in* is how I worded it. I will not allow substitutions, even when they are synonymous."

Jocelyn took another deep breath. "I may breathe in without worry, as I—"

"Watch your posture," admonished Mother. "Drooping affects diction."

The grandfather clock chimed once, twice . . .

"Is it eight of the clock already?" exclaimed Mother. "As the old wives say, 'Time flies when you are having fun.' But Gothelyn, we cannot spend the whole night indulging in merriment. Recite quickly so you can have your cup of tea. Mine is quite good," she added, sipping from her cup.

Jocelyn's heart began to race. *I'm panicking!* she realized.

"Do get on with it!" urged Mother.

"I . . ." Jocelyn's breath had become short, her mouth dry. "I may breathe in, as I—

"Omission!" sang out Mother, though her voice hadn't any mirth in it. "You forgot *without worry."*

Jocelyn cleared her throat. "I may . . . breathe in . . . without worry . . . as I have done . . . my tired . . . no, entire life, because—"

"Your speech," said Mother with a sigh, "should flow, not flounder. Your phrasing is annoying and distracts from the meaning. Skip to the part about the poison."

Jocelyn's mind went blank.

After a few moments, Mother coaxed, "It begins, I am cursed . . ."

I am cursed, thought Jocelyn. "Mother, I think I'm going to faint."

"I am!" scolded Mother. "Do not dare faint until I have critiqued your voice. It does not register the appropriate spirit. Do you believe in what I have instructed you to say?"

"I think I do," answered Jocelyn.

"Do not think!" shouted Mother. "It shows doubt. Proclaim with absolute conviction. Enunciate! Practice in the morning until your performance is flawless and spirited. For now, we must get on with the festivities."

Mother took several pinches of the sleeping powder from the jar and deposited them in Jocelyn's blue pot. "This is valerian root mixed with . . . with something or other. The powder has the smell of dirty socks but will drop you into the abyss of sleep."

Reaching for a dark vial on her bedside table, Mother said, "Here is a novelty. I have not tried it before. It is a solution of deadly nightshade, glove of the witches, and death cap. Why do you look as if you have seen a ghost?"

"Are you putting that into my tea?" asked Jocelyn, mortified.

"I am certainly not putting it into mine. I have no need for it. But you . . . I found a proverb in a Chinese text: poison defeats poison. You require an antidote to the machinations of Mother Nature."

"But won't . . ."

Mother cringed. "This poison will not kill you," she said. "At least, it will not kill what is good in you. To fortify your vital functions, I have mixed in flowers from the elderberry bush, although they may have come from the toxic hemlock; their flowers are similar, you know. But take solace. I seldom make mistakes."

Mother uncorked the vial and poured a measure of the liquid into Jocelyn's pot. "An herbalist must have a good eye for this," Mother said. "A drop too much and it will be your funeral we . . . Oh, you have turned an unhealthy pale! I like you clean but not washed out. I was only joking. Soon I hope you will have the sophistication to appreciate my humor."

Mother stirred the entire concoction with one of the kitchen spoons, then filled Jocelyn's cup with it.

"Cheers," she said, holding out the cup.

CHAPTER 7

'ROUND THE CORNER AND INTO THE WOODS

FEENO WAS STEEPING tea leaves in a pot of boiled water and looking forward to retiring to the cellar when Maag flew into the kitchen.

"Why did Iduress think I purported to do it?" she cried. "I've more in my brain than to thieve off with one of her shinies when it's on the lip of her nose. Does she believe I'm a dodo? It's the skull-knavery of those gleamy baubles taking to me like flies to you."

"That serves you well, Maag," said Feeno, rising to his tiptoes and prying open a cupboard at its bottom edge. "It's a good idea to let her catch you."

"I don't *let* her catch me; she does fine on her own." Maag, who dwarfed Feeno, reached up and took down a cup for him before he could fetch a stool. "Why do you say it's a good thing?" she asked.

"If Lady Idris believes you haven't the wits to steal from her, she won't suspect you of the hoard you've—"

"Hush!" whispered Maag harshly. "Sound may be up to its tricks. We don't know how it's carrying this night." She rotated her head, darting her eyes here and there, as if Sound might be lurking, ready to scamper to within Lady Idris's hearing. "Asides," went on Maag, "I haven't a hoard . . . How many are in a hoard?"

"It hasn't got a number," Feeno answered, keeping his voice soft. "You've made off with most of Jocelyn's grandparents' knickknacks. I'd reckon that's a hoard."

"They're neither knacks nor knicks," she whispered. "They're treasures. Iduress, though, doesn't pay them any brain, and her in-laws haven't any use for them."

"What if they return?" asked Feeno.

"That chance is as poor as Jocie's papa coming to life after succumbling on a bucket."

"But doesn't Lady Idris say that her mother-in-law wanders the woods and her father-in-law—"

"Professor Oldric's 'round the corner. You think I've just hatched from an egg or fallen off the heavens? I know what Iduress says. But Lady Elda's been in those woods near thirteen years, and what corner is it that her husband doesn't come 'round? They show up, they'll be more in shock than us. Asides, they don't dare."

"Why not?" challenged Feeno. "They'd put Lady Idris in her place."

"This *is* her place," said Maag.

"Not so!" he whispered. "Jocelyn's grandparents are master and mistress of this house."

"Was! That was yesteryear. Face up, Feelo. They're gone."

"But they must be near," he insisted.

"Methinks," Maag said, lowering her voice even more, "Iduress is trying to scare us with that ball of yarn. Like if you, me, or Jocie misbehaves, we'll be condemned to forever wander the woods with Elda or be stuck in a corner with Oldric. I liked those folks, what I saw of them, but their fates sound worse than death.

"Oh, I near forgot," Maag went on. "I spoke to her High Muck-a-Muck about you peeping in on the girl this eve, and she said there's no reason for it, because Jocie's aging so, she gets to select if she'll be above the weather or below it."

"But why would Jocelyn choose to be sick?" asked Feeno.

"I asked myself the same. She won't pick to fall sick, I said back. That's maybe why there's no sense of you watching out for the girl. She's able to offend herself."

"Defend," corrected Feeno.

"They're both *fend*. You're picking nits."

Feeno threw out his arms, encircling Maag's waist, and twirled her around the kitchen. "This year we'll have a real birthday party!"

The bell rang twice—a call for Feeno from Lady Idris.

"I wouldn't count my chickadees afore they break out," observed Maag.

Feeno hurried up the back stairs to the hall that led to the Lady's chambers. It was unusual for her to question him after her evening visit with Jocelyn, and when this night she made him wait at her door an inordinate amount of time, his apprehension increased. He couldn't face Lady Idris without fearing she would punish him with severe pain. *Have I done anything I shouldn't have or not done something I should have?* he speculated. When at last she allowed him to enter, he felt as if he were about to pee in his pants.

"I am pleased you came immediately," said the Lady.

"I did not think you wished to play hide and hunt at this hour."

"Not at any hour, unless I choose," she corrected.

"Excuse me, Lady Idris, but I must run outside to the privy."

Lady Idris scowled. "More times than not, this is how you greet me," she said. "Why do you not visit the privy before you come to me?"

"Because I do not need to. But now the need is urgent."

"Good," said the Lady, smiling. "I prefer you uncomfortable. You are quicker in speech, more direct. How I enjoy our chats! Do you?"

"No."

"There is the joy of them!" she exclaimed. "The spell I cast on you is a great improvement over the one I cast on Maag. You cannot lie to me, whereas Maag—at a cost, of course—can. But I get impatient with her writhing and shrieking. Not that I do not take satisfaction in her pain, but pleasure at times must be sacrificed for expedience."

"Lady Idris," implored Feeno, "have you forgotten you rang for me?"

She beamed. "See? Straight to the point. I have questions, Feeno. First, has there been a man in the house?"

"There has," he answered.

"Who?" she demanded, obviously taken aback.

"Your husband, for one."

"You saw him?" exclaimed Lady Idris.

"I did," said Feeno, nodding.

"When?"

"Before he ran off."

"What?" exclaimed the Lady. "He has run off again?"

"There was only the once, I think," said Feeno.

Lady Idris, having looked first alarmed, then puzzled, now appeared as if a light had dawned. "Of course," she said, relieved. "You saw him when Miss Glum was a baby."

"I saw Professor Oldric, too," said Feeno. "That was all the men, unless you count me, though I'm . . . I am not sure. Do you regard a male gnome as a man, my Lady?"

"That is not one of my questions!" she barked. "For one who needs to go to the privy, you are very roundabout."

"Perhaps your questions should be . . ."

Lady Idris was glaring at him. "I do not want advice," she said with an edge. "Keep to answers. That is all the honesty I will tolerate." Gathering herself, she asked, "Have you recently seen the father of Miss Glum? Or did Maag tell you that she has?"

"No."

"He may have looked different," said Lady Idris. "But you have a good nose. Have you smelled him?"

"Recently? No. But, Lady Idris, is your husband not dead?"

"Do not ask me questions! But, yes, I presume he is dead, although we do not have a body. A body would put the matter to rest."

"May I go out and search for it?" asked Feeno.

Lady Idris smiled. "You really are desperate to depart. Hold fast, Gnome. I have but one question more: Did Maag tell you not to check on Miss Glum tonight?"

"She said there was no point to it," he answered.

"That is correct. Now be gone before you wet my floor."

CHAPTER 8

WHAT SIZE THE RISK?

HAVING USED THE PRIVY and picked up his lukewarm tea from the kitchen, Feeno descended the servant stairs to the cellar, candles fixed to the walls lighting his way. He took several sharp sniffs. *How can Lady Idris claim that the air in this house is wholesome?* he wondered. *It's stagnant. And no wonder, what with the Lady's insisting that all the windows and outside doors be kept shut. Thank goodness Jocelyn defies her, and Maag often leaves the kitchen door ajar.*

Unhooking the latch, he opened the door to his room. Once inside, he set his cup and pot of tea on the bedside table. Using his pocket tinderbox, he lit a candle, then returned to the door and closed it.

Toad peeked out at him from its hiding place, the bottom dresser drawer where Feeno kept his dirty laundry. It was a good choice, because Lady Idris would never rummage there for forbidden things.

"Good to see you're not gallivanting about," said Feeno, as he poured a cup of tea.

He worried when Toad wasn't in the cellar room. *If Lady Idris were to capture it, she'd undoubtedly torture . . . No, that was not correctly put. I must watch even how I think,* he cautioned himself, *or else I might let words slip out that the Lady would interpret as rude. She'd doubtless make a trial upon the toad; that was how I should have said it. If I begged her to spare it, as I did on behalf of the mole* (he'd mistakenly mentioned it to Lady Idris, because it was a nuisance to the garden), *she'd say what she'd said after ordering me to trap the creature—that she was ennobling it, making it useful to compensate for its useless life.*

He kept the toad a secret, too, from Jocelyn, because though Lady Idris hadn't said he couldn't share his room with a toad, there was probably an unspoken rule against it—he'd been punished for violating plenty of others—and he didn't want the girl accused of being an accomplice if he got caught.

Feeno also hadn't told Maag about Toad, not only because Lady Idris could have wrenched the truth from her; the housekeeper had an appetite for reptiles and amphibians, and Feeno feared she might be tempted to cook it for dinner.

Sliding out of his short, sleeveless jacket, which had belonged to Jocelyn's father when he was a boy, Feeno sat down on the cot, pulled off his boots, and stretched his toes.

The toad climbed out of the dresser drawer to the floor and padded to the cot. Feeno leaned down, lifted it to his lap, and stroked its head. He had sighted it late last summer while he was attending to his gardening tasks and been struck by how intently it gazed at him with its bulging eyes. Much to his surprise, he'd woken one morning shortly after to find it sleeping at the foot of his bed.

Now, when he picked up his cup of tea, Toad scampered from his lap onto the bedside table.

"I don't spill *every* time," Feeno asserted, but at once he did, right where the toad had been. "Drat!" he cried, patting his trousers with a cloth. "At least the tea's not hot." He pointed at the toad. "Admit that it was your fault!" he jested. "If I hadn't been trying *not* to spill . . ."

Toad stuck out its tongue.

"How rude!" exclaimed Feeno, laughing. "Oh, I haven't fed you, have I?" Setting the cup next to the toad, he stood up and reached into the front pockets of his trousers, pulling from one pocket dried apple slices, watercress, cauliflower, and fresh rhubarb and from the other pocket a balled-up napkin containing a handful of meat. He hadn't bothered to ask what kind it was. Toad liked all types, so what did it matter? Maag insisted on always giving Feeno a serving of it, calling his distaste for flesh an *unnaturality.*

Feeno's diet consisted largely of garden produce, but he preferred wild bilberries, flowering stems of heather, and the fruit of brambles. Maag would have been happy to collect and even preserve them, but Lady Idris forbade her to waste time on such *savage fare.* So Feeno often ventured into the forest to eat them. Now and then Maag would accompany him, not only to eat beetles, salamanders, and the eggs of songbirds—her *dainties,* she called them—but also to add what trinkets she'd collected to her hoard, which she kept inside a tree stump.

Feeno now unwrapped the meat and tore it into bits, laying them on the floor. Toad, having slid down the leg of the bedside table, ate eagerly. So far it had showed no qualms about eating whatever Maag prepared, devouring the leftovers with enthusiasm.

Feeno crossed the room and, from the bottom drawer of the dresser, withdrew the small knife he'd borrowed from the kitchen. Having a knife in his room or on his body was useful but violated one of Lady Idris's spoken rules. *Does she fear for her life?* he wondered. *I haven't the bravery to even menace her with it, much less do her harm.*

I can, however, harm myself—by accident, of course. "Would you enjoy a slice of my hand or a finger perhaps?" he joked, glancing down at Toad, as he chopped the fruit and vegetables into small pieces so the toad, who had no teeth, could swallow them. Feeno puzzled over its omnivorous diet. He'd thought toads dined on insects, spiders, and the like. Not that there were any bugs in the house for it to eat, except in Jocelyn's room. Likely that was why it ate what it did. Now and then he fed it a fly he'd caught and saved for it, and Toad gobbled it down, as if it were a treat. Feeno didn't know how often the toad went outside. There, he probably got his fill of his customary diet.

Having placed the chopped fruit and vegetables on the floor and returned the knife to its drawer, Feeno took up his cup, sat down on the cot, swung his legs up onto it, and leaned against the wall. As he sipped tea, he ruminated about Jocelyn. *I'm so used to fearing for the girl's life this time of year, it's hard for me to believe she isn't still at risk. Are Maag and I deluding ourselves that Jocelyn is safe?*

Toad croaked, and Feeno leaned down, encircled its cool, bumpy body with his hand, and lifted it to his chest. At once it scurried to his shoulder.

"Safer there if you're going to avoid a bath of tea, eh?" he asked. "I must admit you show good sense."

Toad nestled against his neck, and soon Feeno heard faint but regular croaks. *It's snoring,* he thought. He put the empty cup on the bedside table and closed his eyes, feeling he, too, should take a nap. *It might clear my mind,* he thought, *enabling me to decide what to do about* . . . He drifted off.

He found himself in his favorite dream, the one in which he was agile and swift. As he ran, he sensed the wind in his face, the smell of the woods, and the sunlight filtering through the trees. He reveled at being unrestrained, but this exuberance did not make him unmindful of the path. Sure-footed and nimble, he ran faster, just for the joy of it.

This time, however, the dream turned dark. Clouds descended. Storms threatened. He felt pursued. He was running for his life! He took chances, bounding over brush without knowing what was on the other side. He leaped—

The crack of his head jarred him awake. *Have I jumped over a cliff and landed on the rocks below?* he wondered. He rolled onto his back. The light from the candle helped him get his bearings. Toad was gazing down on him from the cot.

"I'm all right," he assured it (and himself), though he wasn't certain.

I threw myself off the bed to escape the . . . the menace, he thought. He checked for blood, sliding his palm across his forehead; he felt nothing wet. *I haven't cracked my head open,* he realized with relief, not wishing to lose more of his memory or, indeed, the whole of his brain.

Feeno didn't know whether the fall had knocked sense into or out of him, but all at once it became obvious that he must look in on Jocelyn. Lady Idris had not forbidden him this birthday eve to *meddle with the girl,* as she had put it in the past; she'd only said there was *no point. Most important, though,* he mused, *Jocelyn fears for her life, and I'm her guardian. It's as simple as that.*

He didn't know how long he'd napped. He had no clock, not that it would have told him anything; he'd never figured out how hands told time. He joked that for him it was always now. *I shouldn't wait to check on Jocelyn,* he thought. *It may already be too late.*

Struggling to his feet, he poured himself another cup of tea, cold now, and downed it in a few gulps. Then he put on the jerkin over his shirt and stepped into his boots. Sliding his hand under the toad, he crossed to the dresser and set it in its hiding place. Immediately, Toad climbed from the drawer onto his wrist and scampered to his shoulder.

Feeno, now erect, looked sharply at the toad. "You want to go with me?"

Toad slid headfirst down his coat into his breast pocket, completely concealing itself, though it made a bulge.

"I can't allow it," said Feeno, removing the toad and placing it back down among the dirty laundry. "I'd welcome the company, if you realized the danger, but I can't imagine you do."

The gnome took a deep breath to brace himself. Life with Lady Idris, he'd learned, required that he take risks, but he tried to limit them to small ones. *What size is this one?* he asked himself. *If Lady Idris catches me, I'll find out in a hurry.*

As he was closing the drawer, he eyed the knife. *Might I need it to defend Jocelyn on this night?* he wondered. Having never checked on her before on her birthday eve, he didn't know what to expect. *Surely a knife would have no use against a sickness,* he reasoned, *but what if the Grim*

Reaper should appear? Or an evil witch? Retrieving the small knife from the drawer, he slipped it into a side pocket of his jerkin. *It's not much,* he thought, *but it's the closest thing to a weapon I possess.*

The climb from the cellar was uneventful until Feeno discovered Jocelyn sprawled partway up the stairs that led to her room in the attic. Illuminated by a candle in a holder that was attached to the wall, she slept, her head lying in the crook of one elbow, her knees drawn up, one foot on a step, the other dangling below.

"Jocelyn," he whispered, shaking her lightly, then more vigorously.

She murmured, "Father?"

Feeno brushed her cheek with the fuzzy hair on his face, but she merely gurgled. *Lady Idris must have given her sleeping powder,* he realized.

He maneuvered her on the stairs until she sat. Her head drooped.

"Jocelyn!" he repeated, lifting her chin and blowing forcefully into her face. She reared slightly, her eyes fluttering, before her head collapsed forward. "You must wake up!" he exhorted, as he grasped her upper arms and shook her from side to side, her head swinging like the pendulum of the grandfather clock.

I must carry her to her room, Feeno thought. Putting one arm under her legs and cradling her back with the other, he tried to lift her. But she was too heavy, and he dropped her down a step. Turning about, he sat in front of her, took hold of her arms, and brought them forward over his shoulders, crossing them before his chest.

"Toad!" he whispered, seeing it below him on the stairs. "Don't follow us." The toad, however, scrambled up past him and Jocelyn. "Oh, so now we're following you, are we? Where has your good sense gone?"

Attending again to Jocelyn, Feeno thought he should be able to bear her weight on his back. *But I'm facing the wrong way!* he lamented. He reared his head, eyeing the landing above. *We're not near it,* he observed. Standing, he slowly pivoted on the step, nearly stumbling, then trudged up the stairs, his spine bent, his nose nearly touching the steps. He caught the scent of rosemary and came across a pile of it.

I've heard rosemary's good for pain, he reflected, his head aching and his nose still sore. Seizing the sprigs with his mouth, he chewed and swallowed them, as he continued up the stairs.

In Jocelyn's room, he pulled back the covers, laid her in bed, and took off her shoes. He wished she were in her nightgown, but because she was no longer a child, that would have to wait until she could change into it herself. Covering her with bedclothes, he kissed her forehead.

Where has Toad gotten to? he wondered.

Collapsing to the floor and lying on his back, he rested, waiting for the rosemary to give him some relief from pain. Gazing into the dark above him, he became mesmerized by what appeared to be stars coming out, then vanishing, then returning. He'd been seeing them since he'd toppled out of bed. Or was it after he'd tripped on the rug and fallen on his face? *At least now I'm already on the floor,* he reasoned. *I can't fall from here.*

CHAPTER 9

WITCHERY

CREAK!

Feeno snapped awake. *Has the floor ruptured?* he wondered. *Has the attic settled? Is the house coming down?* Light from the moon showed Jocelyn asleep in bed. *What made that ear-splitting—*

He heard, then, a more distant, quieter creak. *Sound must have magnified the first,* he guessed.

Again, a creak—one nearer. *Someone is mounting the stairs!*

Feeno scrambled to the closet. Yanking the door open, he dove inside, pulling it closed behind him, but not before a few flies joined him. He heard the knob to the room turn and the door open. The scent that entered was the Lady's.

His heart beat so violently he feared she would hear it. *What's rattling? My bones? No, my teeth.* He opened his mouth to stop their chattering. *Why am I holding my breath? Won't there be a loud blast when I let it out?* He buried his face in one of Jocelyn's gowns, exhaling into it, then inhaling through his nose. Dust tickled his nostrils. To stifle a sneeze, he pinched his nose, nearly crying out in pain. *Breathe deeply and softly,* he told himself. Slowly his body quieted.

Then he sneezed five times in quick succession. He slapped his brow in frustration, forgetting it was bruised. He winced. His nose throbbed. *No matter,* he thought. *I'm found out, and much worse will come.* He huddled in the dark, awaiting his fate.

There'd been no noise! Where had Sound put all the sneezes? In a bottle or a pocket? Had it swallowed them?

He peeked through the slats of the door. The moonlight illuminated the back of Lady Idris, who was cloaked and hooded. She lowered a candle until the flaming wick licked at the girl's chin.

"My biyearly visit, Gothelyn," said Lady Idris. "Are we not pleased? Has Mother Nature given up the ghost?"

Feeno started. *Ghost?*

"And how fare you, Glum?" asked the Lady. "Not well, I expect. You, faint spirit, are only a wisp of smoke from a fire that is going out. Unlike several of your forebears!" she roared, whirling about and raising the candle. "You, Brazen!" she cried, thrusting the flame at the bronze-colored balloon.

Feeno barely suppressed a gasp. The balloon narrowed and stretched, and its surface rippled, as if it were bristling.

"How impudent and shameless you were!" snarled Lady Idris. "You nearly provoked me to wring the neck of the child." She lashed out, whipping firelight across the red and orange balloons. "You, Fury, and you, Smolder! A year of fiery temper, another of suppressed rage, you turned Gothelyn into a fearsome beast."

These are the names she gave Jocelyn, marveled Feeno: *Miss Fury when she was two years old, Miss Smolder when she was four, and Miss Brazen when she was five and six.* Astonished, he watched Fury flare.

"How dare you threaten me with your fire!" screamed the Lady. "Oh, Smolder, do you really think your swelling intimidates me?"

The orange balloon, the most rotund, looked as if it might burst.

"How tempting to tickle with my candle flame the fragile skin that cages all of you," cackled Lady Idris.

"Oh, does that make you cower, Bustle?" the Lady jeered, throwing light on the green balloon, which was quivering. "My first birthday spirit, captured after months of Infant behaving like a fussy slug, then becoming worse—unrestrained, rampant, full of commotion. How would you, Bustle, like all of that uncontrolled energy of yours splattered about the room?" Maag or Feeno would do the cleaning up, never for a moment suspecting the nature of the mess.

"Oh, you do not think you would splatter?" taunted the Lady, pretending the balloon had spoken. "Airy, are you? I do believe, Bustle, you are correct. Your green color would not stick. There would be no trace of you. No mess. You would be dispersed, scattered to the corners of the world.

"But I should be generous," acknowledged Lady Idris. "Gothelyn must have a hand in this. Once Mother Nature dies within you—indeed, she may already be dead—Gothelyn will be of a mind to pop your bubbles, and—bang!—she will blow you all to smithereens."

In the closet, Feeno hugged himself tightly to control his shaking. He felt as if his head were spinning. *What on earth is going on?* he wondered. *Why is Lady Idris talking to pig bladders?*

"At the moment, however," said the Lady, placing the candle on the table next to Jocelyn's head, "I must tend to you, Glum, the last of the malign spirits that shall *ever* inhabit my daughter. You are as unpleasant as your kin, but my contempt for you . . . It far exceeds that which I felt for the others. I detested them, yes, but they prompted my respect. They possessed zeal, pluck, fortitude. You are a mere shadow of the likes of them. Even your predecessor, light-blue Sorrowful, shone in comparison."

Lady Idris rummaged through her satchel, drawing out . . . Feeno couldn't see what the objects were or what she was doing with them. But when she went around the bed opposite the candle and leaned toward her daughter, he saw that in one hand she held a deflated, colorless pig bladder whose opening she'd secured to the end of a . . . *What is that?* he wondered. *Why, it looks like the hollow stalk that Angwyn made into a musical instrument, the reed, which he used to play for the amusement of Jocelyn when she was a baby, much to the displeasure of his wife.*

"Open wide," the Lady cooed as she pulled down on Jocelyn's lower lip with two fingers and pushed up against her upper lip with the index one. "Unlock your jaw!" she barked.

When Jocelyn didn't respond, Lady Idris roared, "Are you dead?"

Feeno clapped his hand over his mouth so he wouldn't cry out.

The prospect that Jocelyn might be dead did not appear to grieve Lady Idris; she seemed annoyed. She placed her hand on the girl's chest, apparently checking her heart, then pumped her diaphragm until Jocelyn gasped.

"Good girl!" the Lady exclaimed. "I feared you had disappointed me by ingesting hemlock instead of elderberry."

How potent the sleeping powder must be, thought Feeno. *The roars and cackles, the pounding on Jocelyn's chest . . . how could she not awake?*

Lady Idris dropped the reed and pig bladder onto the bed (*I must learn to call it a balloon,* thought Feeno). Using both hands to pry open Jocelyn's jaw, she kept it spread by thrusting the fingers of one hand into the girl's mouth.

"Do not dare bite me!" she cried. "If you cause me to bleed . . ." Slipping the free end of the hollow stalk into the girl's mouth, the Lady removed her fingers, allowing Jocelyn's mouth to snap shut around it.

"Gothelyn, we must have another heart-to-heart," the Lady said, as she checked that the balloon was well attached to the reed. "Do not pretend you cannot hear me. Your father spoke to you from afar as you slept, and I am not only present, but I am also more commanding than he. That you are asleep makes my conversation with you more agreeable."

Lady Idris bent closer to Jocelyn.

"I have done more on your behalf than any mother would," she asserted. "But you have shown no gratitude. I could perform magic on you to extract Glum, but that would tire me and compel you; it would not make you a collaborator. Show your consent to this exorcism by acting voluntarily for your own good. Exhale the gloom that resides in you and inhale the joy that surrounds you for which I take full credit." Wrapping her hands around the stalk to close the finger holes, Lady Idris laughingly remarked, "The music you make, as you blow through the reed, should be a funeral hymn." Then she sternly exhorted, "Expel Glum!"

Expel it? questioned Feeno, brushing flies from his head. *But Glum is . . .* He shook his head rapidly to jiggle his brain so that it might work better. *Miss Glum has been Jocelyn's name for the past two years,* he reflected. *Glum is a mood, a temporary but dominant disposition, Lady Idris calls it. Now she is describing it as a . . .*

Oh, my! Feeno realized all at once. *Glum is a bad spirit, and the Lady is urging Jocelyn to rid herself of it. But how can she blow gloom into a balloon?*

Apparently Jocelyn couldn't—or wouldn't—because the balloon didn't inflate.

At length, Lady Idris threw up her hands. "Do you lack the will, Gothelyn, the determination? Or is that vile spirit, weak as it is, too powerful? Glum, do not dare hold on! Let go of my child!"

I never could have imagined it, Feeno thought, *but is Lady Idris, after all, a good mother? Didn't Jocelyn fear that the poisonous spirit inside her, the likely cause of her sick spells, would kill her? The Lady is simply trying to cure her daughter. Odd-year birthdays must be occasions for exorcizing spirits. Isn't Lady Idris, on this thirteenth birthday eve, calling for Glum to depart or for Jocelyn to banish this evil spirit that keeps the girl from health and peace of mind?*

"My patience thins," said the Lady. Her voice, now cold, no longer betrayed feeling. "Once more, Gothelyn, I must save you from yourself. Your debt to me is great. It will take your whole life to repay it."

Fingering the white crystal at her neck, Lady Idris called on Glum to come forth this instant, then mumbled something. *What? The sounds have rhythm,* thought Feeno, *as if she's chanting.* He pressed his ear against the closet door but could not decipher them.

Slowly and fitfully, the balloon filled.

Lady Idris slumped against a bedpost, gasping.

When she had caught her breath, the Lady smiled. "You look colorless, Glum. I believe I have succeeded. You are the evidence that Mother Nature is dead within you." Her hand on the bed, she circled to the bedside table. "I only wish that Gothelyn had demonstrated her loyalty to me by killing Mother Nature herself." Picking up the candle, she brought it close to the balloon. "Do I see a blemish?" she asked. "Has Mother Nature still the power to soil you? Or is it my eyes, bleary from exhaustion, that make you look smudged, like unclean glass?"

Jocelyn coughed.

Lady Idris froze. "Gothelyn, do not dare come down sick!"

Jocelyn's breath labored.

"Mother Nature lives!" wailed the Lady, collapsing to her knees.

Jocelyn wheezed.

"Curses!" screamed Lady Idris. The shout caused Feeno to jump and nearly fall against the closet door.

The Lady rested for a while, then put down the candle and removed the reed from her daughter's mouth. Pulling loose the balloon and tying off its opening, she held the balloon in her hand. It was only half the size of the smallest one, the pale-blue.

"How pathetic you look!" Lady Idris taunted. "Of course, it follows: there never was much to you." She retrieved the candle and shone its light on the ceiling. It lit upon the purple balloon.

"Look, Glum, at Tragic," said the Lady. "It had a melodramatic flair and prose that was high flown, but it gave the child presence. Or behold Smolder," she continued, illuminating the orange balloon. "What a surly spirit! It commanded my attention, though, because it acted as if, at any moment, it might set off a conflagration.

"But you, bleak spirit," she went on, drawing the candle down next to Glum, "are but spent smoke, your color ashen, your pallor cadaverous." She let go of the balloon, and very gradually it rose.

Lady Idris put the reed into her satchel, as she watched Jocelyn throw herself from side to side. The attack was worsening, but it did not wake her.

"Mother Nature is tenacious," said the Lady, "but you, Gothelyn, are complicit, and it has made you ill. Stop this folly. My triumph over Mother Nature, whom I am rightfully supplanting, is inevitable. You are *mine,* not *hers."*

Holding the handles of the bag with one hand and the candle with the other, she swept from Feeno's sight. He heard the door slam.

CHAPTER 10

AFTERBIRTH

"ANOTHER BIRTHDAY RUINED!" As Idris descended the attic stairs, she threw back her hood and shook out her hair, auburn curls exploding around her. "What is a mother to do?"

One thought was to substitute hemlock for elderberry and pour the poisonous mixture down the throat of Gothelyn. That would destroy Mother Nature. Unfortunately, it would kill the child as well, although that was perhaps a small sacrifice to make for the good of the household.

No, Idris reflected, *I should not make such a joke, even to myself. I have invested a great deal of time and energy to perfect this child, and I expect a sizable return. Better to slip a bit of poison into each of the meals Gothelyn eats and hope that Mother Nature dies first.* But even that she knew she would not do.

Idris wished she could return to the attic and extract immediately the budding spirit that Mother Nature must now be nurturing in Gothelyn. But casting spells weakened Idris and her magic. She must first regain her power. Also, the spell was quite specific: once a year until the victim . . . No, that was not well put. Once a year until the *subject* was five years old, then once every two years was all the child could tolerate. Also, the procedure could only succeed on the birthday eve of the subject. The spell was silent about how many trials the magician must make for its fruition, although it warned of *unpleasantries* that could arise if the child proved recalcitrant.

Gothelyn, her mother reflected, *had caused trouble from the beginning.* The child could not be completely blamed for her own conception, but what was the egg doing there, beckoning like a harlot? Husband, too, was at fault, for he had exploited the youthful vulnerabilities of his wife by plying her with spirits. She had vowed that from then on, she would not imbibe liquor. She also would sublimate her juvenile sexual impulse into the mature, civil passion of subjugating others.

But how inconsiderate of the embryo to take up residence in her without even a *May I please?* It acted as if it owned her womb. How audacious to squat like a vagabond who had not the goodwill to pay room and board!

And the pregnancy—what an ordeal! First the morning sickness; she could not even enjoy a hard-boiled egg. She tried to abort the fetus, as her mother, Ceridwyn, had successfully done several times after Idris was born. (Idris always imagined her mother did not want another child because it was impossible to improve upon perfection. There was also the fact that Ceridwyn did not like children.) Idris took heaps of sage and tears of my lady, the first to stimulate her uterus, the second to expel the intruder, but they only gave her loose bowels. She even resorted to unsafe doses of columbine, which made her deathly ill; the uninvited guest, however, remained unmoved.

The fetus weakened her, absorbing her nutriments, as if it were an earthworm taking advantage of fertile soil. Most maddening: while the embryo depleted her, it fattened her; she did not enjoy the irony. No longer could she wear her fine, small-waisted gowns. Was there any better proof of its malice? Idiot Husband would beam as he listened to the heartbeats of the coiled parasite and coo as he stroked the bloated belly of his wife, even as the ingrate kicked viciously at her organs. Angwyn cared more for *it* than her!

The birth . . . No, she could not bear to think of it.

The afterbirth—not the placenta, but that other discard she called *Infant*—fussed and made demands upon her, tempting Idris to abandon it in the forest. Often she took it there, once even leaving it for an afternoon, but each time she relented. *Is this a maternal instinct?* she had wondered. *No, I do not suffer from that sentiment. My reluctance suggests the child has a purpose, namely, to be the subject of a scientific or magical project.* In any case, Idris instead disposed of meddlesome Husband and the indulgent grandparents and handed over the care of the baby to Maag and Feeno.

In the final months of the first year, however, once Infant gained locomotion, it was nearly impossible to evade. Angwyn had named it *Jocelyn* but had insisted on pronouncing it *Joy*celyn just to infuriate his wife. Idris had derived some satisfaction from discovering the name meant *one of the Goths* and had taken to calling it *Goth*elyn to irritate Husband.

The name correctly characterized how disgusting and crude Infant was, but when it became a rampant scourge, Idris was horrified that she might actually have borne a barbarian. It crawled from here to there and up and down stairs, getting into cupboards and drawers, strewing books, even rumpling or ripping pages, and knocking down ornaments from shelves or putting them in its mouth as if to devour them. In short, Miss Bustle, as it became known, proved more of a nuisance than the unborn child and Infant. Idris was astonished that a mere toddler could threaten her domination of the household. Headstrong and irrational, it frustrated and confounded her at every turn.

Vowing to bend it to her will, Idris searched the library of her father-in-law, Oldric, a scientist at the university in Brynmor. She nearly passed over *Birthday Wishes,* certain that the book would nauseate her, but she was curious about it because it was one of the texts Oldric, who was also a magician, had made her promise not to read. Perusing the book, which was written in Gothic (a good omen!) but which she could decipher by using the white crystal as if it were an eyeglass, she became exhilarated by its birthday-eve magic spell. Together with the crystal, it gave her hope that she might reclaim her life.

Indeed, after Idris extracted the spirit Bustle from Gothelyn at the end of her first year, one-year-old Gothelyn (or Miss Gullible, as Idris named her) was easier to manage, although she was foolish, could not enunciate, spoke gibberish, and could not handle a fork or spoon. In the ensuing years, however, things became more difficult. Gothelyn resorted to temper tantrums, relentless questioning, sullenness, impudence, theatrics, and other maddening behavior. It was only in the last four years, when Gothelyn turned first sad and then grim, that it appeared Idris was on the verge of success. She reveled in her imminent victory over Mother Nature, who had spawned these sorry spirits.

Not only will my life become tranquil, she thought, *I will gain more fully the admiration of the Brynmor Society of Benevolent Magicians, which will spread word of my triumph, securing for me everlasting fame among magicians and scientists as well as grateful parents everywhere, for who else in the history of the world has created a perfect, obedient child and can show how to replicate it? Gothelyn will no longer be one of the Goths. I will rename her Perffaith in keeping with her role as the model of perfection.*

Depositing the satchel in her workshop, Idris descended the main staircase. She desired a midnight refreshment, hoping a treat would lessen her ire. Normally she would have rung for Maag to bring it to her room, but she felt a need to unwind after the bad episode with Gothelyn and the spirit, Glum; the light exertion of a short walk might prove just the thing.

I would like to know more about those spirits, she thought. *Where is the locus of their consciousness? And how do they move themselves? I will make a trial on one of them to see if it will reveal the essence of its pungency. But which spirit? Gullible, that is the one! She will be easy to manipulate, because she is almost as good as gold, so trusting and naïve. Too bad she is not brighter.*

CHAPTER 11

GEOMETRIC DECOR

AT THE FOOT OF THE STAIRS, Idris bristled at a bouquet of bluebells, primroses, and forget-me-nots. "Who is responsible for this frivolity?" she grumbled to herself, knocking the arrangement from its pedestal, shattering the glass vase. *Maag, of course. Was this her idea of a birthday surprise for Gothelyn if or when she is able to come down for breakfast? Maag should know I do not want nature—even dying flowers—brought into the house, unless it is required for my experiments.*

These thoughts brought to mind Oldric and Elda's prissy furniture, which was also out of place. Idris strode to the parlor at the front of the house and regarded the pair of matching upholstered chairs with curved legs and three-toed feet with disdain.

"You are not mine," she said. "You are too French. You show the taste of the in-laws." *I have been remiss,* she scolded herself. *I should fashion this house and its grounds completely to my taste.* One example, already in place, was the tidy ornamental garden, manicured by Feeno according to her specifications.

Another example was what she called the *swath of death*—an exact, even path of dead earth. The swath had been created when Angwyn had fled the estate. Enraged, Idris had sent death throes after him, cutting a trail of desolation in their pursuit. She did not know how far the spell had traveled before it caught up with him. She assumed it had killed Angwyn, especially because that fawning horse of his came back without him. It would never have left him had he been alive.

The swath of death, displaying excellent linear preciseness, led across the lawn and into the forest, and for a long time, nothing had grown in that path. It irritated her no end when nature reasserted itself, spoiling the path with weeds. She retaliated by having Feeno spray a solution of arsenic, lead, and garlic onto it and ordering him to treat the path often with these toxins to maintain its fine lines; the forest swath, however, reverted to its former, wild state.

Yes, she thought, *too much in the house and its surroundings remind me of despicable Husband, interfering Mother-in-Law, and pompous Father-in-Law. Has their taste damaged Gothelyn? How dare the in-laws and Husband corrupt the child with their leavings! I created a proper atmosphere of mind and manners, but the furnishings, decorations, and so much else . . . Do they explain, in part, the refusal of Gothelyn to be made in the image I desire?*

Upending the matching chairs, Idris now examined other objects in the parlor, making mental notes of those she felt unsuitable. She cringed at the sight of the paintings by her maudlin husband. She wondered why Oldric and Elda allowed their son to hang them—likely Elda's influence. *The landscapes are false,* Idris observed. *They idealize nature, which contradicts my discovery of its universal pungency. Where are the disemboweled carcasses, the picked bones, the putrid earth, the blight upon plants, and the sap bleeding from trees?* Usually, she ignored his landscapes as trifles, but now they appeared menacing. Angwyn had hung his oils, it seemed, all over the house—not unlike a cur that urinates to mark its territory. *I must dispose of them,* she vowed.

She left the parlor and strolled down the main hallway toward the kitchen at the rear of the house. On either side were portraits of undistinguished, family ancestors painted by artists more skillful than her husband. She paused before a large portrait of Elda's father, whose eyes were obliterated from the countless times Idris had shot them with arrows from the upstairs balustrade. *How accurate my aim,* she congratulated herself.

Her mood soured, however, when she took a few more paces down the hallway and stepped on broken glass and scattered flowers. They had not been swept up.

Where is Maag? she wondered, vexed. *Did she not hear the vase break to pieces? A housekeeper should know when a house needs tidying. Besides, there is no time like the present to begin altering the furnishings.*

She turned into the dining room and rang for Maag, whose small quarters were across from the kitchen. Idris had not been in the dining room for some time. Here were two more paintings by Angwyn that must be taken down. She checked the table and chairs to see if they had feet and was pleased that they did not.

"You rang, my Luminary?" asked Maag from the hallway.

Idris turned. "You sleep too soundly," she scolded. "Stay alert to the needs of the house. Here is your present charge: clean up the flowers and shards of glass. I will not tolerate an unkempt house."

"You rang in the belly of the night to disgust keeping house?"

"Not just housekeeping," said Idris. "But it comes first."

Maag examined the broken glass and cut flowers on the floor. "These flowers . . ."

"Throw them out," said Idris. "They are wild."

"I can see they've been misbehaving—knocking over the vase and strewing themselves about."

"I can tolerate only cultivated ones," said Idris.

"I'll tell Feelo to watch for unruly flowers sneaking into the ornamental garden," Maag assured her. "Would you like me to gather some of the housebroken ones from the ornamental garden and put together a spray of them for Jocie's hatching day?"

"No!"

That's how I should always speak to her, thought Idris. *Why bother with explanation or conversation? It is my civility, I suppose. I am overly patient and too forgiving of idiocy. I must cool my blood. If it were ice cold, I would keep to commands and have the tasks that are required more efficiently executed.* "Now, get busy keeping house!" she commanded in her head-of-the-household voice.

"Wait!" Idris shouted.

"I haven't started," said Maag.

"What are better than cultivated flowers? Artificial ones, of course! We will make straight-edged, symmetrical flowers of cloth from the garments of Mother-in-Law. Unlike natural flowers, they will not need water or—thank the stars—sunshine. Also, their style—I shall term it geometric—will be in accordance with my new decorative design. These flowers will not be fashioned after the inferior ones that nature has produced. They will be ideal!

"But we must clear the way for them and other, correct furnishings!" Idris exclaimed. "After you throw out the wildflowers . . ." She was about to add the hand-decorated dishes to the things to be immediately discarded, but she had just noticed that they were missing. "Where is the pottery Mother-in-Law displayed on the sideboard?" she asked.

Maag hesitated.

"Why are you tongue-tied?" questioned Idris. "Answer me truthfully, and you will not suffer pain."

"I put them in a tree," Maag whispered.

"A tree?" *But of course,* realized Idris.

"At day's crack, my High-minded, I'll fetch them back."

"No, leave them," said Idris. "I desired that you rid the house of them, and you have."

"I have the second sense," said Maag proudly, tilting back her head and expanding her chest.

"Second sight, sixth sense," corrected Idris.

"I've got all that?" exclaimed Maag, her mouth dropping open.

"You have neither," said Idris. "You are a thief."

"Now, where was I?" Idris asked herself. "Oh, yes, your chores. After you sweep the floor, hurry to the kitchen, prepare a delicacy, and drop it off in my sitting room. Third, go to the attic and bring me the golden balloon. Fourth, fetch thyme from the vegetable garden and dandelions from the wild (an exception to my ban) for my bath. I am speaking of thyme the herb, Maag, not clock time."

"Thanks for the expletive, my Linguist," said Maag appreciatively. "Good thing I have your wits about me or I'd be confused. I have thyme in the panty off the—"

"Fresh thyme, Maag. Fresh from the vegetable garden."

"Have you, like Jocie, the testinal ingratitude?"

I must remedy her mind and language! screamed Idris in her head. *Soon! For my sake! But what is the corrective?* She took deep draughts of air, exhaling slowly. *Didn't I just vow to avoid explanations and stick to commands?* she scolded herself. But she proceeded to explain, perhaps out of habit, that thyme was meant to purge Gothelyn of a bad spirit, not move her bowels. "I certainly do not wish to move mine," she commented. "It is disgusting.

"Fortunately, thyme has other uses," Idris went on. "In bathwater, it infuses strength. It invigorates, as bracing air does, but has the advantage of not mussing hair.

"Also, Maag, to be clear: I want you to fetch dandelions the flowers, not—"

"You don't need to clarify the two of those," cut in Maag. "It was only that once, years in the rear, did I scout the woods for those dandy lions. That was afore I upgraded to a hortacultist."

"Fifth," said Idris, trying to keep on task, "throw out the three-toed chairs in the parlor and all of the paintings by my husband. Later, we will make a bonfire of them. Oh, another exception: do not take down the landscape in my sitting room; that one amuses me. Mother-in-Law insisted it was her favorite. She would so enjoy, she often said, to wander in those woods."

"Pity they're not real," said Maag. "Instead, Lady Elda is trodding the grimy woods that bound our asylum. But pardon, my Unnaturalist. My bed beckons. I need to answer it, so I'm ripe for the jobs that have been put upon me . . . if it's all the same to you."

"It is not the same!" hissed Idris. "Clean and tidy the house while I—"

"Now?"

"Most definitely now!" Idris exclaimed in anger. "The disorderliness is not later. Do you expect me to tolerate it until it is more convenient for you?"

"But it's past sunsink and afore the sun's resurrection," protested Maag.

Idris pressed her temples on either side of her head. "Is it too late to unscramble her mind and put her language right?" she asked no one in particular.

"I'd be more upright if I got my sleep," offered Maag.

I must do it tonight—for my sake! It will raise my spirits after the disappointment with Miss Glum. But what are the correctives? I must peruse my books! She took deep draughts of air, exhaling slowly.

"Before the fifth task," Idris directed, "fill my bathtub with buckets of water from the well."

"That makes a hoard of things to do, my Taskmaster."

Idris studied her. "Do I ask too much of you, Maag?"

"Oh no, it's what I've come to suspect, Malady."

Idris bowed her head, shaking it from side to side. *Perhaps Maag is a lost cause,* she thought. *It might be best to dispose of her and start over with a fresh vic—subject.*

Idris turned and walked down the hallway to the library at the front of the house. *Why is it,* she wondered, *that I am surrounded by half-wits? Maag is the prime example. The incessant scrutiny she requires, if she is to accomplish even basic chores, such as tidying, has caused me to neglect the interior design of this house.*

Not this *house. My house!*

Every room should display the geometric style. My chairs will be triangular, hexagonal, spherical. Drapes, rugs, and wall hangings will display geometric patterns. This indoor environment of points and lines will foster mathematical thinking in Gothelyn as well as Feeno, even Maag. Accordingly, tasks I assign them will be carried out accurately, efficiently, and appropriately. What an ideal household we will make!

Unlike the household of my youth, she thought bitterly. Idris had lived with her parents in a house of stone and sod, its roof covered with thatch. Inside, the walls were smoothed with mud. The dirt floor was uneven. There were no windows and but one door. Half the space was given to animal pens, the rest to dining, cooking, and sleeping. The style, if it were to have a name, was *natural*—in other words, primitive and crude. The only furnishings were box beds and chairs with short legs to allow the family to sit below the cloud of smoke from the peat fire.

Having collected a few promising books on the wizardry of language, Idris returned to her chambers, pausing in the sitting room to peer into the romantic landscape by Angwyn. Idris had read that every work of art possessed a magic of its own. *Besides the obvious, what secrets does this painting hold?* she wondered.

Idris turned and regarded the grandfather clock. *And what about contrivances such as this?* she mused. *Have they, too, a magic of their own?*

CHAPTER 12

A BRONZE SURPRISE

FEENO HAD HEARD footfalls descending the stairs, but how could he be sure Lady Idris had gone down them? Might Sound deceive him, enabling the Lady to burst into her daughter's room without warning in search of something she'd forgotten, such as a disobedient gnome? It was hard for him to believe she hadn't found him out.

He knew he could trust his sense of smell, however. So far, Smell had proved reliable in this house. Even so, he waited a considerable time after Lady Idris's scent had dissipated before he poked his head out from the closet.

Jocelyn tossed and turned in the moonlight, gasping for breath and choking. *If all of her birthday attacks have been this bad, how has she withstood them?* he wondered. *If this one worsens . . .*

Using his tinderbox, Feeno lit two candles on the walls. Toad scampered in from a corner of the room.

"Ah, my pet, you're safe," said Feeno, scooping it up and placing it on the bed. "If only I could say the same of Jocelyn." The toad climbed onto the girl's chest. "Have you an idea, Toad? How can we help her?"

The balloons, Feeno noticed, were hovering above them, nearly within reach. *I should grab Glum, a party to this attack, and return its air to Jocelyn's lungs.* He eyed the bellows that leaned against the fireplace.

I haven't got a reed, but could I transfer Glum from its balloon to the bellows and then . . . But what benefit would come from forcing low-spiritedness down Jocelyn's throat?

Indeed, would the airy spirit of any of these balloons do Jocelyn any good? Her mother claimed the spirits were bad. But if so, why was Jocelyn in the throes of an attack? Shouldn't she feel better because Glum had been removed?

Mother Nature must be still alive and potent, thought Feeno. That was how Lady Idris explained Jocelyn's illness: Mother Nature was evil and filling the girl with poison.

But Jocelyn had told him that during the sick spells, she felt as if her breath had been taken from her, and she was trying to retrieve it. Feeno squeezed his eyes, so intently was he thinking. *Might Jocelyn,* he speculated, *be suffering now from a loss of spirit—even one as sorry as Glum?*

Glum was gloomy, of course, and Smolder sullen. Those were bad moods, but Glum and Smolder weren't evil, nor was Tragic or Brazen or Fury or any of the rest. He'd been around Jocelyn when those spirits dominated her. She was a handful, he acknowledged, but he never thought of her as wicked.

If anyone seems diabolic, he thought, *it's Lady Idris.* He found it impossible to believe she was a good mother. For one thing, she wasn't . . . well . . . motherly. She took no joy in her daughter and displayed no love for her. She never hugged her or touched her gently.

Jocelyn's chest now shuddered, and her breathing stopped. Feeno pounced on her, which sent Toad scurrying. Feeno pumped on her diaphragm, as Lady Idris had done (though, perhaps, a bit softer), and sighed with relief as Jocelyn resumed breathing. *Might I remedy the attack,* he wondered, *if I use the bellows to force more of the house's air into her?* No, in spite of his pumping just now, her breath remained short and rough. The so-called virtuous atmosphere the Lady claimed she'd made might resuscitate, but it wasn't a cure.

Looking up, he reconsidered the balloons, recalling that Jocelyn didn't want their air taken from her. Apparently sensing his attention, they retreated and assumed their customary disarray. *Which one, if any,* he wondered, *would best help the girl by providing her with a large blast of hearty breath?* Smolder, the orange, was the biggest, but most of the others were good-sized. Only blue Sorrowful and gray Glum didn't look as if they'd give her more than a puff.

But won't Lady Idris see that one is missing? worried Feeno. *No, she won't—at least, not for a long while.* It seemed she made a visit to Jocelyn's room only once every other year, so the next was a long way off, more distant than he could hold in his mind. By then, who knew what might be?

But wouldn't the Lady notice a change in Jocelyn, which might lead her to inspect the balloons? If, say, he was to infuse the girl with Brazen, how insolent she would become! Or if he were to imbue her with Fury, wouldn't she repeat those thunderous tantrums that Lady Idris complained had shattered her nerves?

Yes, he had to consider not only the amount of air but also the type of mood with which he should fill Jocelyn. Evidence of brashness or a fiery temper would alert the Lady that something was amiss. Purple Tragic also wouldn't do. It was too theatrical; Lady Idris would spot its style in a moment. Green Bustle was reckless, yellow Quizzical overly curious, and Smolder surly. As for Sorrowful and Glum, he'd already ruled them out for lack of substance.

Oh, but I've forgotten Gullible! realized Feeno. That impressionable, good spirit had dominated the child when she was one. That was Lady Idris's favorite year, she'd said, because Jocelyn was relatively submissive and trusting. If he were to fill Jocelyn with those qualities, Lady Idris wouldn't see that anything was wrong; indeed, she likely would cite her daughter's compliant conduct as evidence of the girl's progress toward her mother's goal.

Jocelyn wheezed, her breath whistling. Sitting on the edge of her bed, Feeno turned her on her side and patted her sweat-soaked back, hoping it would relieve her congestion. It did not. Jocelyn rolled onto her back and rocked to and fro, gasping for breath.

I have to replenish her, Feeno decided, pushing himself to his feet. He pulled and shoved the dresser, but he couldn't move it until he'd taken out its drawers. Positioning it under golden Gullible, he clambered up.

"Drat!" he exclaimed. The balloon was beyond reach.

Dropping to the floor, he dragged a stool to the dresser and heaved it onto its top, then climbed up and set the stool upright. Mounting it, he rose haltingly to his feet.

How high I am! he thought. *And how unsteady, especially with nothing to hold onto and the flies pestering me! But the golden balloon is so near, just above me.*

Tilting his head back, he came face-to-face with . . . Brazen! *Where has Gullible gone? There, in the corner. Was it scared off? Or did Brazen shove it away?*

Feeno scrambled down. Throwing aside the rug, he pushed the dresser across the wood floor to the corner. Keeping an eye on the golden balloon, he climbed, his hand on the wall for support, until he was balanced on the stool. Standing on tiptoes and reaching up, he gently took Gullible in his hands. But from behind, a blur shot past his ear and knocked it from his grasp. There before him was Brazen.

"Go away!" pleaded Feeno. "You'd be a disaster for Jocelyn."

The bronze balloon flew into his chest. Buckling at its force, he threw his arms around it, hoping its buoyancy would help maintain his footing. At that moment, there was a knock on the door, immediately followed by Maag rushing into the room. She gasped, and Feeno, teetering on the stool, flipped and tumbled down.

As he struck the floor, his chest sank into the balloon, which cushioned him, but his weight caused it to elongate . . . and then burst!

Out from it, head over heels, rolled a girl who grew increasingly large. She was the color of bronze.

CHAPTER 13

THE UNRELIABILITY OF MAGIC

JOCELYN'S GRANDFATHER heard a pop. *What has Sound delivered to me now?* he wondered. The noise seemed to have come from the attic. In Jocelyn's room, there were pig bladders filled with breath—yes, breath—composed of the various dominant spirits or dispositions the girl had had over the years. Might one of those bladders have popped? If so, what were the ramifications?

He'd heard about the bladders from Sound. Years ago, when Jocelyn was a baby, Oldric had coaxed Sound—largely by magic, of course, but a magic so imperfect it required wheedling on his part—to alert him of any cries of distress the baby might make. He'd feared the property was too big for Jocelyn's voice to carry to every corner of the house and the grounds around it, not to mention the vegetable garden and farmyard, and he'd come to believe he could not trust Idris to respond to the baby's needs.

Oldric's . . . *change* . . . hadn't altered his arrangement with Sound. As Jocelyn grew older, it even expanded its scope, providing Oldric with not only her wails but also her words as well as the words of others and noises that pertained to the girl.

Oldric worried, however, that he'd not sufficiently fostered in Sound a discriminating intellect, which meant it didn't have a good grasp of what might be important for its master to know. The last piece of knowledge he'd received, for example, was that the day before her birthday, Jocelyn had eaten boiled oatmeal for breakfast and at midday, a piece of mutton she could only ingest by keeping it away from her nose. Now, that was all well and good, but why hadn't he been informed how Jocelyn was holding up after she'd been subjected to Idris's birthday-eve spell? It would have been cast an hour or so ago, but Sound hadn't given him a hint about it.

Nor did Oldric know Elda's whereabouts. Was she still taking a walk in the woods, as Sound had reported more than twelve years ago? Why had she not come home to protect and care for Jocelyn? Was his wife—heaven forbid—dead?

And what of Angwyn? According to Sound, he'd run off to save his own skin. What sort of father would do that? Perhaps Oldric should give his son the benefit of the doubt. Angwyn had appeared in Jocelyn's dreams. But what help was that?

Not that Oldric himself had been of much service, especially after having taken on the trappings of a long-case clock (he'd vowed never to call himself a *grandfather clock,* because that was the name Idris had given him).

Daughter-in-Law, ironically, was one source of information. Oldric had died, she'd told him, from a head injury he'd sustained when he was thrown from his horse. "Your fellow scientists and magicians send their condolences," she'd said with a sly smile. Often she would taunt him, especially about her membership in the Society of Benevolent Magicians. How she had managed to become a member of the all-male Society was a mystery to Oldric.

He wished more events occurred here in the sitting room. Why had Idris removed the chairs—all but one? Wasn't this the place people were supposed to sit? How he would enjoy listening in on a conversation! Unfortunately, the sitting room was used almost entirely as a passage. Jocelyn was the only one who sat here, and that was when her mother was not ready to receive her.

Of course, now and then events occurred within the field of his senses, and one of them had been quite extraordinary. On an evening early this past fall, Jocelyn had been very late for her interview with her mother, and Oldric had to slow time in his usual way, which was to resist the falling weights within him by slowing the exhalation of his breath. To his surprise, a toad crept into the sitting room. *What is it doing here, poor fellow?* he wondered. It gazed at Angwyn's painting, probably longing for the woods his son had depicted. Oldric had heard about Idris's dealings with animals. If she should get hold of this toad . . .

From what he could observe, the creature chiefly nosed about the baseboard along the wall that separated the sitting room from Idris's bedroom. *It must be seeking an escape,* he thought. *No! No!* he wanted to shout. *That's not the way!*

Suddenly, the bedroom door opened. The toad froze. Idris, her nose in the air in her customary, haughty manner, stepped into the sitting room and turned to face the long-case clock. She frowned. "Are you keeping good time?" she asked accusingly. "I am certain Gothelyn is late. I will see that Feeno gives you a good oiling." Idris started back into her bedroom but halted, sniffing the air. Oldric had sensed it, too—a foul smell coming from the toad. It would not take Idris long to locate the odor's source.

Oldric could think of no way to help this unfortunate creature. The suspense over what would now befall it made him hold his breath. Oldric stopped ticking. This was a new sensation, and it alarmed him. Had his life depended on his behaving like clockwork? Had he endangered the clock's inner mechanisms by manipulating time? Had he finally broken?

How odd, he thought. *Idris has stopped dead.*

The toad cocked its head, as if wondering why the witch had come to a standstill. Why, indeed? She wasn't frozen in fear. Oldric released his breath. The *tick-tock* resumed, and Idris recommenced sniffing the air. As she followed her nose in pursuit of the odor, Oldric experimented. He stopped exhaling, and again Idris froze.

Of course! My breathing, or the lack thereof. That's the key!

For the sake of Jocelyn, he'd varied the exhalation of his breath to slow or accelerate time, the ticking and hands of the clock acting accordingly. It'd never occurred to him that, by holding his breath, he could stop time altogether. Was this an aspect of Idris's magic spell, one she doubtless knew nothing about? Without time, nothing could happen, which meant that Idris couldn't capture the toad.

But neither can the toad escape, he reasoned. *Wait! Didn't the toad move, cocking its head? How . . . But no matter! If it can do that . . . Run away, little fellow!* he wished he could say. The toad, however, realized its advantage on its own. But instead of running to safety, it scampered behind the long-case clock.

No! No! thought Oldric. *She'll find you there!*

The toad, paying no heed, of course, to a voice it couldn't hear, leaned against the clock's base, as if trying to merge with it. Oldric, frustrated though he was, felt such warmth from it he couldn't help but whirr, as if wheels inside him were spinning.

Thinking it risky to hold his breath for long, he exhaled, allowing the weights within him to fall and the ticking to begin. Idris once more took up sniffing the air until she'd come nearly full circle and was facing the toad's hiding place. Oldric again held his breath, freezing Idris. The toad, apparently perceiving its vulnerability, scurried toward the arched doorway of the sitting room and rounded it, allowing Oldric to continue exhaling. Idris, acting as if nothing unusual had happened, peered behind the long-case clock, then traced the smell partway to the archway before she gave up and returned to her bedroom.

How had the toad kept moving when time stood still, Oldric wondered later? The reason, he speculated, might be why his colleagues at the university rejected magic: it was too unpredictable. Science involved laws that did not change, but magic's laws were of a different sort: they varied case by case. Regarding the toad, magic had made an exception in order to save its life. But why? Could it be that magic had a fondness for toads?

Oldric took advantage of his newfound ability. He began toying with his daughter-in-law, stopping and starting her when she passed through the sitting room. It was solely for his amusement, because she gave no indication of noticing her strange gait. But he took great pleasure in his power over her, however small.

And why shouldn't Oldric take pleasure at the expense of Idris? It was she who had put him in this fix! Not that he didn't bear a large measure of responsibility for his lot. Headstrong and confident in his powers, he had underestimated how ambitious and clever Idris was. He had to confess, too, that he had been smitten by her beauty.

He'd wanted to believe that she had but an innocent curiosity about magic and his scientific investigations. He had been flattered—fool that he was—by her praise and by her desire for knowledge of his expertness, especially because his wife and son were not interested in the least. Elda had a passion for needlework, decorative painting, and herbal remedies, and Angwyn, a student at the university in the town of Brynmor (the same place Oldric taught), was caught up with superficial studies, such as art and literature.

Oldric's grave mistake had been giving Idris access to his library and the white crystal. He remembered so well that fateful conversation before Jocelyn's birth when he was showing her his books from all parts of the world.

"You read Sanskrit?" Idris had asked in surprise.

"No," he answered, "but I have the means to make it intelligible." Telling her about the magical properties of crystals, he displayed on his palm an especially potent one. "In conjunction with an incantation," he said, "which I will confide to you, this white crystal has the power to make texts, whatever their language, comprehensible. It is but one of its powers. I do not dare reveal its others."

"Nor would I hear of them," she asserted. "I desire only to advance my learning. That I may read books in all languages is a godsend. Besides, it will while away my time as I incubate in my womb—glad of the burden, of course—your blessed grandchild."

"Some of these books . . ."

"What troubles you, Father?"

"It's that you're young and innocent," said Oldric. "Your judgment may be flawed. Certain of my books are dangerous."

"Point me away from those!" she cried. "I shall have nothing to do with them." She eyed the stone. "I do confess the crystal draws me to it," she said. "Is that a sign of its trust? Oh, dear Father, may I hold it?"

He let her. He also gave her permission to use it for reading while he was away at the university for the spring term (he was leaving for Brynmor the next day), but he insisted that she not take it from the library, which served as his study.

Oldric did not return to the country house until the middle of June, the start of his summer holiday. Angwyn had arrived in May, a few days before Jocelyn's birth, having begged leave to be with his expectant wife, whom he described to the department authorities as *having complications* (but whom Elda had described in a letter to him as *being insufferable)*.

"Where are the servants?" Oldric asked his son on the day of his arrival.

"Idris dismissed them after you and I left for the spring term," replied Angwyn. "She said they were ne'er-do-wells and that she hadn't the patience for them."

"Lyel a ne'er-do-well?" questioned Oldric. Lyel had looked after the place from the time Oldric's father had purchased it.

Angwyn sighed. "The last weeks of Idris's pregnancy and these few weeks since have changed her disposition, Father. She's not as easy to please as she once was. But she's acquired two new servants, one a housekeeper—"

"That would be Maag," interjected Oldric. "I just met both of them. Peculiar bird, Maag, if you ask me. Certainly, her native tongue can't be ours. As for the misshapen dwarf . . . Feelo, is it?"

"That's Maag's way of saying it," said Angwyn, smiling. "Feeno's his name."

"Seems a good chap but claims he's a gnome. I thought they were mythical."

CHAPTER 14

THAT POTENT BIT OF QUARTZ

THE EVENING OF HIS RETURN from the university, Oldric saw firsthand that Idris *had* changed, becoming haughty and disdainful. Also, she refused to hold the baby. He excused her behavior as a transitory state from which she would recover, as one would from a serious, though not terminal, illness. But the next evening, when Idris remarked that Elda knew nothing about child raising or she would not have produced someone as inferior as Angwyn, Oldric felt compelled, in defense of his wife, to give Idris a tongue-lashing to put her in her place; he even managed to say a good word on Angwyn's behalf. Idris's cold, unapologetic response, however, unsettled him, making him want to run for cover. *Ridiculous!* he thought. *I'm Master here.*

Still, he hurried to the library to find a means by which he could safeguard his granddaughter. Throughout the night, he pieced together fragments from texts on the science of acoustics and the magic of personification. Success, however, eluded him until, at dawn, he added a supplication, which begged Sound to yield to him *for the sake of Jocelyn.* At once he heard Maag grousing from afar, "Why didn't they dig it in the intimacy of the kitten?" Immediately after, there was the sound of water pouring into a pot. Oldric clapped his hands in glee at having charmed Sound into granting him its services. But what was Maag saying? And did it have anything to do with Jocelyn? Obviously, there were a few things he had to work out.

Weary but wanting to give himself a treat for his mastery of Sound, Oldric decided to get his cherished white crystal—his talisman, which augmented his powers—and feel its strength before he retired to bed. Standing up from his desk, he yawned and stretched, then crossed to one of the bookshelves. He removed Arwel Prydudd's *The Tomfoolery of Magic.* Having feared the servants might discover the crystal, he'd hidden it behind the book, thinking he was clever to choose such an ironic spot. Only Idris knew the hiding place.

Where is the crystal? he wondered, pulling out several books that surrounded *Tomfoolery.* He grew increasingly angry. Idris must have defied the conditions of its use. He checked the time. *She won't be up yet,* he realized, but he rushed from the library, determined to haul her out of bed and force her to relinquish the crystal. At the bottom of the staircase, he took hold of himself. *I mustn't imagine the worst or think so ill of her,* he thought. *She may have mislaid it. Or perhaps she took the crystal for the convenience of reading while she tends the baby. I shouldn't have been so strict over the whereabouts of its use.*

Instead of climbing the staircase, he went to the kitchen.

Maag, who was stoking the fire, looked up and said, "You're up afore the night crawlers sink to bed."

Oldric laughed. "I haven't slept a wink, so I must be one of your night crawlers."

Maag clapped her hand to her chest, and her eyes widened. "I'm mortifried and panic-whacked!" she cried.

"You're on the mark, Maag. I'm a sort of worm, a bookworm, and last night I had my fill."

Maag pondered this.

"Bookworm and *eating up books,"* Oldric explained, "are figures of speech. They don't mean I literally—"

"Ahhh, I get it," she interrupted, slapping her forehead. "You're speaking the highfalutin dialectic. It's so choked with delusions, illiterates, and gibberygooks it oft overpasses me. I best understand the homely tongue."

"What are your origins?" Oldric asked.

"Beg pardon?"

"Where do you come from?"

"That's an unrelentful bafflement," answered Maag. "An intruded egg, I suppose. Speaking of . . . Do you want me to hard boil a chicken egg for you like I do Junior Lady?"

"I'd prefer a bowl of porridge," he replied. "And a couple of biscuits with honey. But first a cup of tea."

"I have a pot made-ready. Waddle a mite, and I'll pour you a jug."

"When does my daughter-in-law rise?" asked Oldric.

"Not afore noon. She says late-rising is a sigh of mobility." Handing Oldric a mug of tea, Maag said, "I'll bring mush and breadcrumbs soon as they're repaired; the nectar's fixed already."

When Oldric entered the dining room, he heard the baby's cries. *She's fairly near,* he thought, *so it's probably not Sound's doing but Jocelyn's great set of lungs.* She had wakened, undoubtedly hungry and in soiled diapers. Idris would sleep through or ignore the crying, but Elda right now would be on her way to succor Jocelyn.

Oldric sat down at the dining room table and sipped his hot tea. It wasn't long before Maag came in with his porridge and biscuits.

"What do you know about the sheep?" he asked.

Maag replied, "I know they're nearly all-purpose—rudders milky, flesh tasteful, and they have fluff that Old Lady—"

"My wife," interrupted Oldric, "would not appreciate being called *Old Lady."*

"That's what she was telling me 'til she gave up," said Maag. "Methinks her stomach now is set with it. I pretend no discurtsy."

Oldric studied the housekeeper. *She doesn't mean to offend,* he decided. "Since you call Idris *Junior Lady,"* he suggested, "why not call Elda *Senior Lady?* It shows that my wife is superior and—"

"Methinks Junior wouldn't favor being underneath a superior," said Maag.

"I agree," acknowledged Oldric. "But call my wife *Senior* anyhow. It's a polite way of indicating she's older."

"Oh, it's a nicety—one of those eufeminisms," said Maag, again striking her brow. "That's like those surreptitions Junior Lady's always accusing me of."

Oldric, attempting to restore the subject from which they'd been diverted, said, "When I checked the livestock yesterday, three sheep acted strangely."

"Strange is a hazard here," commented Maag. "But I don't adventure among sheep no more; you have to ask Feelo about them. Speak of the revel!" she exclaimed, seeing the gnome pass by in the hallway on his way toward the kitchen. "Feelo! Old... No, *Senior*... Are you *Lord,* Sir?"

"No, I'm *Professor* Oldric."

"You sound certain," observed the housekeeper. "I'm glad one of us knows who we are." She turned to the gnome. "Senior Professor has a quest, Feelo, about sheep that haven't proper etiquette."

Feeno, having come back, leaned into the doorway, a hand on the doorjamb. "Have sheep gotten loose?" he asked.

"No," Oldric assured him, motioning for him to come in, which Feeno did, though reluctantly it seemed. "Three sheep—a ram and two ewes—encircled me," said Oldric, "and bleated plaintively, as if they wished me to relieve them of some misery."

Maag interceded. "Maybe they're afright. But they needn't be. Junior Lady more often than not execrates and dissembles lambs.

Senior sheep don't suffer that fate much on account their meat is musty and rugged."

"So, you do know a thing or two about sheep," complimented Oldric.

"That's from tasting them raw. You get to know an animal when you chew on it. Junior Lady and Jocie don't want to know the lambs, so for them I roast. Feelo won't touch meat any which way. That's why methinks he's good at shepherding. The sheep don't have to fret about him eating them for lunch."

"But they *are* fretting," pointed out Oldric. "Perhaps you could—"

"Oh, but I couldn't. I'm retired as a sheep hand. Already I hold two jobs, which is one more than I'm supposed to. I had three when I got signed up here. Plus housekeep and crook, I overlooked the animal kingdom afore Junior Lady carted Feelo in from the wood to look after the frock."

"He was carried?"

"Over her shoulder," said Maag. "Methinks Lady Iduress was bent on a meaty supper, but the lambs had gotten a hint one of them'd be digested, so they scattered with their tails up. Her Bulls-eye wasn't about to chase them all over the sidecountry. Instead, she went into the wood with bows and arrow and came back with Feelo bloody from an exaggerated rent; she'd penetrated his leg. Thought he was a badger or auk."

"I wondered about your limp," said Oldric, turning toward Feeno. He gave the gnome a long look. "You seem frightened," he observed.

"He's timid around masters, jesters, mischiefs, and whatnots," answered Maag. "See how he doesn't talk much? I don't know why. Maybe it's because Junior Lady brought him low to show who's the bully here. She manhandles him with cramps and aches. Conjures them for me, too."

"Conjures?"

"That white crystal is her staymain," went on Maag. "She savages the household with it. Never slips it off her neck, though she oft hides it 'neath her louse."

Oldric thrust himself up from the table and rushed from the room. At the staircase, he met Elda, who was holding Jocelyn and likely on her way to get milk.

"Idris is using the white crystal in ways I didn't sanction," he said.

"Why does that not surprise me?" Elda retorted sarcastically.

"Yes, yes," conceded Oldric. "She's become a danger to us all. Is Angwyn up?"

"I'll check the parlor," said Elda. That, Oldric had learned, was where Angwyn had been sleeping ever since he'd returned to be with his wife before the baby was born.

"No hurry," said Oldric. "I don't need him to deal with Daughter-in-Law."

"I wouldn't be so . . ."

But Oldric didn't hear the rest of what Elda said, because he was rushing up the stairs. At his daughter-in-law's bedroom door, he rapped loudly.

"The help knows better," Idris answered. "Is that you, Father-in-Law?"

"It is," he declared. "I must have a word with you."

"You disturb me," said Idris.

"Not as much as you disturb me," he retorted.

Idris became quiet.

"Open the door!" insisted Oldric.

"Not until I am at my best," responded Idris evenly.

She made him wait in the sitting room until he lost all patience and banged his fists against the door.

"No one is in," said Idris from behind him.

He wheeled around, realizing she had left her chambers through the nursery door and come down the hall and into the sitting room. She wore a dressing gown.

"Were you looking for this?" she asked, opening her hand and revealing the white crystal on her palm, then cradling it in her fingers and rubbing it in a circular motion with her thumb. She spoke words that to almost anyone else would have been nonsense, but to

Oldric were the vocabulary of magic—specifically, of transformation. Alarmed, he sought to wrest the crystal from her, but his feet had become fixed to the floor.

He roared, "Unbind me!"

"You are bound by your makeup," said Idris triumphantly, "which is changing."

"To what?" he cried, his arms rising and crossing at the wrists. He felt his legs come together and his torso lift and narrow as if it were being forced into a long box. His skin turned wooden. His face swelled behind his hands. He tried to speak, to protest, but he had no means. In terror, he waited for his breath to expire and his heart to stop. Instead, he felt movement inside, a swinging to and fro, a release of weight, gears turning. He heard the *tick . . . tock . . . tick . . . tock* of a clock. Surely that wasn't . . .

"I will call you *Grandfather,*" said Idris. "*Grandfather clock.* Is it not a clever improvement on long-case clock? And how appropriate! Perhaps the name will become commonplace."

Later that day, Maag and Feeno tugged and pushed the clock into place. In the full-length mirror opposite him, as he'd expected, Oldric beheld a long-case clock. Still, it was a shock, causing his pendulum to waver; *tick-tock* came out *theck-thuck.* In spite of his situation, he couldn't help admiring himself. *Handsome clock,* he thought. *But I can't remain like this!*

There he stood, however, year after year. He had to admit that life in the guise of a pendulum clock wasn't as bad as he would have thought—if, indeed, he could have imagined such a thing. He took great pleasure from Maag's dusting. The gentle feather duster did more than clean; it soothed him, except when it was applied to spots that so tickled him, he felt he might warp. Another treat was Feeno's occasional oiling. Unlike balms used on humans that must penetrate the skin to relieve joint aches, this oil directly lubricated any interconnected parts that grated, allowing him to run smoothly.

He even found comfort in being wound. The first time, he'd been afraid when Idris turned the key that lifted the weights. He felt as if his lungs were being filled with air; surely, if she turned the key too tight, his lungs would burst. But then Idris removed the key, and as the weights fell gradually, he exhaled, great calm pervading him as he unwound.

Sad that he hadn't been able to be much of a grandfather, Oldric relished the opportunity to be of service to Jocelyn, however small, by slowing or accelerating time. Other than that, he could only observe, as she waited for permission twice daily to enter her mother's bedroom—the first time for afternoon lessons and the second for the evening interrogation. He took great pleasure in watching his granddaughter grow up but worried over how little joy and laughter she exhibited, which was due, of course, to her mother's parenting.

Especially troubling was how eagerly Idris had embraced the birthday-eve spell with its promise of an obedient daughter. Excited by the prospect, she hadn't grasped the implications of the magic. For if a child is perfect, it is not a real child. Jocelyn's life depended on her perpetually rekindling her spirit, even as Idris sought to extinguish it and turn her daughter into a handmade doll.

Oldric wanted to shout, "You are killing your daughter!" But he could not, and perhaps it didn't matter, because Idris had no use for a youth who was alive.

So how is Jocelyn faring on this birthday eve, he wondered. He hoped that Sound would soon deliver news on that pop he'd heard.

CHAPTER 15

SPIT IN THE IMAGE

THE BRONZE-COLORED GIRL stretched her limbs. "I'm Brazen," she announced.

Feeno saw that she was about the size of Jocelyn and so like her that he grabbed a blanket to cover her nakedness.

"She isn't full of bash," said Maag.

Feeno stopped. *"Bash?"*

"Modest she isn't," said Maag. "Maybe cold."

"I'm not," said the girl calmly. She eyed Jocelyn, who was asleep and gasping for breath. Rising to her feet, she walked to the bed and sat on its edge, then placed her hand on the girl's chest, which quieted her.

Feeno let the blanket drop, agreeing that this . . . this other Jocelyn didn't appear bashful over her nakedness, much less ashamed.

"Are you astonished that I tumbled out of a balloon?" she asked Maag and Feeno, as she gently rubbed Jocelyn's chest.

"That's a weak way to prescribe it," said Maag.

"What then?" asked Brazen.

"Fuddled," suggested Maag.

"Wondrous strange," said Feeno, whisking flies from his face.

"For me, too," agreed Brazen. "A few moments ago, I was a mix of fumes, but now . . ." She gazed down at her body, then touched her face. "Do I look like Jocelyn?"

"Spit in the image," said Maag, "except for . . ."

"The color," said Brazen. "Mine is rich, I'm sure you'd agree. Jocelyn is much too pale. You should take her outdoors more often to play in the sun."

Feeno, feeling censured, spoke up in his defense. "Her mother says—"

"She shouldn't play," cut in Brazen, "because it's frivolous. She shouldn't go outdoors because it's not as safe as being shut in. She shouldn't be exposed to the sun because . . . What's the reason for that?"

"It's not good for her skin," said Feeno.

"But it brings out freckles," retorted Brazen.

"Iduress hates them," said Maag. *"Blemishing* she accuses them of."

"They give color," asserted Brazen. "If Jocelyn were covered in them, she'd be a mosaic of browns. Instead, she looks sick."

"She *is* sick," said Feeno.

"Oh, but even when she's well, she's pale," said Brazen. "It's not just from the lack of sunshine. That . . . That *witch* . . . She's taken bold colors from her." Brazen pointed toward Fury. "Isn't her red impressive? Have you seen her flames?"

"I haven't," said Maag, as Feeno nodded that he had.

"Compare Fury to Glum," went on Brazen. "Glum's pure black was diluted by our mock-mother, producing a drab, grayish color. I don't care much for the golden or blue—too soft. But you need only look at me! Is it any wonder that Jocelyn is failing when she's deprived of reddish brown?"

"Are you a real girl?" asked Feeno.

"Are you a real gnome?" Brazen asked in turn.

"I think I am."

"How can you tell?"

He tapped his arm.

"Touch mine," she said.

He reached out his hand. She felt more like a force than a substance, as if she were a fair breeze or the sun's warmth.

"Maag?" offered Brazen.

The housekeeper gave her a push, and the girl absorbed it. "You haven't the feel of the stuffings Jocie and us do," said Maag.

"I'm not surprised," said Brazen. "I'm her spirit, not her playmate."

"A sprite?" exclaimed Maag, taking a step back.

Jocelyn moaned. All of them turned to her. The girl's lungs sounded as if they were grating against her ribcage.

"That's not normal," said Maag.

"She'll be over the crisis once her new spirit gets her footing," Brazen asserted.

"She'll be all right, then?" asked Feeno.

"She won't be *all* right. How could she be," Brazen declared, motioning at the balloons, "when so much of her is up in the air? But I'm a start."

"And what a get go!" cried Maag excitedly. "Why not pop the gold loon, too? There's a sprite-girl in it, isn't there? You two'd be Iduress's menacis, the zing we've craved for. Won't her Highball be flabberfounded when I present her with sprites instead of the gold loon?"

"Is Lady Idris expecting the golden balloon?" asked Feeno.

"About a while ago. Why did you think I came all the way up here? Wasn't to be the speculator of a bronze sprite popping out. No, Iduress directed me to fetch the gold loon afore she laundered and fumigated her carcass in the bath I'm supposed to fix for her. I don't know why she wants Goldie. Doubt it's to make merry.

"But now, I've got my own idea," Maag went on, "and it's marital. Pop out *all* the sprites so they can be Jocie's gang. Her Illustrated Highbrow, why, she'll be put to rout."

"I wouldn't wager against her," said Brazen.

"Aren't you supposed to be the brassy one?" challenged Maag.

"I *am* bold, but I'm not foolish. Gullible hasn't grit. Glum and Sorrowful are weak. Tragic is full of hot air. Quizzical isn't a spirit of action. Bustle is flighty. Fury is irrational. Smolder is moody. I wouldn't count on them to overwhelm the witch, especially so long as she holds the crystal."

"Then we need to snatch it," said Maag. "That's a talent up my sleeve."

"Maag," cautioned Feeno, "you're good at stealing what's not being attended to, but if you couldn't make off with Lady Idris's silver box, how are you going to steal a crystal that she always wears on a chain around her neck?"

"That's a puzzle," said Maag.

"What needs doing," said Brazen, "is to return a fearless spirit to Jocelyn, one brave but also insolent, defiant, brash—namely, me!"

Feeno sensed the balloons stirring and looked up through the flies that hovered over him. The balloons seemed agitated. Pointing at them, he asked, "Don't they agree with you?"

"They would if they were objective and had any regard for facts," said Brazen. "Glum and Sorrowful probably would defer to me, but they'd concede anything. Tragic hasn't merit because she's false—always acting in her melodramatic way. Gullible is hopelessly naïve, and Quizzical is—"

Feeno chuckled. *"Why is there sky? Why is it blue? Why is blue blue?"*

"Nosy, Iduress said she was," said Maag.

"Also, *uncontrollably curious,"* added Feeno. "Miss Quizzical nearly drove Lady Idris mad."

"My influence," interjected Brazen, "made Jocelyn's questions pointed. *Mother, how do you know what's good for me? Why won't you let me have a playmate? Why do you make me practice being pleasing when you aren't?* Jocelyn wasn't curious like Quizzical; she meant to needle and challenge. *Cheeky,* her mock-mother said she was. *Too smart for her own good.* She was right about my presence making her smart. I'm more clever than the others."

Smolder and Fury swooped in, the first puffed up, the second fiery, and boxed Brazen's ears.

"You scalded me!" complained Brazen to Fury. "Cool down."

"You don't get along?" exclaimed Feeno, appalled.

"Not particularly. Fury! Smolder!" Brazen shouted as she batted them away. "Contain yourselves!" Addressing Maag and Feeno, she said, "It may surprise you, but we spirits don't know one another very well. It doesn't help that in the balloons we can't speak. Now and then we run into each other. Or one might approach another—have a bump."

"A bump?" questioned Feeno.

"A crude way of communicating, to be sure. How does one interpret a bump? Is the spirit being friendly or pushy? There are misunderstandings, and fights break out. At times we play a game of tag, darting and dodging. It's meant—on my part, at least—to be fun, but it's hard to tell how each spirit is taking it; I'm sure there are bruised feelings. Not mine. I always stay calm and calculating; I don't lose control. Bustle, Fury, and Smolder, though . . . Smolder! Don't expand like that!"

"Is she angry?" Feeno asked.

"She's always angry, like Fury, but usually she's more restrained."

"Isn't she trying to burst out?" asked Maag.

"She wouldn't be that foolish . . . Oh, but she might!" Brazen cried, slapping her own head. "She knows she won't splatter or scatter; I've proven it. Smolder, you mustn't burst! We don't know if it's a good idea; my coming out may be the death of me. Don't overstretch! Idiot, you're going too far!"

There was a loud pop, and an orange spirit-girl spun in the air, increasing in size as she dropped to the floor. She bounced up faster than she'd fallen. "*Idiot,* you called me? If I'm an idiot for bursting out, what shall we call you? Idiot the First?"

"I'm the one who takes risks!" retorted Brazen. "You're the spirit who runs from danger, then fumes. The balloon was the perfect place for you. But I'll accept your name for me. It shows I'm foremost. You, Idiot the Second, followed."

Smolder glowered at Brazen.

"Now, now," Feeno said, trying to calm them, "you're both idiots."

They looked askance at him.

"Not that *I* think you're idiots," he hurriedly added. "But it's something you can agree on. It's a step toward cooperation."

"I don't cooperate," said Smolder. "It's not in my nature."

The bell rang once, a call for Maag.

"That's our Imperiousness!" exclaimed Maag. "I've got to wisp Goldie to her, or else she may come up and bring us all down."

"Take her at once," said Brazen. "The witch is having a bath, didn't you say?"

"She's planning on making abnormal flowers, too," said Maag. "I don't know when. She has it in her brain to turn the tired house downside up. And on account of my tongue being misaligned, which is frustrating to her scientific expedition, she wants to put me right."

"I may have time, then, to come up with a plan," said Brazen. "Maag, do whatever you can to steal the crystal. Gullible . . . Where are you? Come out from hiding."

Slowly and hesitantly, Gullible emerged from the darkest corner of the room.

"Go with Maag," Brazen instructed her. "You needn't fear. If the witch should pop you, she'll find you so agreeable that even she won't have the heart to harm you. You're her favorite, don't forget."

Showing fewer signs of reluctance, Gullible floated to the housekeeper, who held her gently at her breast as she tiptoed from the room.

"Just so you know," grumbled Smolder, "I don't agree to any of this."

CHAPTER 16

NEARLY A CROOKED GOOSE

BRAZEN SAYS IDURESS *hasn't the heart to wrack and ruinate Gullible,* thought Maag, as she made her way down the attic stairs. *But hasn't she that very heart—if heart she has?* "Iduress's fancies tend to meander," she whispered to the spirit inside the golden balloon. "She's crazy as a loon. Not your *loon;* I mean the bird. If she pops you out a girl, we need a plot that'd detain her some. I'll make a flap, you grab her behind, and I'll scratch out her eyes and rip off the crystal."

At Idris's bedroom door, Maag knocked.

"Come in! Come in!" Idris shouted impatiently.

Maag steadied herself, then swung open the door. Idris was reading in bed. Books were scattered over her quilt, some having fallen to the floor.

"It has been one half of an hour," said Idris testily.

"On my chastity, my Watchtower, I did hasten—well, not *hasten,* but I did sweep with rigor and ambulate up, down, and crosswise, as if with wings." Maag felt a slight ache in her belly, but Pain apparently couldn't make out if she'd lied or not, so it let her be. "Asides, I dumped on you afore I went to the attic the hay-berry to dillydawdle over."

"The strawberry tart was sickly sweet and warm," complained Idris. "I wished it ice cold."

"Lackadaisy, that pasty was far beneath your expectancy."

"Beyond measure, Maag. Tonight, I wished my sweets bitter."

Maag pondered this. "I don't mean to be pertinent," she said, "but why then didn't you ask for a bitter? A sprig of mugwort . . ." *No,* reasoned Maag, *this night, likely as not, she'd fancy her bitters sweet.* "Untamed mustard's a lenient bitter," she noted, "but I'd have to go into the woods to—"

"I do not want a wild-mustard tart," said Idris, clearly disgruntled.

"I've got yarrow in the house. It's bitter but with a tang of sweet. If you hanker, quick as a pigeon I'll pace to the kitten and get—""

"Stay!" commanded Idris. She pressed her fingers against her brow and leaned her head back.

"Is my clatterwaggling muddying you?"

Idris nodded. "My head aches," she said. For a moment or two she didn't speak. Maag wondered if she should slip away. But at last Idris seemed to gather herself. Sitting upright, she looked directly at Maag. "I do not want yarrow," she said. "That is not one of the tasks I listed for you."

"Oh, I forgot about them . . . What's the secession, my Head-throb?"

"First," Idris bellowed, "hand me the balloon!"

"I have it here cuddled in my fairy hands," said Maag, as she hurriedly tiptoed to Idris, who yanked the golden balloon from her arms.

"What have we here?" Idris said, peering into the balloon.

"It . . . It's a . . .

"I did *not* pose the question to you!" snarled Idris.

Maag slapped her hand over her mouth. *It's the first ever,* she thought, *that Iduress saved me. I was nearly a crooked goose. I have the debility to lie to her, but . . . if I do, I'll be smitten to my knees by violet cramps.*

Idris had risen from her bed. She said to Gullible, "Once I complete my research and correct Maag, I will investigate you, my trusting spirit." Idris narrowed her eyes, creasing her brow. "But how will I accomplish it? If I pop the balloon to probe its contents, and the spirit is airy, as I suspect, how can I contain it without a container?"

Maag rotated her head, searching the room.

"There is no one else," said Idris to Maag. "I addressed the question to myself."

"I don't wish to intrude while you defer with yourself," said Maag. "If you're having a clandestine consummation, maybe I ought to dispatch my tasks."

"You should, Maag. At once. When I find from the books how to fix you, I will ring."

Idris crossed the room to her workshop and opened the door. "For now," she said to Gullible, "I will set you adrift in these unlit confines. Feel free to poke about. Be careful, though, because there in the dark something sharp might poke back. Later, if you would like, we can have a hide and hunt contest. I love a good hunt." Idris closed the door and turned back toward her bed and the books that awaited her. "Why are you still here?" she asked Maag.

"I'm scratching my brain, my Lady-a-Waiting. The tasks are jumbled there. Take down the woodscapes. Harvest thyme. Sweep and mope. Drag out redundant chairs. Fetch yarrow. No, no, dandelions instead. What was that about perpendicular flowers? Where are they in the lineup?"

"Maag." Idris spoke the name as if she were trying to bring the housekeeper to her senses or maintain her own composure. "You are confused."

"That's a randy obfuscation. I'm oft fused, and this day's like no other."

"My bath," said Idris.

"That's next?" cried Maag.

"No, first bring me dandelions so I may distill them. I want to squeeze the essence of cold from them. Then I will drink the essence, and it will chill me to the bone."

"I'll bring a casket of it, my Coldhearted," said Maag, rushing off.

Egads, she thought, *I near forgot! I'm supposed to let go Jocie's gowns so they'll refit her. Come to think on it, I need, too, to dress the sprites. Iduress doesn't approve of anybody, but if the body is denuded, her Judgmental will be notarized.*

CHAPTER 17

CONTENTIOUS SPIRITS

FEENO WET A CLOTH and wiped Jocelyn's brow, while Smolder pouted and Brazen paced because of the words they'd had with each other.

"She's breathing easier," observed Feeno.

"Her new spirit is quickly filling her," explained Brazen. "We all began like that—lively and full of energy. I hope this one proves rebellious."

Smolder spoke up: "Considering how Jocelyn's spirit has been crushed in recent years, I doubt the new one can hold her own against the witch's power."

"Which is why we must fortify her with a large infusion of spirit," said Brazen. "But how can we do it in our present form? Neither you nor I can even get a foot into Jocelyn's mouth."

"We've been shut out," said Smolder. "Nothing good can come of us."

"Especially with that sort of attitude," retorted Brazen.

"My attitude?" exclaimed Smolder. "Your think *yours* is better? You're brash. You strut and blare."

"I do not *strut and blare!"* protested Brazen.

"Yes, you do!" insisted Smolder.

Brazen closed in on Smolder, the latter holding her ground; their noses nearly met. "You're morose," Brazen said. "You sulk and mope."

"I do not *mope!*" retorted Smolder.

"Girls, please!" interrupted Feeno. They stared at him, as if expecting he would go on, but he hadn't any idea what to say. *I called them girls,* he thought, *but they aren't girls. How does one reason with a pair of contentious spirits—one brassy, the other sullen?* He recalled four-year-old Jocelyn, whom Idris named Miss Smolder, and how he and Maag had had to put up with her abrupt changes of mood and her resistance to sharing what was on her mind. In her mother's presence, she had been even more difficult—surly, quick-tempered, hostile. Miss Brazen, too, when Jocelyn was five and six, had been more challenging for Lady Idris than for Maag and him.

"I brood," said Smolder. "It's Glum who mopes; she's the one who's dispiriting. I brood over our revenge on the witch. Now isn't that positive?"

"Yes," agreed Brazen. "But malicious thoughts aren't enough; actions are needed. Jocelyn's spirit has to be daring and throw caution to the wind."

"You're too rash," scolded Smolder. "Her spirit must wear the witch down, exasperate her by being contrary and stubborn, until she wants nothing to do with Jocelyn."

Brazen turned to Feeno. "Which strategy would you use against the witch—mine or Smolder's?"

Feeno was at a loss. *I can't pick one without offending the other,* he thought. "Maybe someone else's strategy, say, Fury's, or . . ."

They were looking at him as if he were out of his mind.

He then had a turn of thought which made him rather pleased. "I wouldn't confront Lady Idris," he said. "I'd run away like Jocelyn's father did. Whether the girl is saucy or sulky or full of fury, it comes to the same thing: She's no match for her mother."

The two spirits were silent for a while. "The witch does have the advantage of magic," acknowledged Brazen.

"And is the adult," added Smolder.

"Pardon me," interjected Feeno, "but shouldn't we attend to a more urgent matter?"

They looked at him blankly.

"Jocelyn's recovery?" he prompted.

For the first time since her entrance, Smolder took a good look at the girl, who had resumed some of her restlessness after Brazen left her side. "What's the toad doing on her?" Smolder asked.

"Toad!" cried Feeno, who had lost track of it after it had dashed off when he'd pumped on Jocelyn's chest to revive her breathing. The toad was resting on Jocelyn's shoulder.

"I don't trust it," said Smolder.

"The toad's with me," explained Feeno, smashing a fly between his hands and holding it out for Toad, who lapped it up. "I sort of adopted it. It keeps to the cellar for the most part."

"It's often here," said Smolder.

"It is?" Feeno exclaimed. "Jocelyn never mentioned it."

"She hasn't seen it," said Brazen. "It only comes at night when she's asleep."

"It's crossed my mind," said Smolder, "the toad might be the witch."

Feeno staggered, as if kicked in the midsection. He'd spoken freely to Toad as if it were a confidant. What had he revealed? *Calm yourself,* thought Feeno. *Likely Toad is a toad, just as I am a gnome, though in some ways Toad is . . . Well, it's not like a toad. It has an appetite for lamb and cauliflower, for example. Also, it sought me out as a companion. But perhaps toads and gnomes have a natural affinity that I don't know about because I have so little knowledge of gnomes.*

"Mother is too vain to disguise herself as a toad," asserted Brazen.

"But it could be the witch's spy," persisted Smolder.

They gazed at Toad.

Finally, Brazen shook her head. "There's no evidence of the toad's treachery. Quite the opposite: it's been affectionate toward Jocelyn.

When it visits, it snuggles next to her on her pillow while she sleeps, as it's doing now."

"Toad has been friendly to me, too," asserted Feeno, even as he resolved to watch what he said around it.

"Don't say I didn't warn you," said Smolder.

Jocelyn was overtaken by a fit of coughing.

"I thought she was improving," said Feeno.

"She is," affirmed Brazen. "When Glum was removed, the witch's so-called wholesome spirit—"

"I call her *Prim,*" interjected Smolder.

"And a good name it is," agreed Brazen. "Prim moved in, but now the new spirit is supplanting her and clearing her out. Smolder's right, though. Our mock-mother will soon overpower the new spirit and take the air out of her unless we intervene."

"You agree!" exclaimed Feeno.

"We're not completely contrary," said Brazen. "There's some overlap."

"A tiny bit," acknowledged Smolder.

Brazen proceeded to pace back and forth across the room, deep in thought, her wrists crossed behind her. Smolder sat down on the bed and stroked Jocelyn's hair. Toad still rested near the girl's ear.

Frowning, Smolder declared, "The toad's disgusting. It's covered in warts. Doesn't like cause like? Jocelyn will soon have them."

"I haven't gotten any warts from it," protested Feeno.

"I'm not taking any chances," said Smolder, taking hold of the toad.

"Don't hurt it!" pleaded Feeno.

All at once, Smolder began disintegrating, turning into orange particles. Feeno reached for her, trying to hold her together, but the cluster of particles, rapidly losing the shape of a girl, passed through his fingers and penetrated the bedcovers. Brazen, having raced to the other side of the bed, threw back the cover as the last of Smolder seeped through Jocelyn's gown and skin.

"How did that happen?" questioned Feeno, aghast.

"I haven't any idea," replied Brazen.

Feeno leaned over the sleeping girl. "Wake up, Jocelyn . . . Smolder? . . . Whoever's there."

"Maybe the sleeping powder hasn't lost its strength," reasoned Brazen, "or Smolder is sulking and won't rouse her."

Jocelyn burped loudly, then gave off an enormous fart whose wind ricocheted off the walls, putting out candles.

Brazen laughed. "Prim's been forced out. What a lot of her! And she's so clean. Immaculate she is. Why, she hasn't any odor!"

Jocelyn's eyes shot open, causing Feeno to jerk upright. "Feeno!" she cried. "I was dreaming about my father, and he . . . Oh, my! What's this doing here?" Jocelyn lifted Toad from her shoulder with her thumb and forefinger and held it away. "Mother will have a fit. And I'll get warts. Put it out the door." Handing the toad to Feeno and turning her head from it with disgust, she came face to face with Brazen. "And who are you?" she exclaimed.

CHAPTER 18

BECOMING SQUAT

TOAD STOOD OUTSIDE Jocelyn's door, where Feeno had deposited him with a whispered apology for having to put him there. *How,* Toad wondered, *did Smolder dissolve into Joycelyn?* He suspected he'd had something to do with it, but when Smolder grabbed hold of him, all he'd done was clutch Joycelyn more firmly. Was it possible that, given the seemingly magical power of a toad to change from a tadpole into a toad and live on land rather than in water, he'd inherited the capability to serve as an intermediary to transform one form of spirit (a girl) into another (a cluster of particles) and set in motion the crossing of the particles from outside Joycelyn to inside?

He didn't know, but one thing he was sure of: he was no use to Joycelyn outside her door. She had rejected him, but she was in good hands. Gullible, however (once Maag delivered her to Idris) was not. He didn't know if he could rescue her. He had perhaps a better chance of stealing the white crystal, and that was slight.

He scampered to the top of the attic stairs and hurried down, slipping and sliding—not the most graceful of descents. His short legs were not made for leaping; indeed, they weren't even good for hopping. It was at a time such as this that he wished he were a frog. Its powerful hind legs ...

How peculiar that wish, he thought. Many times, though, for the sake of jumping or swimming, he'd made it. He'd given up wishing he were a human, nearly thirteen years of being a toad having lowered his expectations.

But if it were a choice among amphibians, in the end he was content to be a toad. True, frogs had sleek, narrow bodies, whereas toads were hunched and stubby. But frogs were slimy. He preferred having dry skin, even if it was thick and bumpy.

Besides, he'd never have made it back from Brynmor if he'd been a frog. Lots of animals ate frogs, but most of them stayed clear of him because, when anxious, he'd secrete through his skin a milky poison that irritated their mouths. The toxin also stank. Like a skunk, he could ward off snakes, foxes, raccoons, hawks, and other predators with a caustic smell that burned their eyes and nostrils. He'd had plenty of experience.

He wished there were some way to use his poison against Idris. Probably, though, it would only annoy her; certainly, it wouldn't kill her. Indeed, it might even enhance the toxins that already resided in her, making her more dreadful. But what chance had a toad, anyhow, against a sorceress? Look at how he'd fared as a man on the morning he heard his wife and mother arguing in the nursery and hurried in from the hall (the door was kept unlocked in those days) to intervene.

Idris was finishing chanting a magic spell and ignored his intrusion.

"Where's my mother?" Angwyn demanded.

"I feel faint," responded Idris. "Have some regard for your wife. Elda went for a walk in the woods."

"I don't believe you. I just heard her voice coming from in here."

"Spare me from contractions!" cried Idris, clapping the palms of her hands over her ears.

"Don't change the subject!" shouted Angwyn. "What have you done with Mother?"

"Calm yourself, Husband. She ran off in a huff, when once again I won our daily battle over how to raise a child."

"She wouldn't have left the baby alone with you," argued Angwyn. "You were chanting when I came in. Are you dabbling in magic these days? What spell did you cast upon her?"

"One that fulfills the desire of her heart."

"I strongly doubt that," retorted Angwyn. "I'll get Father. His magic will more than match yours."

"He is not here," said Idris. "A messenger arrived by coach before dawn, informing him of a crisis in his department. Sadly for you, he has left for Brynmor. You are defenseless," she said with a sly smile.

He eyed his father's crystal, which hung from a chain around her neck. "Give me that!" he exhorted, reaching for it.

She curled her upper lip. "Take away your arm, or I will wither it."

He hesitated, then drew back.

"Father-in-Law entrusted me with this crystal," she declared.

"Certainly, he did not intend for you to harm anyone with it," said Angwyn.

"I do not *harm;* I make right," insisted Idris. "You, for example, are a blunder. Your appearance is wrong. You are not a man; you are a toad."

Angwyn backed away, as Idris fingered the crystal, bowed her head, and mumbled an incantation. When she raised her head and gazed at him, her face dropped and she collapsed, sitting on a chair.

"You are not a toad," she said, sounding both surprised and disappointed. Then she brightened and asserted, "But you have a red wart on your cheek."

He clapped his hands against his cheeks and felt a rough spot on one side.

"Oh, and your fingers are slightly webbed!" she added with enthusiasm.

He looked at them and gasped, not just because of the webbing; there were only four fingers on each hand.

"Remove your shoes so I can see if you have six toes!" cried Idris. "And take off your shirt; there should be a yellow line down the middle of your back. I chose the natterjack over a common toad because of that. A yellow streak suits you." She paused. "Perhaps I should have changed you into an invertebrate—a louse. But you might have gotten into my hair; it would be just like you. No, a toad is what you are." All at once she scowled, sticking out her lower lip. "But the magic has not fully worked," she said. "You are still a man, and that will not do. Do not try to escape!" she shouted after him.

But Angwyn quickly fled the house. He raced to the stable, saddled Ceffyl, his faithful horse, and rode hard toward Brynmor. He believed that Maag and Feeno would keep his little Kettle safe, that Idris surely would do no serious harm to her own baby, and that only his father's magic could retrieve his mother and protect them all.

Angwyn knew a shortcut to Brynmor. It had no trail, but he'd traveled the route before, as had Ceffyl; even if he should lose his way, his horse would find it. They arrived without incident at his parents' home in the middle of the afternoon. His father wasn't there.

After leading Ceffyl to a stable where he would be cared for, Angwyn hurried on foot to the university. There didn't seem to be anyone about.

He went to the house of his father's colleague and closest friend, Martyn.

"But surely you know," said Martyn. "Oldric is at your country house—dabbling in magic, I suspect."

"What about the crisis?" asked Angwyn.

"Crisis?" questioned Martyn.

"I've been told there is a crisis in your department, and my father has been called here," said Angwyn.

"I dare say, you've been misinformed."

Angwyn wanted to shout at his wife, "Liar!" and choke the truth out of her.

"Pardon, my boy," said Martyn. "My eyesight isn't what it was, but . . . your skin is the color of ocher. You're especially yellow around the mouth. And your eyes . . ."

Angwyn hurried to a nearby mirror and gasped at his reflection. His eyes were bright green with horizontal pupils and double eyelids. Several reddish warts had grown on his face. Reaching behind his neck, he felt bumps on his upper back. *Am I imagining it,* he wondered, *or am I becoming squat?*

Bidding Martyn farewell, Angwyn rushed to the stable. Idris's spell was working slowly, but it *was* working. He must ride like the wind (one blowing vigorously) so that he'd reach the country house before he was reduced to a toad. Then he'd . . . He'd have to leave the details till later.

Retrieving his horse, he galloped through the town and into the countryside. Ceffyl sensed his rider's urgency and gave his all, as Angwyn pressed him to go faster. Realizing, however, that the horse might run itself to death, Angwyn reined him in next to a creek. Gazing down over the valley, he was surprised to see a path that led across it. It was so uniform it appeared to have been cut by a scythe. *What luck!* he thought. *Now Ceffyl can travel with greater ease and speed—at least as far as the trail leads.* A question nagged at him, however: why hadn't he seen the path on the way to Brynmor?

Angwyn dismounted and collapsed on his back in the grass. His clothes seemed oversized, but he didn't dare examine himself closely. Time was against him, but he must give the horse the opportunity to drink, eat, and rest. As for him, he needed rest, too, if he were to . . . to . . .

All at once, Ceffyl jostled him with his muzzle, then grabbed his coat by his teeth and pulled.

"Let go!" Angwyn shouted, ripping free. Ceffyl had never been so rough with him.

First he heard its sound, faint but distinct—a groan. Then he saw it, which made him gasp. The path was advancing toward him! No one was wielding a scythe; rather, something invisible was on the move, causing the grass and brush to wilt behind it. Ceffyl had been trying to drag him clear of the oncoming . . . *What is it?* he wondered with alarm.

He scrambled to his hands and knees as the path passed beneath him. It came to a stop, as if *he* were its destination. Ceffyl reared and struck his front hooves against . . . *What?* The horse was outside the path, banging against the air as if it were a solid. The groan was louder now. The air had turned filmy, clouding Angwyn's vision and impairing his breathing. In a panic, he slogged his way on all fours through the heavy, suffocating air, desperate to escape the path. At its edge, he reached out to the horse, but his hand, which he could barely lift, encountered the invisible barrier that kept Ceffyl at bay. It was no use. Collapsing onto his back, he gave in to death, allowing calm to pervade him. He was irked, however, that Idris must be behind this killing. It wasn't just that she'd gotten the better of him; he worried that Kettle wouldn't be able to hold her own against her mother. *Idris will destroy her,* he thought, as he blacked out.

"Sorry I'm late."

Angwyn opened his eyes. It was twilight. A cloaked figure with a large scythe hovered over him as he lay there in the path.

"Alis succumbed to an infection in her big toe," said the Grim Reaper. "Glaw choked on a bone of mutton. Ffion died from being poisoned by her husband, Elar. All in the past hour. Glynnes is having a difficult labor. Bledden is cornered by wolves. Eurig is on his deathbed from living so long. In short, I expect I'll have to be off at any moment." The cloaked figure shook his head. "I try to be prompt, but when several deaths occur near the same time . . . Thank goodness there are many of us in this calling and I have only one region to serve."

"I'm dead?" asked Angwyn, alarmed.

"Not as a doornail, as people like to say," replied Reaper, "but dead nonetheless."

Angwyn tried to digest this. "You look just as you do in drawings and paintings," he said.

"No, I don't think so," countered Reaper. "They render the trappings—the skeletal features, the dark robe with the hood, the scythe. But by and large they make me look too grim. In truth, I should be called the Cheerful Reaper; I always bring a smile. But when an artist gives me one, it makes me look grotesque." He brandished his scythe. "This won't hurt. I have to sever your spirit from your body so I can accompany what's left of you to the other world."

"What world is—"

"We mustn't dally," interrupted Reaper. "Glynnes just gave birth to a boy but is losing a lot of blood, and the midwife can't seem to stanch it. I fear she's about to give up the ghost."

Angwyn considered this. "In the interest of time and considering your workload," he offered, "maybe we could . . ."

"Negotiate? It's frowned upon. And don't try to trick me." Reaper pulled from his robe what looked like an hourglass and examined it. "What's this?" he exclaimed. "The last grain should have fallen, but . . . a great deal remains."

"I'm not dead?" exclaimed Angwyn.

"Let me feel your pulse." The Grim Reaper bent over and pressed the back of two fingers against Angwyn's neck. "My, your heartbeat is racing!" Reaper straightened up. "I guess Idris's magic was at cross-purposes: the death throes she sent after you were meant for a man; they must have been trumped by her transformation of you."

"Is it obvious I'm a toad?" asked Angwyn.

"Just look at yourself," said Reaper.

Angwyn raised his head and beheld the body of a toad, his underbelly cream-colored with green spots. He saw, too, that he was the size of a toad—four inches long, give or take a bit. His transformation was complete. He was mortified, but at least he was alive.

"Idris's magic is hit and miss," said Reaper. "Once in a while she gets it right. You, for example, are an excellent facsimile of a toad." He turned Angwyn onto his side. "Idris tried, I see, to make you into a natterjack, but you're not a true one. You have characteristics of other types, but to all appearances, because of that yellow streak down your back, you seem to be a natterjack."

Angwyn croaked.

"There goes your human voice," said Reaper. "Obviously, our conversation has come to an end. Perhaps next you'll adopt the sensibility of a toad. But who knows? Idris is prone to bungle her magic one way or another. Take Maag and Feeno—they're not exactly what she expected."

Angwyn tried to ask the whereabouts of Oldric, but he could only produce variations on a croak. He tried to croak louder, but his throat inflated, becoming larger than his head, and he feared that it might burst. In any case, loudness did not appear to improve his intelligibility.

"As a magician," went on Reaper, "Idris is a novice, one whose arrogance won't allow her to abide a teacher. She so annoys me. She discovered in Oldric's library an obscure book containing a passage that told how to summon me. She's horribly afraid of death—her own, not anyone else's—and calls me to her, not for her amusement, as she claims (I say as little as possible and grind my teeth), but to show her power over death. She doesn't have any, of course, any more than Glynnes does, no, *did*; just now she died. I must go to her. There's nothing to hold me here." He stroked his chin, which removed some of its skin, revealing bone. "Your situation is most unusual," he said. "I wish you luck." He turned and sauntered off.

CHAPTER 19

THE ESSENCE OF COLD

AFTER DELIVERING the dandelions for Idris's bath, Maag slowed her pace. *I'm not about to tumble down the stairs,* she thought. By the back door, she picked up a pair of empty buckets and went outside to the well. *Thank gods for a gorged moon,* she thought, *so I don't have to dangle a lit lantern from my teeth and get smoke in my eyes and nose.* Lowering one bucket at a time into the well, she filled both and walked—heavy-footed now—back to the house.

Why's Iduress so set on renovating me? she wondered. *I'm not perfect; I'm last to confess that. She's inspired to straighten my tongue, I guess. It's slipshody, she says, or some such. She desires to make my words and their meanings coincidental.*

But don't I speak plain? Jocie's grandma, Elda, said I talked quaint. I asked what that is, and she said it's a condiment. I wish Feelo was wrong about Elda never coming back and putting down her feet here. But Feelo and me excavated the woods and found no symptom of her.

Having climbed the stairs to Idris's floor, Maag toddled down the hall and through the sitting room into Idris's bedroom. Idris, engrossed in reading, paid her no heed, for which Maag was grateful; the less Idris engaged with her, the less chance of additional tasks. After emptying the buckets of water into the tub, the housekeeper tiptoed toward the door, but Idris spoiled her escape by asking if she had seen any toads about.

"In the house, my Spyglass?" she asked, careful not to lie.

"Of course not!" snapped Idris. "Outside on the grounds or in the woods."

"They're there," said Maag. "Are they for a potion you aim to wreck me with?"

"Not *wreck; correct.* But no, the toads are for the benefit of Gothelyn. Listen to this passage*: Strip a live toad down to its bones.* Now does that not sound amusing?"

Maag made a face, but Idris didn't see it.

Idris continued reading: "Take the bones to a stream and float them until one goes against the current. This bone is the magic one. It enables the witch . . . That is poorly said. It enables the magician to summon spirits whenever it pleases her. I would not need to wait until birthday eves."

Maag realized Iduress was talking to herself again.

"I could purge Gothelyn daily," went on Idris. "Yes, I must have one of those bones." She turned to Maag. "If you come upon a toad while you are doing your tasks, bring it to me."

"I'll keep my eyes pruned," said Maag.

"That reminds me. Have you seen a man on the premises? Not one in the past, but recently?"

Maag shook her head.

Idris eyed her carefully, probably to see whether Maag showed discomfort. Apparently satisfied that the housekeeper was not lying, Idris changed the subject. "Oh, I almost forgot to ask, when you fetched the balloon, was Gothelyn breathing?"

Maag nodded. "Ragged it was. Came in starts and fits and thens and nows. But Jocie has a hoard of sprite."

"Too much for her own good," said Idris, resuming her reading.

As Maag continued hauling buckets of water, one circuit after another, she became increasingly weary. She ached all over. *It takes way too many rounds to water Iduress,* she thought. I *poured more tubs when Elda and the rest were here, but I was heaps younger. Asides, I never minded because they were grapeful I hugged those buckets. I liked Elda. I dismember way back how Iduress—she was fully pregnated—deduced me to her.*

That goodly Lady Elda threw up her hands, happy as birdsong. "At last, you've uncovered a keeper!" she whooped. *At least her words were something like that.*

"I'm calling her Maag," said Iduress.

"Isn't that her name?" asked Elda.

"That's what I said," said Iduress.

It seemed like Iduress named me there. Like Feelo, I haven't any recommendation of my life afore this house.

I dismember meeting Angwyn as well, a week or so afore Iduress vacuated Jocie. His mother gushed to greet him, pulling me along. When he asked about his wife, Elda explained she was in her chamber and out of sports.

"My poor chickadee," Angwyn said (but in his own discrepant dialectic). "This pregnation's hard on her, isn't it?"

"It's wacking us all," I said.

"And who are you?" he asked.

"I'm a late acquaintance," I said.

Soon after, Feelo joined this holdup. Angwyn and Elda were glad he was here, in spite of the leg wound, but they were in a dither over him being a misshapen dwarf—a gnome, Iduress called him—because they hadn't seen the like. I hadn't any druthers what he was as long as I got some resuscitation. Apparently, Iduress had the notion gnomes make decent nannies, are fair at keeping grounds, and have farm hands. I wished they were good housekeeps—crooks, too.

Maag shuffled into Idris's bedroom with her sixth round. "Methinks the tub's efficient," she said, as she lugged the water behind the screen.

"You always underestimate," said Idris, putting aside her book. "One more bucket, at the least."

"So this might be the terminal circus, my Ringmaster?"

"Unless I find your underestimation gross. But here, take this basket and fill it with more dandelions. The essence of cold is nearly distilled, and I will shortly pour some of the extract down my throat and chill my very core. Even so, I want to immerse myself in water that teems with raw dandelions. Also, don't forget to fetch thyme from the vegetable garden, or my bathwater will be incomplete. Oh, did you capture a toad?"

Maag shook her head.

"That will give you something to do the evening of this day," said Idris. "You can scour the woods until you find one."

Maag hauled what she hoped was the last bucket from the well, then went into the woods with a basket and picked more dandelions. Instead of stopping at the garden to pick thyme, she proceeded to the kitchen, sat down, and ate a lizard, a store of which she kept in a jar. Then she added to the basket handfuls of thyme from the pantry. *There's hardly a chance,* she thought, *that Iduress can tell the disagreement between inexperienced thyme and the few-days-old type, especially because she'll be sitting in it instead of munching on it. I haven't time to grabble in the garden if I expect to sleep this night. Asides, I don't want to step on a toad for the sake of her Highness's debauchery.*

Upon returning, Maag was pleased to find Idris reclining in the tub; there would be no more hauling of water. Idris held a book in her hands. More books were in a pile on the floor within her reach. Maag was careful not to spill on them as she emptied water into the tub. She added dandelions and thyme, leaving some dandelions in the basket in case the Lady desired to ingest them.

Idris moaned with pleasure. "I feel icy throughout," she murmured. "My blood circulates near freezing."

"We all have our idiotcentrics," said Maag. "Feelo likes to rub his hind against the jamble of a door, and I like to—"

"Attend to your tasks?" suggested Idris.

"Your urgencies take presidents," said Maag quickly.

"The thyme should soon make me crisper," said Idris. "Is it fresh?"

Maag hesitated. "It was fresh afore I picked it," she replied. "After that, its bite might be more a nip." She felt intimations of a cramp, but Pain seemed to decide she hadn't lied and returned to the place it rested. *I've my words with ways,* she thought proudly.

Crossing the bedroom to the door, she noticed the dishes—cups, saucers, and pots—from evening tea. *I near forgot to dismember them,* thought Maag, picking up the tray. *Iduress will demand them clarified. Oh, but not these silver spoons—least by me. Aren't they pretty how they gleam?* Maag wiped them with her apron. *Now, they're shiny as anything in my hoard.*

"Maag," called Idris from the bath behind the screen, "don't steal that silver box you coveted earlier today."

"I wasn't thinking of it, my Treasury," replied Maag. *But come to think of it,* she thought, *what a good idea! Not the silver box; Iduress would notice right away. Something else.* Looking around the room, Maag spotted on top of Idris's desk the wooden box that held the silver cutlery. Quickly she took the two spoons over to it and opened the box. *Look at all these treasures!* she marveled. *There are countless spoons, long as Iduress doesn't count them. But I can get away with one, can't I?*

"You failed to take the dirty dishes to the kitchen," called Idris. "Do so at once."

"Yes, my Immaculateness." Inserting the silver spoons into the box, Maag added, "I've heretofore wiped the silver spoons and put them in their coffin."

Idris was silent for a while. "Did you steal any of the other silverware?" she asked.

"No, my Constable." *Not yet,* she thought.

"Leave the wooden box where it is. I do not want you rummaging in my drawers."

"Yes, my Lady of the House," answered Maag, tucking a silver spoon into her bosom and closing the lid of the box. She picked up the tray of dishes and tiptoed from the bedroom. *I got away with it!* she exulted. *Methinks my cleverness is next to nothing.*

In the sitting room, Maag noticed that Angwyn's painting was crooked. It had once hung in the nursery, but when Idris had turned the nursery into her proving ground, she'd moved the landscape to the sitting room. "It's near a rook's throw but not over my shoulder," Iduress had said (or something like that).

As Maag straightened the painting, it came off its hook. She fumbled with it but managed to lean down and keep it from crashing to the floor. *I've dropped my spoon,* she realized. Looking about on the floor, she couldn't find it. She shook herself, thinking it must be caught in her clothes. *Shinies don't banish,* she thought. *It'll jiggle loose. I'll just keep an outlook for it.*

Peering into the landscape, she turned it this way and that. *Her Benightedness mislikes how Elda tastes,* she thought. *Why doesn't she have me cremate this scrape of woods with the others? But I'm no art cricket.* She put the painting back on the wall.

CHAPTER 20

A WALK IN THE WOODS

An earthquake?

Elda picked herself up off the ground. *I've never felt the like,* she thought. *The whole woods shook. I'm surprised that the trees didn't uproot or that the earth didn't split open. But now everything seems calm again.*

And here she'd come out for a respite! At least, that was why she thought she was in the woods; it seemed the most logical explanation. Nothing relaxed her like a walk in nature. *Don't I need refreshing after my upset with Daughter-in-Law?* she reasoned.

When Oldric had rushed up the stairs to confront Idris over her use of the crystal, Elda had roused Angwyn in the parlor, alerting him of his father's anger, then chatted with Maag in the kitchen while she fed Jocelyn. After that, Elda climbed the staircase to the nursery, entering it from the hall. She thought she'd heard pounding on a door upstairs, but now all was quiet. Perhaps Daughter-in-Law had willingly handed over the white crystal, though it didn't seem likely. Elda changed the baby's diapers, then sang to her, and soon Jocelyn fell asleep.

No sooner had Elda retired to her bedroom than Jocelyn began to cry. Returning to the nursery, she found Daughter-in-Law standing by the crib.

"Has it been changed and fed?" asked Idris.

"She has," affirmed Elda.

"Then it wants for nothing," said Idris.

They both watched as the baby squalled.

"Perhaps she suffers from colic," ventured Elda.

"Its unruliness is at fault," asserted Idris. "It pesters me with it. It needs to cry it out. It does it good."

"But she'll become hysterical!" exclaimed Elda.

"It is not your place to interfere," said Idris. "I will not tolerate your spoiling it."

Spoiling her? Anger surged in Elda, filling her. She subdued it, but her voice caught as she said, "I wish only to comfort her."

"I refuse to raise a child that complains if it does not get its way," declared Idris.

"She's in distress," insisted Elda, her voice rising. "I'll fetch Angwyn."

"I will not allow him to indulge her," vowed Idris.

"He does not *indulge* her," protested Elda. "He shows sympathy and patience."

"You think those are virtues?" jeered Idris.

Elda nodded vigorously.

"Acquiescence, too?" scoffed Idris.

"He's being kind," Elda explained, showing exasperation.

"If Angwyn has his way, he will create a monster," said Idris. "He is not fit to father the child. Behold his influence," she declared, pointing at the baby. "Infant wails like the child of a beggar. This urchin cannot be a relation to me."

"I wish she was not," retorted Elda.

"Damn you!" shrieked Idris. "You are a bloody nuisance!"

Elda supposed the words had struck her like a blow, dazing her, because she found herself in the woods before she came to her senses.

As far as she could tell, she was on a path she'd never been on before, which surprised her because she thought she'd traveled all of the trails in the vicinity of the country house. In fact, she herself had fashioned a good many of them. The others had been made by animals, especially deer and fox. *How did I miss—or forget—this one? Oh, but it makes for a bit of an adventure, this not knowing where the path may lead!* And she was in a part of the forest that was especially lush, reminding her of the radiance of the landscapes Angwyn painted rather than the sparser, softly colored woodlands she ordinarily traversed.

It was near the summer solstice, the longest day of the year. *I must take advantage of this opportunity to more fully enjoy the lovely weather,* she thought. The air was a slight too warm but cooled by a mild breeze. The sky, patches of which she glimpsed in spite of the foliage above her, was clear.

She heard the fast drumming of a woodpecker and spotted it only a few yards off, clinging to the trunk of a silver birch. The bird was green with a bright-red crown, a telltale black stripe under its eye revealing that it was female. The tree didn't seem bothered by the pounding, its graceful, pendulous branches swinging gently.

Oh, if only I *wasn't bothered!* Elda thought. She couldn't get the discord with Idris out of her mind. *Why does the young woman annoy and worry me so?* Was there good reason, as Elda believed? Or did she suffer from jealousy, as her son, Angwyn, had once declared? Was it because Idris had become the apple of her husband's eye as well as that of her son? Though of late, Angwyn *had* shown misgivings.

Elda had tried to welcome Idris into the family—really, she had—when they'd first met in their home in Brynmor.

"She's reserved, Mother," Angwyn explained, taking her aside at the first chance after his betrothed had regarded Elda's open arms with scorn. Idris, looking statuesque, had sat on the small sofa, and Oldric, having presented himself with a polite bow, had sat down beside her. "She thinks it ill-bred to express affection in public," Angwyn added.

"Ill-bred?" questioned Elda. "She insults me."

"Mother!" said Angwyn in a hushed voice. "She cloaks her past for reasons she won't reveal, but I have come to believe she has blue blood in her family line."

"It's made her cold," said Elda.

"I can vouch for her passion," said Angwyn, blushing as he grinned.

"Indeed," said Elda, observing that her husband and Idris had become engaged in rousing conversation.

"Oh, they're getting on!" whispered Angwyn, giving his hands a quiet clap. "She could hardly wait to meet him. That nature has secrets offends her, and she won't rest until she finds them out. When I mentioned that Father was a professor of science . . . I told you she's an herbalist."

"I thought good of her for it," said Elda. "We'd be kindred spirits, I supposed."

"And so it shall be," whispered Angwyn. "That at first meeting she didn't embrace you doesn't mean the both of you won't find common ground."

"But our family doesn't come from nobility," said Elda. "If her ancestors are aristocratic . . ."

"She has modern ideas, Mother. I told her our family history, and she is most impressed that Father's father became a rich merchant and bought this country house, making us as good as gentry, she said."

"But *my* father was but a provincial banker," said Elda, "who failed because of bad loans. Her behavior toward me shows that in her eyes I'm not worthy."

"Not so, Mother. When I told her about your father's ruin and how, having earlier been schooled, you were apprenticed out as a dressmaker's girl, she broke down in tears. Misfortune, too, befell her family. Like you, she had to find her own way in the world. It made her humble, she said, and it gave her an independent spirit. She's most resourceful, just as you. And she's very excited about Father's profession, especially his membership in the Society of Benevolent Magicians. The questions she's asked! If I were the jealous sort . . . Thank goodness, she has high regard for me. She praises as noble my study and practice of art because art, she believes, is essential to the human spirit."

From the love seat, Idris, obviously responding to something Oldric had said, cried, "I adore magic!"

Angwyn and Elda turned in the direction of the couple and took a few steps toward them.

"That it is regarded with disdain by your colleagues is a grave error," said Idris to Oldric. "Natural science is knowledge of nature; magic is the control of it."

"Well said!" exclaimed Oldric. "If I turn base metals into gold, am I not employing both science and magic?"

"And" said Idris, "if I make use of my knowledge of common plants by turning them into remedies . . . "

"You are a magician!" affirmed Oldric.

"Also a scientist," added Idris, "as you."

"I investigate art as well as make it," interjected Angwyn, causing Idris and his father to look over their shoulders at him. "Am I not, too, a . . ." Oldric was peering at him disapprovingly. "I suppose not, according to you, Father, since I'm occupied with superficial pursuits, I believe you said, and my art is—"

"Frivolous," declared Oldric.

Elda frowned.

"I tire of arguing with you, Father," said Angwyn. "I wish my learned professors could have a go at you. I understand and applaud your passion for science. Why won't you do the same for my heart's desire? Neither Mother nor my betrothed agree with you. Isn't that so, my dear Idris?"

She gave no sign of a response.

"Speak freely," urged Angwyn. "Don't be intimidated by my father's—"

"It is not my place," interrupted Idris, "to take sides in a dispute between a father and his son."

"But . . ."

"She's a diplomat!" observed Oldric, chuckling.

Angwyn threw up his hands, obviously disappointed that Idris wasn't an outspoken partisan, no matter how devoted she might appear to him in private. As he turned away, Elda caught Idris watching his retreat with a derisive smile. Elda blinked hard to clear her eyes. They were closed for only a moment, but when she opened them, Idris was regarding her without expression. That, too, was fleeting, for at once Oldric drew his new admirer back into conversation.

Had she misinterpreted Idris's show of contempt for Angwyn? If she told her son what she'd seen, he'd say she was wrong. Even if he were to witness it, he'd deny what he saw, so besotted was he. Such a sensible boy he'd been until . . . There was no delicate way around it: Idris had seduced him as she would Oldric, one way or another.

After their first meeting, Elda had sought excuses for her future daughter-in-law's behavior. Idris was young, she told herself, though she was of uncertain age—probably a few years older than Angwyn. Be that as it may, her youth could account for her self-centeredness, which in time she might outgrow.

Also, it appeared that Idris hadn't had a normal upbringing. Her superior ability with bow and arrow implied a strong male influence. Angwyn confided that she always concealed upon her person a dagger.

"Don't startle her," Angwyn had joked—or warned; Elda couldn't tell.

Idris claimed she had acquired her deep knowledge of herbs (though Elda hadn't seen evidence of it) from her mother, indicating a female presence in her past. But of what character? About her mother, Idris had said, "She was neglectful," then added offhandedly, "She was a bit of a witch." She hadn't clarified whether she meant she was a shrew, a sorceress, or both.

I mustn't dally, thought Elda as she continued along the way. *The sun, though, hasn't made much progress, if any. I have plenty of time to savor the forest's restorative powers and gather some of its charms before I need to turn back. Idris may be familiar with herbs, but I know a thing or two about them myself, including nature's protections against evil. Oh, I do hope the baby has stopped crying or fallen asleep! I'll make this walk short in case I'm needed, even if Idris insists I'm not.*

Ash trees grew among the birch. Through the canopies of both, sunlight filtered to the forest floor, nourishing gorse, hawthorn, holly, and juniper as well as ground ivy and wildflowers—bluebells, pale-yellow primroses, violets, and poisonous foxgloves with their maroon, trumpet-shaped flowers. The gorse had yellow blossoms, while the hawthorn, interwoven with hazel, sported flowers of white, pink, and red. *Tempting though they are,* thought Elda, *I shan't collect hawthorn blossoms. They invite doom into a house. Juniper, though, now that's a different matter.* She gathered a few of its needlelike leaves and aromatic twigs, which she added to the pockets of her skirt in which she'd been depositing protective charms. Later, at home, she'd burn the juniper to keep evil from their house.

But doesn't evil already reside there? reflected Elda. *Or is my perception of Idris colored by my fear that the young woman is usurping my standing as the female head of the family? Am I, as Idris suggests, a busybody who is meddling in my daughter-in-law's affairs?*

No. Evil is present in that woman, she thought. *I'm more and more certain of it.* She checked her pockets and was assured of ample kindling from the ash, which was an even better wood than juniper. Burning ash would remove evil spirits from their house. It was possible that then, Idris would be freed from the bane that Elda believed possessed her—unless her evil nature was her own, in which case, Elda hoped, she would disappear altogether.

On the bank of a small stream, a pair of young red squirrels tumbled among fragrant hostas and ferns with blue-green fronds. One chased the other up an alder, then the other chased the first one down. Elda laughed at their play but quickly moved on, fearing the tree that, when cut, bled; alders were said to embody malign spirits.

Soon she spied with relief a rowan, a small tree with yellow-gray timber. From it she broke off a spray of leaves, which she put into one of her pockets. Rowan leaves, she'd been taught, warded off witches. *Even if Idris proves not to be a witch,* thought Elda, *I'm not about to return to the house without being amply loaded with forest charms to protect the family—even from one of its own.*

Oh, but I shouldn't think of such things. I've come out for a respite, nothing relaxing me like a walk in nature. Don't I need refreshing after my upset with Daughter-in-Law over the baby's crying?

The conflict had grown hot. It was waged in words harsher than usual.

"You are a bloody nuisance!" Idris had shrieked.

Elda supposed the words had struck her like a blow, dazing her, because she found herself in the woods before she came to her senses.

As far as she could tell, she was on a path she'd never been on before, which surprised her. It was very near the summer solstice . . .

CHAPTER 21

SPIRITED!

When Jocelyn had asked who was standing next to her bed, the reddish-brown girl had stepped back, as if she were expecting a quarrel. Jocelyn hadn't meant to sound hostile. But she'd never met another girl before, and hadn't Mother warned her to keep her window shut? Otherwise, she'd said, "Something unacceptable might get in."

"My name is Brazen," said the girl.

Jocelyn felt uncomfortable. She hadn't any experience of being sociable with a stranger. The girl didn't seem threatening. *Perhaps she's imaginary,* thought Jocelyn. *That's it! I've made her up.* "Feeno, is someone here with us?" asked Jocelyn.

"There is," he answered. "She's been with us for quite a while."

Then she must be real, thought Jocelyn. *I should be friendly, but I'm not in the mood. I'm feeling unsociable, which Mother said I often was when I was Miss Smolder. Still, I should find out more about this girl.*

"You look very like me," said Jocelyn, "except for your tan. Do most girls look like me?"

"I don't think so," said Brazen. "But then, I don't have any more experience of the world than you."

"Mother called me Miss Brazen when I was younger," said Jocelyn. "She said I was rude. Are you rude?"

"Very."

"Then why did Mother let you in?" asked Jocelyn. "Or was it you, Feeno? Or Maag?"

"Maag and I had nothing to do with it," replied Feeno, as he waved a hand to fend off flies.

"Mother doesn't know I'm here like this," said Brazen.

"But Mother knows everything," said Jocelyn.

"That may be what she says," said Brazen, "but you know it's not true. For example, she doesn't know you leave the window open."

"Is that how you got in?" asked Jocelyn, certain now that this girl was an intruder.

But Brazen shook her head. "Mother doesn't know you sit on the windowsill and breathe in the fresh air. She doesn't know you go out onto the roof."

"You must have seen me from the out-of-doors," said Jocelyn. "Is that it?"

"No, not from there," said Brazen. "But I have been *in the neighborhood,* so to speak. I know all about you."

"All?"

"At least from the time you turned five," clarified Brazen. "I know only bits and pieces of your early years."

"Oh, so you must have heard about me from Feeno," Jocelyn said, looking at the gnome.

Feeno shook his head.

"Then from Maag," concluded Jocelyn. "Did Maag want me to have you as a playmate?"

"I like to play," said Brazen.

Jocelyn was puzzled. "I wonder why Maag didn't tell me you were nearby. Probably because she knew Mother wouldn't approve of us meeting."

"What else doesn't Lady Idris know?" cut in Feeno, obviously excited by this line of inquiry.

"Yes!" exclaimed Jocelyn. "I want to hear, too. It makes me feel . . ."

"Stronger?" suggested Brazen.

"And a bit naughty," confessed Jocelyn. "But I don't feel ashamed. I feel . . . Help me, Feeno."

"Spirited?" he suggested.

"Yes, that's it," affirmed Jocelyn. Indeed, she'd felt her mood shift from somber and distrustful to excited and inquisitive, as if one mood had elbowed past another. This new temper was very like how she felt the first weeks following her odd-year birthdays (once she got over her sick spell).

"Let's make a game of telling what Lady Idris doesn't know," suggested Feeno.

"What a good idea!" exclaimed Jocelyn. "We should take turns."

"You go," Brazen said to Jocelyn, "since I've already had one."

"More like three or four," asserted Jocelyn.

"But nearly all of them had to do with the open window," said Feeno in Brazen's defense. "I'd say she had two turns at the most."

"I'll be quiet for a couple of rounds," conceded Brazen.

"Let's see," said Jocelyn. "Mother doesn't know that when I was younger, Feeno and I would balance a slat from my bed on a stool and sit on opposite ends and bounce."

"We called it *Titter Tatter,*" said Feeno with a smile. "We should play that again."

"Aren't I too big?" questioned Jocelyn. "And you've put on weight. We'd break the board."

"Don't worry about that," Feeno assured her. "I can find a slat of strong wood, or I can fashion a board for us. I'm next, aren't I?"

Brazen nodded.

"Lady Idris doesn't know we bat balloons," said Feeno.

"Not my favorite sport," remarked Brazen. "Mother doesn't know you pretend," she continued, addressing Jocelyn.

"You were supposed to lose a turn," objected Jocelyn. "Oh, but no matter. I want to hear about pretending."

"You like that, don't you?" said Brazen. *"You be the father,* you'd say to Feeno in your Miss Tragic period, and you'd take the part of the daughter. There'd be a heart-wrenching scene in which he'd blame you for something you hadn't done—or *had* done for a good reason—but he wouldn't listen. He'd drag you off to an orphanage and abandon you there to be raised by an evil headmistress."

"I didn't like playing *that* father," said Feeno.

"Your turn, Jocelyn," said Brazen, urging her to go on.

Jocelyn thought for a moment. "Mother doesn't know we make up games like *Pick up Twigs."*

"Jocelyn can take one from the pile without moving the others," said Feeno. "She wins all the time. I'm too fumbly."

"May I take your turn?" Brazen asked Feeno. "Then I'll give you mine."

"That sounds fair," said Feeno.

"Mother doesn't know that you and Feeno play tag," said Brazen, "and that you race—running, hopping, or walking backwards. There isn't room here, so you go down to the ground floor when it's morning and Mother is sleeping and frolic to your heart's content. You did that especially when you were daring, but even later to shake off some of your sadness and gloom; I imagine you did so earlier, too."

"She did," confirmed Feeno. "She also had an imaginary friend."

"Ceri!" Jocelyn blurted.

"I'm surprised you remember her," said Feeno. "You were only two or three—two, it was."

"The name just popped out," said Jocelyn. Maag recently had reminded her about the imaginary friend—a *delucination* she'd said Mother called it.

"You liked having company," said Feeno. "I had my outside tasks, Maag her inside ones, so lots of time you had to make do on your own. But you told your mother how much fun Ceri was, which put an end to her. Your temper was often flaring then—Miss Fury you were—and you had fits over it. But Lady Idris said Ceri would lead you astray. She demanded you stop playing with her."

Mother shouldn't have done that, thought Jocelyn. *Even now it makes me mad. I gave up the imaginary friend, Maag told me, because I was afraid not to.*

"But I didn't give up playing," Jocelyn asserted. "When Mother questions me about play, I lie to her. It's hard for me to believe she doesn't notice when I lie; I don't think I'm very good at it. Are you sure Mother doesn't know about the games and the rest?"

"If she did, she'd have put a stop to them," answered Brazen.

"I think I missed my turn," said Feeno. "Lady Idris doesn't know Jocelyn paints with brushes and paper Maag takes from Jocelyn's father's supplies."

"They aren't being used," said Jocelyn in Maag's defense.

"There's nothing wrong with it," Feeno assured her.

"And there's nothing wrong with reading books Mother hasn't assigned to you," said Brazen to Jocelyn.

How fortunate, thought Jocelyn, *that Maag found children's books!* They had been in a chest that had once belonged to her father's sister, Lynette.

"Lady Idris also doesn't know Jocelyn reads to me," said Feeno. "My favorite book is *Cobwebs to Catch Flies."*

"The one I like best is *Adventures of a Pincushion,"* said Jocelyn, smiling. "But it's for children. Now I read grown-up books." These Maag borrowed from Jocelyn's father's study and her grandfather's library. They were a strange assortment, because Maag couldn't read the titles. Jocelyn immediately put aside a text on alchemy (alchimia), because it was written in Latin. She found *The Sceptical Chymist,* which declared that matter is made up of clusters of corpuscles in motion, much too . . . well, too much. "I like the novel for adults I'm reading now," she said. "It's about a young woman named Clarissa whose parents try to control her life."

"That story sounds familiar," remarked Brazen with a wink.

"Whose turn is it?" asked Feeno.

They looked at each other blankly.

"We don't have to keep to the order," said Jocelyn.

"That's my spirit!" exclaimed Brazen. "I'll go next. Let's see: Mother doesn't know that you make music by imitating birds, and that you dance with a step and a hop with each foot alternately."

Jocelyn, feeling energetic, sprang up from her bed and demonstrated the dance with Feeno by her side, his hand on her shoulder and hers on his. She loved the way her feet tapped the floor, allowing her body to flow in concert with itself and her partner. At dance she wasn't ungainly; she was light and free.

"You're feeling better," observed Brazen.

Jocelyn stopped, causing Feeno to stumble. "Did I have an attack tonight?" she asked.

"The worst I've seen," replied Brazen.

"I don't feel any of the consequences," said Jocelyn. "Usually, it takes more time for me to recover. I wheeze and cough and sniffle and sneeze and am short of breath and tired out—at least for a few days."

"You usually don't have a dose of Smolder," said Feeno.

"Smolder? Is that one of Mother's restoratives?" asked Jocelyn. "Last evening she put ash in my tea to help me survive the night, and poisons to kill Mother Nature. Is that why I feel well?"

"Smolder is a restorative," said Brazen, "but it's not Mother's; it's yours."

"Mine?" exclaimed Jocelyn. "I don't have any such . . . Wait! Mother used to call me Miss Smolder."

"That was during one of your angry periods," said Feeno.

"Mother said I scowled for a whole year."

"Not with me and Maag," corrected Feeno. "That's another thing Lady Idris doesn't know. You'd be out of sorts, but you couldn't keep a frown when Maag and I played with you."

Why was I more horrid with Mother? wondered Jocelyn. *Was it . . . Oh, it must be. It was because she was horrid with me.*

Brazen said, "Speaking of frowns, what's that scowl upon your face?"

"Mother," said Jocelyn. "I was thinking about her."

"Does she make you angry?" asked Brazen softly.

"Mostly she makes me feel sad and worthless," said Jocelyn. "I try to please her, but I'm never good enough." Jocelyn looked at the window. "Say, is it after midnight?"

"It's way past," said Brazen. "Mother came just before midnight."

"Mother was here?" exclaimed Jocelyn with amazement. "Did she come to see if I was all right?"

"Not exactly," said Feeno.

Brazen said, "She came to see if you'd gotten rid of your gloom. You hadn't, so she did it for you."

"Was she angry that I hadn't done it myself?" asked Jocelyn.

Feeno spoke up. "She was upset with you for coming down sick. But it was Lady Idris who caused the attack."

"Mother is to blame?" questioned Jocelyn. "But . . . it's after midnight. It's my birthday! And I'm feeling tip-top. The bad spirits are gone."

"Here's Mother's gift—your latest spirit," said Brazen, pointing to the balloon whose color was a light gray and seemed to be struggling to keep itself from sinking.

"Mother gave me that?" exclaimed Jocelyn. "It looks as if it's in an awful state. But it's the latest *balloon*. Why did you say it's a spirit?"

"Glum's in there," said Brazen.

"In there?" exclaimed Jocelyn. "Are you teasing me?"

"She isn't," affirmed Feeno.

"That's good, isn't it?" asked Jocelyn. "Who wants to be glum?"

"But you had good reason to feel glum," said Brazen. "All your life, Mother has been taking away your genuine feelings, those that make you alive, and replacing them with artificial ones that deaden you. She wants to turn you into Miss Prim. *Prim* is the name Smolder gave the straitlaced spirit Mother is trying to inspire in you."

Jocelyn felt the truth of what Brazen was saying. Still, it was hard to believe. "Isn't she doing it for my own good?" Jocelyn objected.

The bronze spirit bristled. "When you turned seven, Mother took brazen out of you—me! How could that have been good for you?"

"I don't mean to be rude," said Jocelyn carefully, "but, when Mother called me Miss Brazen, she said I was bigheaded, a show-off, noisy, stubborn, shameless—"

"Yes, yes," agreed Brazen, nodding impatiently, "but you also wouldn't be kept down; you were brave and confident."

Jocelyn sat down on her bed. *I should resist these accusations against Mother, but there must be truth in them, or Feeno would have objected.* She started to heat up, as if she were about to burst into flame; she felt rebellious—not against Brazen and Feeno but against Mother. *Is this on account of the dose of anger Feeno said I'd . . . But how did I swallow Smolder?* She surveyed the ceiling. Sure enough, the inflated orange balloon was missing, as was the bronze. She spied their popped remnants on the floor.

"Where's the golden balloon?" Jocelyn asked.

"Lady Idris told Maag to come and get it," said Feeno.

"Maag was here?" said Jocelyn, surprised.

"It's been a busy night," said Feeno. "She had to take the balloon to Lady Idris."

"Another thing Mother doesn't know," said Brazen, "is that if a balloon is popped, a spirit-girl will tumble out."

"I can't believe you could have come out of a balloon," said Jocelyn, shaking her head. "You're much too big."

"I saw Brazen roll out head over heels and Smolder spin down from the air," said Feeno. "Maag also saw them fall."

So Maag, too, can vouch for this marvel, thought Jocelyn. "I want to see it with my own eyes," she said.

CHAPTER 22

MY POLLIWOGS!

IMMEDIATELY FOLLOWING his transformation into a toad, Angwyn was inclined to give up, so impossible appeared his situation. How was he ever to reach the country house? It seemed, now that he'd become a toad, so much further away. But he had to try, mostly for Joycelyn's sake.

Do toads undertake long treks? he wondered. *They don't migrate, do they?* He had little knowledge of them; indeed, he'd never paid any attention to them. *I may be the first toad to have a distant destination,* he surmised. *But at what rate does a toad travel?* He gave a leap, testing his mobility, but fell on his chin. Pushing himself up with his arms *(or are they front legs?),* he made a few hops, but they proved pathetic. It wasn't from lack of practice; he hadn't the legs for them. He tried walking, which he found more suitable. Increasing his speed, he broke into a run. *Amazing! I'd never have suspected that a toad could move so fast.* Soon, however, he tired. *Short spurts won't take me far,* he thought, *at least in any reasonable amount of time. It will take weeks, maybe months, for me to reach the country house.*

Ceffyl sniffed at him. Angwyn grabbed hold of his muzzle, hoping that the horse would lift him and swing him onto his back, but Ceffyl, obviously wanting nothing to do with a toad, shied away, shaking him loose, and cantered off toward the country house.

Unfaithful horse, thought Angwyn.

But he forgave him at once. A toad hadn't the appearance of the sort of creature Ceffyl would carry, and as for his smell . . . He pinched his nostrils shut with his facial muscles. His skin still had traces of a white, stinking substance that had oozed out of him here on the path. The odor would put anyone off, including himself.

Now what? wondered Angwyn. *Take one step at a time. Keep a good pace. Follow the cleared path home.* He set off on his journey.

In spite of the long day he'd endured, the nighttime invigorated him; he felt . . . nocturnal. He scurried off the path into a patch of daisies, breaking off a leaf with his sticky tongue and gulping it down. Spotting a grasshopper, he threw his tongue forward, caught the insect mid-hop, and hurled it back into his mouth. It rattled about, and he choked, having insufficient saliva to swallow it, but his eyes squeezed down into the roof of his mouth and propelled the insect down his throat.

How did I know to do that? he wondered.

Then he realized it must be because he was not only a toad in appearance, he had the instincts of a toad.

I just ate a grasshopper! he marveled.

It had happened so fast he hadn't had time to weigh the pros and cons. Actually, it didn't taste bad; indeed, it hadn't any taste, probably because he didn't have teeth to grind the juices from his prey. His stomach felt a bit uneasy, but the twitches there soon subsided.

The path ran along a creek, and Angwyn observed shallow pools of water on its bank where lots of toads and frogs had congregated and were making quite a racket—not only croaks but chirps, whistles, peeps, clucks, barks, and grunts. Several were calling out, "Ribbit. Ribbit."

I must hurry along, he thought, though he took time to nab a dragonfly and a couple of pond skaters. He feared the toads might detect he wasn't one of them, and the big ones looked as if they were ruffians.

Then (he couldn't help himself), he suddenly shouted out, "RrrrrrrrrrrrrrrrrrrrrrrrrrrrrrrrRUP!" What had he said? He was beside himself with embarrassment. But there was no stopping the impulse. "RrrrrrrrrrrrrrrrrrrRUP! RrrrrrrrrrrrrrrrRUP!"

A toad bounded to him, halting just short of a collision. It was larger than he, but Angwyn knew immediately (he couldn't have said how) it was female. Rather than be repulsed, he felt . . . *No, it isn't possible. I can't be attracted to . . . to* her. He was flabbergasted. *She's a common . . . No, she's not common; she has a yellow streak from her head to . . .* He peered around her. *Yes, it goes down her back. She's a natterjack toad. And she came to me, as if choosing me for a dance.* He couldn't help noticing that she had the most beautiful eyes, like polished, deep-green jewels.

But she's a toad! he protested. *I'm a . . .*

What am I? I have more than the features of a toad; I have its nature. He could counter it with his mind, which remained human, at least for now, but . . . what use was the mind when he was mesmerized by such beautiful, deep-green—

Bumping came from all sides. Other toads were jostling for her attention. He pushed them away and, with his rear legs, kicked up mud, splattering the rivals at his back.

She only has eyes for me! he wanted to shout. Instead, he rasped, "RrrrrrrrrrrrrrrrRUP!"

The others tried to imitate his voice, but theirs hadn't the volume. They fell back, defeated. He turned his attention on her, taking full measure of his prize.

She's a toad! he rebuked himself. *How can I even entertain the idea?*

She inched past him, flaunting her figure (or so it seemed); he was enamored by its fullness, its roundness. She squatted in the pool near its edge, and he scrambled to her, placing his fingers' black pads on her shoulders.

I'm ill-equipped for this! he feared, peering at his underparts and finding nothing recognizable. Nonetheless, he climbed onto her back.

Into the water she let go strings of . . . *What are those dark specks?* he questioned. *Eggs? They must be. A double row of them. There are thousands!* He felt a surge welling in his nether region, and he discharged a fluid that trailed after and soon mixed with the eggs.

I've fertilized them!

Her body began to vibrate, and he sensed she wanted him off her back. But he must have been slow to jump, because she whipped around, throwing him beyond the pool and into the stream. Struggling to the surface, he thrashed.

Don't panic! he thought. *Surely toads can swim.*

Apparently, though, they weren't very good at it. Maybe he was unique because he hadn't been a tadpole. A frog glided past him, and he wished for the first time that he were a frog. He tried to imitate its kick, but he wasn't any good at it; the toad-kick was manifestly inferior. He floundered, pitching and plunging, until, thankfully, he touched bottom. His nostrils in the air, he heaved himself forward until he stumbled onto the shore.

Fortunately, the current wasn't strong, so it hadn't carried him far. Though he was winded, it didn't take him long to walk upstream to the pool of water where he and his mate . . .

Where is she? he wondered, looking about. *Has she run off? What sort of mother abandons her eggs?*

Idris! That's the sort. Did he have a predilection toward mates who weren't nurturing? So it seemed. Or was this female just doing what a female toad did? He somehow knew she wouldn't return. It was *his* job to look after the eggs. He peered into the shallow pool. There was no denying the impulse. He felt an overwhelming need to protect their spawn.

He tried to reason (to no avail) against this compulsion to stand watch against dragonflies, diving beetles, and insects he couldn't name. He'd splash the water, scaring them away, or eat them, depending on his appetite. Several times he made up his mind to get on with his travels, but he couldn't seem to follow through.

He also kept an eye out for predators who wished *him* for a meal. Sure enough, he soon had an encounter with one—an owl. Angwyn was off his guard because of his skin, which had begun to feel tight and ill fitting, as if it were a sweater he'd outgrown. He was stretching and humping his back when the owl swooped down, got its claws into him, and lifted him into the air. He twisted, trying to get loose, and his skin split. He fell through it, as if the owl had pulled it over his head. Fortunately, he wasn't far off the ground and landed in soft mud. He was shocked that he'd lost his skin (not to mention nearly his life), but he had only to look himself over to see that he had a fresh, new exterior. But the mud . . . *Already I need a bath,* he thought.

Then there was the magpie. For several days it harassed him, hopping sideways around him with its wings slightly opened. Was it a war dance? Only after it nipped at him did he realize it was seeking a position from which to peck out an eye. *Are mine as inviting as the gem-like eyes of my good-for-nothing mate?* he wondered.

On the seventh day after their fertilization, the eggs hatched.

My polliwogs! he congratulated himself, excited.

But he was equally thrilled he could be on his way. *I must hurry to my country home,* he thought, *to do what I can to safeguard my other offspring—the human one.*

CHAPTER 23

AN EPIC JOURNEY

AFTER SCAMPERING ONLY a short distance toward home, Angwyn felt a strong sensation—a tug—which drew him back to the pool. Apparently, his job here wasn't complete. He had the same overwhelming impulse he'd had with the eggs, namely, to protect these offspring until... *When? Must I wait until they metamorphose into baby toads? Will I be free then? Or must I nurture them until they mature?*

There was so much to take in! He was surprised, for example, when only a few days later he once more shed his skin. It turned out that every five days or so he acquired a new outfit. *Toads are certainly a dapper species,* he decided.

About six to eight weeks later (it was hard to keep track of time), fully formed baby toads, changed as if by magic, took their first steps from the pool. In spite of his diligence, there were far fewer than the number of tadpoles had been, not to mention the thousands of eggs. Even so, there were lots of baby toads.

Thank goodness I don't have to name them, he thought.

But he worried that they were so tiny—less than a quarter of an inch in length. How would they survive without him?

But, he reminded himself, *I have responsibilities to my human family—Joycelyn and my mother and father; also to the servants, Maag and Feeno. I can't babysit toads, even if they are of my blood. I must let myself leave.*

Tentatively, he backed away from the pool. He felt no tug to return. Only his mind and what must have been a *human* sense of guilt caused him pause. *I should father my little toads,* he thought. *Or should I?*

Not if I'm a toad, he realized, for he experienced no further impulse to attend to these offspring. Quite the opposite: he felt footloose. It was natural, he was certain, for baby toads to look after themselves.

Angwyn scurried off, keeping to the path, eager to make up time. But it was broad daylight, and soon he felt sleepy. The summer sun took a toll on him, causing him to overheat. He eyed a shrub with yellow catkins and leaves that brushed the ground—a hazel, he thought—and plunged into it, sprawling in its undergrowth, cooled by the shade. It offered, too, a hiding place from predators. He yawned and shut his eyes.

He had a dream. It began with the sensation of something enveloping his head. It was as if he were being squeezed back into his mother's womb. He awoke to the horror of being swallowed headfirst by a grass snake. At once, toxins oozed from him, making him slippery, which helped him yank free, though the snake perhaps did not put up a fight because of how much he reeked.

It was dusk. Angry with himself, not for allowing a snake's attack (how could he have foreseen that?) but for having slept the day away, he picked up his pace, resolving to travel all night.

But I'm hungry, he realized. *I can't get far if I don't replenish myself.*

He stole a fly from the air and tossed it down his throat. He caught a moth. A meandering worm was an easy picking. As he went forward, any prey that crossed his path he devoured—beetles, ants, spiders, snails, and slugs. He ate flora on the side, such as mallow leaves, flowers of nettles, mushrooms, and wild garlic. By morning his belly was full, and he was ready for a good day's sleep. He regretted, however, that he'd gotten only a bit of the way toward home.

The following days and weeks passed similarly. Encounters with predators became routine and were always unnerving, even when he proved to have the advantage. They engendered in him a fear of the wild that caused him to dart for cover at every shadow, movement, and noise. This made for delays.

To make matters worse, he discovered that toads hibernate. One fall night, when he should have been most active, he began to feel extraordinarily sleepy. He buried himself in leaf litter and mud, even burrowing into the ground with his hind legs. When he woke up, he was astonished that it was spring. *I've slept almost half a year*, he thought. *This toad behavior has to stop, or I'll never reach home.*

But I'm feeling procreative!

It was no use. The years passed, and the cycle remained: hibernate in late autumn and winter, then mate and look after offspring, then hunt and hide from predators in spring, summer, and early autumn. That was his existence, and he could find no way of escaping it.

One bright morning, Angwyn stumbled onto a farm. Settling down in a patch of rhubarb for a day's sleep, he heard sounds of hoofbeats and rattling. Peeking through the foliage, he saw a cart, laden with produce, passing by on a wide and well-maintained road.

It has to be the one to Brynmor, he realized.

He had but a short wait before a carriage came down the road, traveling away from Brynmor and toward the country house. Scurrying to intercept it, he took hold of an underpart and hoisted himself up, then managed to climb to the mudguard. Holding fast, he bumped along toward home.

Within a few days, he was there. Spotting Feeno in the garden, Angwyn followed him to the house, slipping inside behind the gnome without being seen. He went immediately to the nursery, only to discover, by peering beneath the door, that it had been turned into a workshop. *Idris must keep certain of my father's books of magic there,* he thought. *If I can peruse them, I may find an antidote to the spell Idris cast upon me, though the chances are slim. Which book? Which page? Have I the dexterity to handle a book?* In any case, there wasn't an opening into the workshop.

Proceeding to the sitting room, he was surprised by Idris, who came out of her bedroom. He held still, and she did not notice him. Instead, she turned away to check the time on the long-case clock. *Where,* wondered Angwyn, *has that come from?*

The change in Idris was striking. The symmetry of her face was distorted by a sneer, her penetrating eyes were like daggers, and her luminous skin had been whitewashed with cosmetics. Rather than beautiful and alluring, she looked grotesque and frightening.

As Idris stepped away from the clock, she sniffed the air, and Angwyn realized he was seeping toxins. He scurried behind the clock and hunkered down. At his touch, the clock quivered, making it feel alive.

As she approached his hiding place, she froze, as if she were a statue. *How odd!* Angwyn thought. Taking the opportunity, however, he scampered out of the sitting room. It was then, for the first time in nearly thirteen years, that he saw Joycelyn. She was coming (he would later learn) for her evening interview.

Doubtful that she would receive him with open arms in his present state, Angwyn again hid, this time behind a storage bench in the hall. *So big Joycelyn has become!* he thought. He grieved over how much of her growing up he'd missed but surged with joy at the wonder of her and the love they could share if only he could figure out how to make himself known to her.

As Joycelyn turned into the sitting room, she sniffed the air and made a face, shaking her head in dismay, then crossed to Idris's door and knocked. She didn't seem surprised when her mother didn't respond, as if this, like a disgusting smell, was a frequent occurrence.

Peeking around the corner into the sitting room, Angwyn had a good view of his daughter. *Tall for her age,* he thought, *and slender; she's somewhat like her mother was in appearance when I met her, but Joycelyn's eyes are soft and her features rounded. Oh, how I love her freckles and bright-red hair!*

But she wore a frown upon her face and looked out of spirits. She also seemed morose, increasingly so as the minutes passed and she had nothing to do but slouch in an uncomfortable chair.

Idris called out, "Come in, Miss Glum. I can suffer you for a while."

Miss Glum? wondered Angwyn. *Suffer?*

Before Joycelyn closed the door to her mother's bedroom behind her, he heard Idris say, "List the things you did today that were proper."

Angwyn had a bad feeling about what his wife would consider proper, not to mention the things she would regard as improper, which surely Idris would want listed next.

At that moment, Angwyn noticed Maag coming down the hall toward the sitting room. *Maag!* he thought excitedly. *Maternal, amiable, hilarious—how I enjoyed her company.*

The housekeeper didn't turn into the sitting room. But as she passed the entrance, she sniffed the air, obviously getting a whiff of his foul smell (he was making quite an impression). Like Joycelyn, she didn't seem surprised and muttered, "What's my Odoriferous up to now?" before continuing on her way.

To Angwyn's surprise, Maag left behind a disturbing scent of her own, one he'd smelled before but couldn't place, which caused him thereafter to regard her with suspicion.

So what now? he wondered. *I need an ally, someone who, at the very least, can turn the pages of Father's magic books. Joycelyn? Besides this repulsive guise of mine, she may not be receptive to me if, as I suspect, Idris has filled her with lies about my running off. Unfortunately, my severely limited vocabulary will not allow me to explain my absence.*

Feeno? Unlike Maag, he has a fine scent. From my encounters with him years ago, I found him gentle and compassionate. He is the one I must befriend, if I am to have any chance of success.

But months later, on this night before Jocelyn's thirteenth birthday, Angwyn was no closer to transforming himself into a man or saving his daughter than when he'd first arrived.

CHAPTER 24

A SURGE OF FEELING

SITTING ON THE SIDE of the bed, Jocelyn watched as Brazen and Feeno conferred over which spirit should be released next from her balloon.

Is this a joke? Jocelyn wondered. *A birthday trick they're pulling on me to brighten a day that's usually dark? It isn't very funny. But so much they'd said had been uplifting, especially that she wasn't always at fault and that, just maybe, she wasn't a bad daughter but had been cursed with a bad mother.*

Brazen turned to Jocelyn. "Is there a spirit you would like to have join us first?"

"It doesn't matter," said Jocelyn dejectedly.

At once, Bustle swooped down and banged on Jocelyn's head until she giggled.

Batting the balloon away, Jocelyn said, "Green is as good as any other."

Brazen took the balloon and fiddled with its knot. "My fingers aren't deft," she said.

"Don't look at me," said Feeno.

Brazen bit the balloon. There was a pop, and Bustle burst out. She hit the floor running.

"I'm so excited!" she cried as she raced toward Jocelyn, then leaped into her arms with the force of a strong wind. Jocelyn fell backwards onto the bed, the blow having knocked the air from her.

"Bustle!" scolded Brazen. "She'd just started breathing normally."

Bustle, straddling Jocelyn on her knees, leaned forward. "Sorry," she said. "I had such a surge of feeling, I . . ."

". . . hit Jocelyn like a tornado," said Brazen.

"Would you please get off me?" asked Jocelyn in a strangled voice.

"Oh, pardon!" exclaimed Bustle, dismounting. She took Jocelyn by the shoulders and pulled her into an embrace.

It didn't take long for Jocelyn to regain her breath, but it was a while more before she pulled herself together. *Am I dreaming?* she wondered. She pinched her arm to wake up, but everyone was still there, Bustle even touching her, which caused her to feel some of this spirit-girl's excitement. *How is such a thing possible?*

Trying to be sensible, Jocelyn disentangled herself from Bustle and declared, "This can't be Bustle. She's bigger than Brazen and talks as well as she. How can she be a one-year-old?"

"I'm a spirit," Bustle said into her ear. "You don't measure spirits in years. You can *bustle* when you're one, thirteen, twenty-five, or ninety-nine. Well . . . perhaps not when you're ninety-nine."

There must be magic here, thought Jocelyn. *"What's bustle?"* she asked.

"When you act like this," responded the green spirit-girl, bouncing on the bed. "And this," she said, leaping down and careening around the room. "Mother named you Miss Bustle because I inspired you to romp. You wouldn't be still. You were into everything, making a mess of her household. You flustered her. And you *exuded cheerfulness,* which from Mother's mouth sounded as if you'd soiled your diapers. You were exuberant, wild."

Feeno spoke up: "Lady Idris would often complain, *Miss Bustle's on the loose again,* blaming me for not restraining you."

"I made you high-spirited," said Bustle to Jocelyn. "Mother couldn't tolerate that. She had to get rid of me. But here I am! Won't you join me in *Follow the Leader*? I'll be the leader."

Feeno shushed her. "We don't want Lady Idris to hear us," he explained. "You're being very noisy."

Bustle pressed a finger against her lips, but she remained as bubbly as before, and her animation was contagious. Jocelyn was feeling sprightly. She couldn't help but follow the spirit-girl, imitating her movements. Brazen and Feeno joined in. They all pranced and twirled. Bustle did a cartwheel. When Jocelyn attempted the same, she lost balance and fell to the side, which made her laugh. But remembering how Feeno had toppled over when he'd tried to stand on his head at supper that evening, she cautioned him to be careful.

"I'll give the cartwheel a pass," said Feeno.

Bustle led them over the bed, then tried to worm back under it but was too big. So she vaulted onto the bed, and the others joined her. Pointing at the door, Bustle whispered loudly, "Let's go downstairs!"

"I'm sure Lady Idris is still up," cautioned Feeno.

"We don't want her spoiling our fun," agreed Jocelyn.

"Then let's stay here and have a birthday party!" cried Bustle. She again put a finger to her lips. "A quiet one," she whispered.

"A party needs sweets," declared Jocelyn.

"Lady Idris forbids cakes, hard candies, barely sugar, and such," Feeno reminded her. "She wants to keep you slight."

"It's *my* birthday!" whispered Jocelyn emphatically. "I will not be fed cucumbers!"

"We haven't time for parties and sweets!" interrupted Brazen, showing considerable vexation. "I don't know what came over me—skipping about as if I hadn't a care."

"But it was such a delight to play," protested Jocelyn.

"Yes, yes!" agreed Brazen. "But Gullible's in danger. We're all in danger, including you, Jocelyn. We need to get more of us inside you, so you have the wherewithal to stand up to our mock-mother."

"Inside me?" questioned Jocelyn, hardly believing her ears. "I really took Smolder in?" She looked at Feeno, who nodded in agreement. "But how?" she asked.

"We don't know," said Brazen.

Bustle pushed Feeno and Brazen off the bed and firmly laid Jocelyn down on her back, then sat next to her. "You were lying there," she said to Jocelyn, "and Smolder was here where I am when she dissolved and passed into you. I want to see if the same thing happens to me."

This is ridiculous, thought Jocelyn. But unlikely things were occurring right and left. And Feeno and Brazen were so serious, Bustle so eager.

They waited, Bustle fidgeting.

"Maybe if you sat still like Smolder did?" suggested Feeno.

"I did that," retorted Bustle.

"Only for a moment," said Feeno.

Bustle folded her hands and rested them on her lap. But soon she was taking them apart, then clasping them. She banged her hands against her thighs. She crossed and uncrossed her legs, then crossed them again and raised her feet. She wriggled her buttocks, causing her to slide off the bed onto the floor.

"Being still isn't in her nature," observed Brazen.

"Why don't you take her place?" Feeno asked.

"But if *I* were to disappear, who'd supervise?"

"Feeno could," said Bustle, turning herself in circles, as she sat on the floor. "And he'd do better. You're too bossy."

"I'd manage," asserted Feeno. "As Jocelyn's nanny, didn't I keep Miss Bustle from hurting herself? Didn't I calm Miss Fury? Didn't I get a smile now and then from Miss Sorrowful?"

"Feeno's a good nanny," affirmed Bustle, nodding her head.

"Besides," said Jocelyn, "Brazen seems the sort of spirit I need in me if I'm to face Mother."

"You've hit the mark," Brazen congratulated her. "I'm vital to—"

"Along with Smolder, of course," added Jocelyn.

Brazen made a face but otherwise did not retort, as she sat down on the bed.

Bustle sprang up from the floor and leaned expectantly toward Brazen, her eyes wide, her mouth open. After a few moments, she fussed, "You're not doing any better than I did."

"I just sat down!" barked Brazen.

"Patience isn't one of my virtues," sniffed Bustle.

"Smolder stroked Jocelyn's hair," Feeno reminded Brazen.

"What could that possibly have to do with it?" asked Brazen.

"Maybe it caused me to dream about her," suggested Jocelyn, "and . . . I don't know but if I liked her . . ."

"How could you like a spirit who's so ill-tempered?" questioned Brazen.

"I like you," retorted Jocelyn, "and you can be quite unpleasant."

Brazen bristled, but she stroked Jocelyn's hair as they waited . . . and waited, Bustle keeping busy by dashing, leaping, and tumbling.

Suddenly, Quizzical swooped down in her balloon and hovered in front of the bronze spirit-girl.

"Of course!" cried Brazen. "Who better to solve a puzzle than one who asks questions?"

"One who has answers?" suggested Feeno.

Brazen glared at him, as she squeezed the balloon until it popped. A yellow spirit-girl tumbled out. Jocelyn lifted herself on one elbow and took in with amazement this brightly colored likeness of herself, who was sprawled on the floor. She still found it difficult to believe her own eyes. *Surely I'm dreaming,* she thought.

"What if the magic wasn't only our doing?" asked Quizzical, getting to her feet. "Maybe the toad, there on Jocelyn's shoulder," she said, pointing, "played a part."

"How could a toad do that?" questioned Jocelyn. "And why?"

No one had an answer.

Finally, Brazen said, "We might as well give Toad a try. Feeno, would you please bring it in from outside the door?"

The gnome soon returned. "Toad's gone," he said. "Likely it's in the cellar. I'll fetch it."

CHAPTER 25

A COMPLETE MAKEOVER

EXILED FROM JOCELYN'S room, Angwyn had hastened to the sitting room and was now within striking distance of Idris (if only he could strike). He was pleased that, when his daughter woke up after the expulsion of Prim, she'd said she'd dreamed about him. His nightly attempts to impart his thoughts to her appeared to be succeeding. *If only I could reveal myself in the flesh . . .*

But one thing at a time. First, I must rescue Gullible. Then I will steal the crystal. And then I must gain access to the magic book that contains the spell that transformed me into a toad. That these were close to impossible tasks, he would not dwell upon. As with his epic journey, he must try. His daughter's nature was at stake. Having witnessed Idris's extraction of gloom from Joycelyn and his wife's testimony that she'd stolen their daughter's natural moods, he was desperate to restore Joycelyn to herself and redeem himself as a father.

Angwyn nestled up against the long-case clock, whose warmth comforted him. He felt a kinship with this clock, though he couldn't explain why. He puzzled, too, over its presence. *Father must have ordered it before Idris took over the household,* he reasoned. *Otherwise, it would not be in the French Regency style with its deer's feet, bulging panels, decorative scrolls, and gold leaf. But why would Idris have accepted it? She hated Father's taste. And why had she put it in her sitting room and not in a place more distant?* Answers to these questions only time would tell.

Angwyn heard the ring of the bell for Maag to come to Idris's chambers. When the housekeeper rushed into the sitting room a few minutes later, she was breathing heavily and muttering. "How can Iduress have uncovered so quick the anecdote to the blemishes of me and my speech?" she asked herself. "And if she hasn't, how can a body get anything done if it's always being bothered?" She hesitated at the door to the bedroom, apparently to gather herself, then knocked.

"Come in," Idris uttered in a surprisingly weak voice.

Maag opened the door and took a few steps in. Angwyn, who had hurried from his hiding place next to the grandfather clock, scooted under Maag's housedress, which nearly touched the floor.

"Your voice sounds decrepit, my Bugle-horn," said Maag, "Are you sick?"

"I am weary," Idris replied.

Angwyn peeked out and saw that his wife was lying on her bed.

"That bath did not invigorate me," Idris complained. "You said the thyme was fresh, and you did not cramp, so it must be true. I just took another swig of distilled dandelions. Its chill already is making my blood brisker. Come," she said, rising and taking hold of a lit candle. "We have work to do."

"Pardon, my Taskmaster. I also—"

Idris waved her hand impatiently for the housekeeper to follow her into the workshop, and Maag tiptoed quickly across the bedroom. Angwyn scrambled to stay hidden under the housekeeper's dress and not get stepped on.

"Make sure the door is properly shut," said Idris. Maag made a sudden change in direction, and for several moments, Angwyn was uncovered. As with the owl, he risked a predator—this time a human one—spotting and swooping down on him.

"Where is Gullible?" Idris taunted, as she lit the wall candles in the workshop. "Ah, my green half-wit, you want me to play the hunter. You must wait. I have one of my prey. I do not feel, at the moment, like hunting another."

Angwyn peeked out again from under the hem of Maag's dress, looking for a more secure hiding place. Maag stopped abruptly, and he ran into her heel.

"What's that thump?" cried Maag, lifting her dress and looking down. Maag's eyes and Angwyn's met.

I'm doomed, thought Angwyn.

"Is it Gullible?" questioned Idris, who was lighting the candles on the worktable, her back to them.

Maag let go of her dress, and the hem dropped around Angwyn. "It's out of my sight," she said.

We haven't met, thought Angwyn. *Why is Maag protecting me?*

"That foul odor . . . Where have I smelled it before?" exclaimed Idris.

My glands! thought Angwyn, horrified. *They're giving me away again.* Frantic to stop them from secreting more of their poisons, he tried to bring optimistic thoughts to mind, but none came.

"Is it leftovers from the mole you fricasseed?" asked Maag.

"No, that smell was disgusting; I loved it. This one is loathsome."

"That's a fine distinguishment," observed Maag.

"The stench is male, that is certain," declared Idris. She hesitated. "Could it be . . ."

Is she thinking about me? wondered Angwyn.

"Later, I will have Feeno search for whatever sort of vermin it is," said Idris. "What gall it has to leave its odor behind! Maag, you must give my workshop a good scouring. Where are you going?"

"To get scours."

"Not now!" scolded Idris. "You are to be made over. I will not deny for another minute the pleasure we will share in that."

Taking a peek, Angwyn saw that Idris was busy clearing things off the worktable. He scurried into the fireplace, hiding in the ashes beneath the grate. Here he ceased oozing toxins.

"Undress," said Idris to Maag.

"Pardon? It's not my privates that need appraisal."

"Do as you are told," said Idris. "You will look peculiar in clothes."

"Methinks I look peculiar without them," retorted Maag, as she stepped out of her dress and shed her underwear.

"You are shivering," said Idris. "Should I light a fire?"

Angwyn's eyes widened.

"If Gullible is where I suspect," observed Idris, "it would smoke her out. But that would distract me from my task. Besides, the cold suits me, and I am the only one who counts.

"Now, sit on the worktable," Idris commanded, "and I will rub you with this ointment. It will soften your skin and make it pliable." Once she had applied the lotion, she told Maag to curl herself into a ball. "Here, I will help you."

"That's rare," observed Maag.

Idris shoved Maag's knees up against her chest. "Hold yourself together with your arms," she said, wrapping them around her legs. "Pull in your feet, lean forward, and bow your head."

"I feel like I'm inside an egg," said Maag.

"Exactly! You are about to be hatched anew."

"My tongue only," protested Maag, "not the whole assembly."

"Oh, but we must have a complete makeover," insisted Idris. "Defects in your first language may have been the cause of the impediments in your second. To correct your speech, I must put you as you were."

"I am as I were."

"You are in for a surprise," said Idris with a smile.

Angwyn, from years of having to be always on the lookout for predators, sensed a presence near him. *Probably Gullible?* he thought. He looked up into the chimney but saw only darkness. The damper, of course, would be closed to prevent Gullible from escaping into the world.

Idris, he saw, was walking around the table, checking Maag from every angle. "Relax!" she demanded, as she pressed Maag more into the shape of an egg.

"I'm about to crack!" cried out Maag.

"Sink your elbows," demanded Idris. "Loosen your shoulders. There! Do not move."

Idris was now on the far side of the worktable, facing the hearth. Angwyn didn't dare so much as wink. If Idris should detect any movement or noise . . . *I wish she'd use this magic on me,* he thought. *Is it possible that the spell she's casting on Maag will overreach, returning me to my former shape?*

Idris rubbed the white crystal and chanted gibberish (at least to Angwyn).

Shrieking, Maag convulsed. Her body collapsed, as if falling into itself, then filled out in a new shape. Feathers sprouted, wings unfurled, a tail extended, legs protruded, feet scuffled, a bill poked out, a black head followed, dark-brown eyes blinked open.

"My magpie," whispered Idris, beaming with pride, as she steadied herself by placing her hands on the worktable.

Maag's chest and back were black, her belly white, her wings iridescent with white tips, her long, black tail purple-banded near its end.

"Pretty bird," conceded Idris. "Why did you not become as fair a housekeeper?"

Angwyn buried himself deeper in the ashes, trying to contain his secretions. Toads were a common prey of magpies.

CHAPTER 26

FIE ON THEE!

WHILE THE MAGPIE lurched and staggered, Idris slowly recovered her strength. In spite of her many successes, she always marveled at her skill as a magician, discounting her failures as aberrations. There was not a feather out of place. *Oh, if only I had had an audience,* she thought.

Maag, gaining her balance, took high steps. Flapping her wings, she tried to launch.

"No flying," scolded Idris, folding in the wings of the magpie and grasping her with both hands.

Maag struggled, chattering, "Chack! Chack! Chack!"

Idris whisked her into a wire cage.

"Queg! Queg!"

"Your voice is jarring," complained Idris, "and your vocabulary tiresome." *But are your grammar and word choice correct?* she wondered. *How can I tell?* She held the crystal to her ear in hopes of understanding what Maag was saying. *If I hear the sounds in English,* she reasoned, *perhaps I can tell if they have imperfections.* But the crystal, an excellent translator of texts, did not serve as an interpreter of the spoken word. Of course, the sounds of magpies may not be language as humans know it and, therefore, incomprehensible to the crystal.

"Aag? Maag? Aag?"

"Quiet down, or I will wring your neck."

"Yak! Yak!"

"I am threatening you, birdbrain!"

"Chack! Aag? Queg!"

This chattering must stop, thought Idris. *She squawks like an infant. I cannot think!* She peered through the crystal, running a finger down the page of her book. *At last! An incantation with some sense to it. Too bad I must recite it seven (seven?) times.*

"Yak! Yak! Yak!" cried Maag.

"There will be no more yakking!" scolded Idris. Using the crystal as a lens, even as she rubbed it between her thumb and forefinger, Idris recited,

Untwist your tongue!
Bind the urge
to be ironic or sarcastic,
to utter half-truths or ambiguities.
Henceforth,
be plain-spoken,
using proper words in proper places.

After the seventh recitation, the magpie turned her head toward Idris and said, "Você é uma bruxa má."

"What?" cried Idris. "What are you saying?"

"Você é egoísta. Suas ideais são erradas, e suas ações são perversas."

"What language is that? French? Spanish? A dialect of one or the other?" Idris was short of breath, the magic having taken a toll. "Why are you not speaking English?"

"Anguish? O que é anguish? Eu não entendo você."

Idris flipped to the frontispiece of the book. She seldom bothered with the particular language of a text, because the crystal always showed it in English. *Printed in Sao Paulo,* she read. Maag was speaking Brazilian Portuguese! Correct Brazilian Portuguese, perhaps, but that gave little consolation. Idris did not understand a word of it—well, perhaps a few words, such as "egoísta" and "perversa." *Are the references to me?* she questioned. *How rude!*

Although Idris needed rest, she wanted first to amend the incantation, which had not specified English as the language Maag should speak. *It is not necessary to repeat the entire incantation,* she reasoned (seven times seemed beyond her present strength), *only the part about the use of appropriate words in appropriate ways.* The rest, which had to do with "untwisting the tongue," would apply in any language and should already have taken effect. Idris vigorously rubbed the crystal and spoke the incantation, substituting *the English of the Queen* for *proper words in proper places.*

After seven repetitions (or six, Idris having lost count from boredom) of the relevant lines of the incantation, the magpie regarded Idris sharply. "Verily I shalt discourse. 'Tis thou, foul creature, that hath done me wrong. Fie on thee!"

Idris collapsed onto the worktable, her elbows supporting her. "The English of the *present* Queen," she gasped, "not that of sixteenth-century Queen Elizabeth!"

"By my troth, thou art a scurvy wench," said the magpie. "Thou dost infect mine eyes."

Idris had not the energy to retort; she was exhausted. *I must lie down,* she thought, *before I do another correction, not to mention transform Maag back into a housekeeper.* Securing the cage with a padlock, she tossed its key on her worktable.

"Wither goest thou?" called out the magpie. "I am hungered and parched. Be aidant in a good maggot-pie's distress."

"Be thankful I do not put you out of your misery for good," said Idris weakly, though managing to slam the door behind her, the exertion, however, causing her to fall onto her bed.

I am worn out, too, from not having slept, she thought. *Look at how the light of dawn creeps around the edges of the drapes. Of course, my exhaustion is primarily due to the spells I have cast. The lot of a magician,* she supposed.

CHAPTER 27

OLD WIVES' TALES

*T*HAT WASN'T THE DRUMMING *of a woodpecker,* thought Elda. *That was the slam of a door. But why is there a door in the woods? And who shut it?*

Of course, there might be a cottage nearby. She hadn't known of anyone living in the area, but perhaps someone had recently discovered an abandoned house or built a new one. Or, because Elda was on an unfamiliar trail and in a part of the woods she'd never explored, a person or family might have been living here all this time.

Certain that the sound had come from behind her, she peered back along the path she'd been following.

That's impossible! she thought. *The trail . . . Where is it?*

Turning in the direction she'd been going, she saw that the path continued as far as she could see. She looked again at the way from which she'd come, confirming there was no trail—just woodlands thick with trees and shrubs.

I'm going mad! she thought. *Or is magic at work? Oldric's? But he wouldn't . . . not against me, unless . . . No, he'd never forsake me at Idris's bidding, no matter how strong his infatuation. Besides, he's angry with her for . . . Of course! She stole the white crystal. It's her use of it that's led me here and concealed the path home.*

But baby Jocelyn . . . She needs tending.

I couldn't have come far, she reasoned, the seemingly motionless sun indicating that hardly any time had passed. *It should be easy to find my way back, even without a trail.*

But wait! She checked the pockets of her dress and found that they were chock-full of the twigs, bark, and leaves that would ward off or sweep away evil spirits. She'd stopped, however, at just three trees—an ash, a juniper, and a rowan—and taken only a few of their charms. How could she have such a large collection of them? *Have I forgotten other stops I made?* she wondered. *Have I traveled a greater distance than I imagined? I must be very far from home.*

But the sun . . .

Confused, she sat down in a heap, her dress billowing around her. *Am I very near or very far from home?* she wondered.

"Why not both?"

Elda turned toward the voice and saw an old woman at the side of the path. She was dressed in an apron over a long, woolen tunic, her shoes were made of leather, and she wore a shawl and a round cap. She was perched on a large stone.

"How can it be both?" asked Elda.

"How can it not?" replied the old woman. "You've walked a great distance, but you haven't gotten far. Your pockets prove the one, the sun the other."

Can she read my thoughts? wondered Elda.

"I can't read," said the old woman. "Have you eaten fish today?"

"Fish?"

"It helps the brain put two and two together," said the old woman. "Or, in this case, one and one. Surely you know that. You're not a young woman."

"You're speaking of an old wives' tale," said Elda. "Are you an old wife?"

"I would be if I had a husband," answered the old woman. "That I don't, shows I'm wise."

"Wise? Then you must know where I am," said Elda.

"I do."

When the wise woman didn't continue, Elda asked, "Must I wrest it from you?"

"You've crossed into another world," said the wise woman.

"You jest."

"I do not," insisted the wise woman. "I'm here at great risk, and for what? Certainly not to amuse a stranger who doesn't belong here. Besides, sitting on a cold stone gives a person piles—or *hemorrhoids,* as some call them."

Another wives' tale, thought Elda.

"That doesn't mean it isn't true," said the wise woman.

They were silent for a while, each looking the other in the eye to prove that they weren't liars.

Elda broke the silence. "What is the *great risk* you've taken by coming here? Surely it's not piles."

The wise woman laughed. "No, it's more dangerous than that. This area is a borderland, a place where worlds meet. I risk being drawn into your world and becoming as lost as you are in mine."

"If there is risk here," asked Elda, "why have you come?"

"No one else volunteered," explained the wise woman. "From the beginning, we've kept an eye on you. We'd never had a stranger in our world, and we feared you'd cause us harm."

"Me?" exclaimed Elda.

"And others of your kind, should they follow," said the wise woman. "But none have, and you've stayed to yourself and not strayed from this borderland. We regard you now not as a threat but as a curiosity. I've come to ask what you're doing here."

"I'm having a stroll in the woods to get over an argument I had with my daughter-in-law."

"A stroll?" questioned the wise woman. "It's been a rather long one, hasn't it?"

"Has it? Then I must hurry home to look after my baby grandchild." Elda looked behind her, and her shoulders slumped. "It won't be easy without a path."

"Then go forward," suggested the wise woman.

Go forward to get back? thought Elda.

"It's no wives' tale," said the wise woman. "You're circling, and if you continue, you'll return to where you started. The trail keeps opening up before you. Follow it until . . ."

Elda leaned forward expectantly.

". . . until you find something misplaced but familiar," said the wise woman. "The year you came, a brave fellow explored this area, staying out of sight of you, of course, and discovered a baby's nursery."

"A nursery?" exclaimed Elda. " There's one in my house."

"Ah, ha!" exclaimed the wise woman. "I thought as much. But most everyone laughed at the fellow. *A nursery in the woods—how preposterous!* they said. He replied it was no laughing matter, especially when a wind nearly pushed him into it. I wondered at the time if he'd spied a portal to your world."

Oh, no! thought Elda. *That slam of a door I heard just a few minutes ago . . . Have I been shut out of my world?*

"On the contrary," said the old woman, "you've been alerted to the way in. The sound of the slam was intended to disrupt your endless, trance-like circling and enable you to find the portal to your own world. But you required more direct instruction, which is why I am here. The presence of the door indicates that the spell you've been under has weakened."

"It's the magic of my daughter-in-law that must have cast me here," asserted Elda.

"Is she a witch?"

Elda nodded.

"It's never good to have a witch for a daughter-in-law," said the wise woman.

CHAPTER 28

A TEA PARTY

FURY AND TRAGIC crowded Brazen, each apparently wanting to be the one whose balloon was popped next. They knew who was boss.

"Pick Glum," said Jocelyn, trying to take the initiative. Glum had floated off to a corner of her room.

"Glum needs more time to herself," asserted Brazen. "See how aloof she is, as far from us as possible?"

"Isn't it her nature to be withdrawn?" asked Jocelyn.

"Angry and gloomy, too," said Brazen. "But being yanked out of you is a wrenching experience, Jocelyn. Glum has to become used to the new world of the balloon and get herself together. Besides, like Smolder, she's dejected. I don't want to deal with that mood just now."

Brazen eyed the pale-blue balloon. Like Glum, Sorrowful was showing reserve, keeping a fair distance. But when Brazen reached out for her to come, she complied.

"Isn't Sorrowful low-spirited like Glum?" asked Quizzical.

"Yes," said Brazen, "but I don't want to start now with Fury or Tragic; I want one who won't cause an uproar."

"I like uproars," said Bustle.

"You'll have one soon enough," answered Brazen, elbowing Fury and Tragic away and popping the blue balloon with a pinch.

Sorrowful came out weeping, which caused everyone to break into tears. Sorrowful was small and her blue was faint, as if color had been washed from her, which made her all the more pitiable.

"I thought we were having a party," blubbered Bustle.

"Oh, am I spoiling it?" cried Sorrowful.

"She's dripping on the floor," observed Brazen.

"I have a cloth," said Jocelyn, wiping away her own tears as she rose from her bed and crossed to the washbasin.

"Hand it here," said Bustle. "We don't want to slip when we dance at your party."

"I don't feel like dancing now," said Jocelyn.

"Sorrowful has dampened our spirits," said Brazen. "It should be the other way around: we should raise hers."

Bustle got up from wiping the floor and took Sorrowful by the hands. Pulling gently, she moved backwards, drawing Sorrowful after her, then swung her in circles, increasing speed until they were whirling.

The others clapped together and chanted, "Clap hands! Clap hands!"

Sorrowful giggled, then whooped.

Bustle sang a traditional folk verse:

Sugar nor honey nor cakes
Have we none,
Yet we will be merry
'Til Mother comes.

Blue Sorrowful shook off Bustle's hands, sending the green spirit-girl careening, and slumped to the floor, burying her face in her arms.

"Might you have made up a happier ending?" suggested Brazen.

Bustle, having regained her balance, hurried to Sorrowful and pulled on her. "I'll leave Mother out of the second verse," she promised.

"All is hopeless," whimpered Sorrowful.

Fury began circling the room, then plunged into the pile of sticks for playing *Pick up Twigs*. Her balloon popped, and she shot forth like a fireball, striking the floor hard. Pounding the wood, she cried, "Let's throttle the witch!" She shot to her feet and bolted for the door.

Brazen and Bustle tackled her.

"Sorrowful! Quizzical!" shouted Fury. "Get them off me!"

Instead, they piled on.

Furious, Fury bucked, roaring for Jocelyn to help her. "These haven't the fighting spirit!" Fury howled. "But Smolder is inside you, and she's—"

"Smolder knows how to resist," interrupted Brazen, "but she isn't the sort to attack."

"Coward!" hooted Fury.

Jocelyn snapped, "I'm not a coward just because I don't do what you say. Besides," she went on, "I can think for myself, and I don't want Mother harmed."

"Humph!" snorted Fury. But she was panting from her exertions and ceased struggling. After a while she said, "Let me up. I think I can behave—at least until I get my second wind."

Quizzical and Sorrowful rolled off, and Brazen and Bustle loosened their hold.

Relaxing her fists, Fury turned over and sat up. "Maybe I got carried away," she conceded.

"You certainly did," agreed Jocelyn.

"But I have another idea that we all might find agreeable," ventured Fury. "Listen to this traditional rhyme:

Mother said I never should play.
If I did, she would say:
Naughty girl to disobey!
But I had me a knack
And was off in a crack!
Tell Mother I'll never come back.

"I like that!" cried Brazen. "I bet even Glum brightened over it. Maybe she's in the mood now to join us." Brazen hurried to the corner of the room where the light-gray balloon still floated, never having risen far from the floor.

Jocelyn wavered. *Run away? How can I even consider it? I've never been beyond the estate. Feeno and Maag used to ask if I could accompany them when they made a foray into the woods, promising to hold my hand, but Mother refused to allow it.* Gothelyn has a perfect life as a homebody, *she always said.*

Jocelyn was certain her life as a homebody wasn't perfect, especially if it meant staying inside the house. Her occasional visits to the garden and farmyard were a joy. Undoubtedly, exploring the world beyond the estate would be exciting.

But might it be too exciting? She felt her heart beginning to act up, beating rapidly. *It's not an attack, she told herself; I'm anxious. Even just the idea of running away has set my heart off.* She tried to calm it by reasoning that she was pretty grown up at thirteen, but to no avail. *I suppose if Maag and Feeno came, too . . . No, Mother has some sort of hold on them. Maybe the spirit-girls, both those inside and outside me, could give me the strength to escape from this place.*

Jocelyn's thoughts were interrupted when Brazen popped the light-gray balloon. Glum, who was the smallest of the spirit-girls and looked frail, dropped to her feet, then sank to the floor.

"She doesn't seem to have much spring in her step," observed Bustle.

"She won't have to," answered Brazen. "Jocelyn won't be in any condition to run away until we've all re-entered her, and then Glum won't need to run on her own; Jocelyn will carry us all."

"But won't Mother chase after me?" asked Jocelyn. "Surely she'll capture me, then punish me horribly."

"You're forgetting us!" shouted Fury. "We won't let Mock-Mother deprive us of our freedom."

At that moment, Tragic made a dive toward the pile of twigs but bounced back to the ceiling, her balloon undamaged. Her purple turned magenta, as if she were blushing.

"Why not give fire a try?" suggested Quizzical.

Tragic sidled up to a wall candle and brushed against its flame, which burst the balloon. She vaulted up, flipping twice in the air before landing on both her feet, arms spread.

In spite of the theatrics, the others couldn't help acknowledging Tragic's entrance, giving her a round of applause.

She bowed. "Please," she said, holding up a hand, "I'm not up to an encore."

"But I so liked how you bounced off the twigs!" cried Bustle. "It was—"

"Embarrassing?" suggested Brazen.

"Don't make fun of me!" Tragic rebuked her. "You know my sensitivities."

"They are several," Brazen said dryly.

"Alas!" swooned Tragic, the back of her hand on her brow. "I'm feeling suicidal."

"They were only joking," said Jocelyn, though she realized how hurtful one feeling could be to another.

"I find no humor here," Tragic retorted. "Our lot, directed by Mother, is tragic, and I am the spirit of doom."

"The life of the party," teased Brazen.

"I'm the heroine in this tragedy," declared Tragic, "unloved, unaccepted, and wanting."

"I feel the same as you, Tragic," affirmed Glum. "I'm just not nearly as important."

"Not so!" protested Brazen. "Tragic is just puffing herself up."

"But she's right that Mother despises us and that our future is bleak," said Glum.

"That's why we must take to the road!" exhorted Fury.

"Where will it lead?" asked Quizzical.

"Into the dark," replied Glum.

Indeed! thought Jocelyn. *We have no knowledge of what lies beyond the grounds of this house. Better to stay here and keep Mother from having her way. I'll be unbearable, that's what. I'll sulk and brood. I won't cooperate.* I'm not in the mood to do my lessons, *I'll say. If Mother insists I do, I'll scream,* won't, won't, won't, *in her ear. I'll wear her down until she comes around or leaves me alone.*

"In my opinion," volunteered Bustle, "life on the road would be exciting."

"I think," countered Tragic, "it would be disastrous."

There was an awkward silence.

"I have some ideas of my own," said Jocelyn. "But for now, let's get on with giving ourselves some cheer. I want to celebrate my birthday with a tea party. Maag gave me a teapot and teacups to play with when I was little. We haven't enough cups, but we can share."

Glum pointed out that they hadn't any tea.

"We can pretend," said Jocelyn.

"What about costumes?" asked Tragic. "We can't very well have a tea party if we spirit-girls are naked."

"And I must change into a fresh gown," said Jocelyn. "We needn't pretend about dressing up; my closet has enough gowns, I think, to fit us all."

"What fun!" cried Brazen, rushing to the closet. "I want something bold."

"Mine should sparkle," said Bustle, sidling up to her.

"I claim the princess dress," declared Tragic, tearing into the closet and removing it from its hanger.

"I want a flashy one," Fury asserted, as she wedged her way in, rifling through the dresses.

From outside the closet, Sorrowful asked if there were a blue dress that would fit someone petite like her. Glum said to grab any old thing for her, then amended her request by asking for the smallest dress in the closet. Quizzical couldn't make up her mind, trying one on after another. Jocelyn chose an orange gown with a floral pattern in white.

When they were all dressed, Quizzical settling on a bronze-colored dress that Brazen insisted complemented her bright-yellow skin, they sat on the floor in a circle. Jocelyn pretended to pour cups of tea from the teapot. There were only four cups, and the spirit-girls quarreled over who would have to share until Jocelyn pointed out that since there were eight of them, including her, each could share with another. This caused an argument over who would share with Jocelyn. Since she sat between Quizzical and Glum, Jocelyn suggested it be one of them. Fury declared that the circle was unfair. All of them rushed to Jocelyn to be nearest to her, crowding around and falling over her.

At first, Jocelyn sought to untangle herself and push them away. *We should get back to our tea party,* she thought, *or the tea will get cold.* She laughed at her jest. *Seriously, though, I want to celebrate my birthday, even if it's more like playing at having a party than really having one.*

But as the spirit-girls converged ever closer, touching her however they could, she felt, amidst the tumult, a warmth and calm she had never before experienced, and she didn't want any of them to let go of her.

CHAPTER 29

AN AERIAL THIEF

ALL WILL TURN OUT WELL, thought Gullible in her golden balloon. *Jocelyn will regain her spirits, Mother will have a change of heart, Maag will become a natural magpie, and Feeno . . . There isn't anything the matter with Feeno,* she thought, *except for his loss of memory, his deformities, his awkwardness . . . Oh dear, will Mother try to change him, too?*

Gullible lowered herself down the workshop's chimney. *Why is the toad here?* she wondered, as she hovered just above the ashes. She couldn't believe it was Mother's spy. During the past several months, she had observed its nightly visits to Jocelyn's room, trusting that it meant to comfort the girl or be comforted by her. What's its purpose now?

Gullible turned her attention to the magpie. Maag was studying the padlock Mother had fastened to the cage door. The key was on the worktable but out of the magpie's reach. Sliding her head through a pair of vertical bars, the magpie turned and picked at the lock with her beak, but after a few minutes, she stepped back and surveyed the cage.

She's looking for a weakness, Gullible supposed.

The toad scooted out from beneath the grate, scattering ashes onto the golden balloon, and scampered to the worktable. There, it climbed one of its legs, moving more slowly now, pausing often, as if to test a finger hold, until it reached the tabletop.

"What goest thither?" asked the magpie. "A toad? Erst I ate a toad. Was dungy fare, bestowing upon me unbraced bowels. Yet I hath not seen thee afore this hour. When didst thou enter this abode? Dost thou not wit that Iduress craves thy bones? Hath thou a dialect? Nay? Then be a useful wag. Pray procure the key."

The toad whipped out its tongue, landing it on the key, but it couldn't jerk it back to its mouth, probably because the key was too heavy and slippery. Using its hands, the toad groped clumsily, able to pick it up for one moment, then dropping it the next.

"Edge the key nigh," said the magpie.

Lying flat on its stomach, the toad propelled itself with its back legs, sliding the key with its outstretched fingers toward the magpie.

"Nigh! Mine neck be short."

The toad stopped its advance.

"Why dost thou forestall?" asked the magpie. "Didst I not say I hath none stomach for thee? Thou as yet dost not credence me. Yet I dost not reproach thee, for mine beak and claws art keen."

The toad seemed to consider the risk, then pushed the key closer.

"Thou art a goodly acquaintance," said the magpie. She snatched the key with her beak, then flipped onto her back. Unfortunately, the keyway was on the front of the padlock, and no matter how much she stretched and twisted her neck, she couldn't insert the key with her beak. At last, she rested her head and let the key fall next to it.

"Toad, dost thou laugh at me?" inquired the magpie. "I would'st, were I in thy stead. Thou hath been of employment, yet I surmised more aidance. Thou hath pickers and stealers. Expend thy fingers anew. Prithee, I importune thee. I hath none other than thee."

Yes, you do, thought Gullible, rubbing her balloon against the rough stone of the fireplace. The balloon burst (but without sound, just like Feeno's sneezes), and the golden spirit-girl somersaulted out.

"Mine savior!" the magpie shouted, springing to her feet. "Oh, I didst bellow soundly," she whispered. "Hath Sound betray'd us so soon? Thy dame mayst come. Shroud thy self!"

"I won't hide!" whispered Gullible loudly. "I'm not afraid of Mother."

"Thou art odd," the magpie whispered. "Hark!"

They all listened.

"Blessedly, Iduress didst not ear mine loud pipe," said the magpie. "Prithee, Gullible, acquit me from this grate."

As Gullible retrieved the key, she asked, "Are you truly a bird or a woman?"

"I was born a fowl—a maggot-pie—Iduress sayeth. That be square. I was not a dame 'til Iduress transfigured me by her art. Abide me wing from this witch."

Gullible thrust the key into the lock and turned it. The padlock sprang open, and the magpie burst from the cage.

"I hath bare begun mine delivery from limbo," said the magpie. "Thou, too, mine gilt imp, art within peril. Why else hath Iduress bereaved thee from Jocie? She desires to quell thee."

"Quell?" inquired Gullible.

"Extermine!"

"But she said she wants to play with me," insisted Gullible.

"Hunt and wrack the sprite?" scoffed the magpie. "That be for her disport."

"But she flatters me," insisted Gullible. "I'm her favorite, Brazen said. Mother even wants to know more about me."

"She shalt dissever thee."

"Dissever?"

"Dissect," explained the magpie.

"Oh."

"Iduress mayst come within at any hint," said the magpie. "She revives from her infirmity pertly. Hide thee behind the tapestry! Toad, too. I shalt pervert her."

"Pervert?" questioned Gullible.

"Thou hath a sixpenny stock of words," said the magpie. "I quoth I shalt distract her."

Gullible hurried behind the drapes but immediately peeked out. The toad slid backwards down the table leg and scurried to where Gullible hid. The magpie launched into the air and perched on top of the frame of the door that led to Mother's bedroom.

I wish the other spirits were here, thought Gullible. *I haven't their experience of being naughty. It's against my nature. But perhaps I'm good as gold because I'm foolish and dimwitted. Mother said as much, even as she praised me for not speaking up for myself.*

Mother opened the door and strode in.

The magpie plunged, her claws spread and landed hard on Mother's upper back. Mother screamed and raised both hands to grab the bird. But already the magpie was taking flight, lifting over Mother's head the silver chain that she'd clasped in her beak.

"My crystal!" cried Mother, lurching after it.

The magpie circled sharply, reversing direction, and flew into the bedroom, the crystal dangling just above Mother's reach.

"You cannot escape!" shouted Mother, chasing after the bird. "My bedroom and workshop are sealed."

Gullible rushed from behind the drapes to the door to the hall, hoping to flee to Jocelyn's room in the attic, but the door was locked and required a key to open it from the inside. She crossed to the doorway the magpie and Mother had passed through, keeping to the side so that she'd remain out of sight, and peered into the bedroom.

"Where are you hiding, Maag?" Mother asked impatiently. "Do not require me to open the drapes to let in the morning light." She removed a lit candle from a wall holder and scanned the room. "There!"

Gullible saw that the magpie was perched on the chandelier. Maag swung the chain over her head, then let go of it with her beak so it hung now from her neck.

"And thither thou art," observed the magpie. "I hath Oldric's shiny. Thou stole it and hath none patent to it."

"I conspired for it but won it fairly," protested Mother. "It is mine!"

"Thou art frantic," observed the magpie. "Temper thyself."

Mother glowered but took a deep breath, exhaling slowly. "I will negotiate," she said. "Give me my quartz, and I will release you to the wild."

"I shalt not parley," said the magpie resolutely. "I shalt be freed, aye, yet with a shiny for mine cupboard."

"No, the crystal will adorn mine . . . *my* neck," insisted Mother. "If you will not bargain, you will stay my servant."

Gullible wondered if she should offer to mediate. *There must be a way to help the magpie but not disappoint Mother,* she thought. *Oh, I'm being naïve!*

"We art at a still-stand," said the magpie.

"Not for long," answered Mother, crossing to the bed and ringing for Feeno to come. "The gnome will catch you or rue the day."

"Then rue the day he shalt," said the magpie. "He cannot wing."

"A ladder will be his wings," asserted Mother.

"Dost thou deem I shalt abide hither while he climbs it?" asked the magpie, incredulous.

"Then I will give him wings," retorted Mother. "Of course!" She rubbed her hands together with anticipation. "I will transform Feeno into an eagle, a white-tailed one."

"Yet how, mine iron-willed wench," asked the magpie, "shalt thou enact this art sans the ivory crystal?"

Idris paled to a color close to Glum's. "I . . . I still have my books," she stammered.

There was a knock at the door.

The magpie screeched, "Open the portal betime!"

"No!" shouted Mother.

But Feeno was already hurrying in.

CHAPTER 30

A MAGGOT-PIE

FEENO NEARLY JUMPED out of his skin, as a bird swooped over his head and through the doorway.

"You let it out!" screamed Lady Idris.

"I did not know there was a bird I should keep in," said the gnome in his defense. "Did you not demand I enter with great speed?"

"Fool!" shouted the Lady. "You mistook a magpie for me."

"A magpie?" questioned Feeno. "I have heard the cries of many a magpie, but none spoke words that I could—"

"Feelo," screeched the magpie, "thou art mine garland."

"Speak of the devil," said Lady Idris, striding into the sitting room.

"Devil?" repeated Feeno, thinking there was no limit to what might turn up in this house. He followed Lady Idris into the sitting room. The bird was circling, and the Lady was glaring at it, her arms crossed. *How does the magpie know my name?* Feeno wondered. *But* Feelo *it said, not* Feeno. *It must have spent time in Maag's company.*

"Mine inept witch," taunted the bird, "thou shalt not latch me!"

"The house is tightly shut," Lady Idris responded evenly, as if she were in full control. "In due time, I shalt . . . I *will* have in my hands both you and the crystal."

Feeno noticed that her hands were trembling.

"The hour mayst not favor thee," said the magpie to the Lady, "for I vouch anon to find an outlet." The bird sailed out of the sitting room.

What was hanging from the magpie? questioned Feeno. He looked at Lady Idris's neck, confirming the improbable. *The white crystal. The bird stole it!*

Lady Idris leaned down so that her mouth was next to Feeno's ear. "Inspect the dampers in all the chimneys," she whispered harshly. "I ordered Maag to close those not in use, but she has proved unreliable. Check, too, the windows and doors to the outside, although I am certain they are secure; they always are."

Except Jocelyn's window, thought Feeno, holding his tongue. *But is it closed now? I must make sure her window is open—her door, too—so the magpie can escape. The bird will carry the crystal from the house, and Lady Idris won't be able to regain the power it's given her. Also, I should tell Maag to leave the back door ajar. She'll be thrilled! She so wanted to steal the crystal from Lady Idris, and here a magpie has done it.*

But where did this bird come from? Lady Idris must have captured it to make trials upon it, as she did the mole. The magpie speaks a sort of English—one that is flawed. Lady Idris must have cast a spell on the magpie as a test before casting it on Maag to correct her mind and speech. The Lady still doesn't have it right.

"Why have you not left?" questioned Lady Idris, ushering Feeno into the hall. "Go first to the kitchen. Maag sometimes leaves its door open to the outside. If you spot the magpie, try every means to catch it—alive or dead—and bring me the crystal. Given the likelihood you will fail, I will get my bow and arrows from my workshop." Turning around, she marched into her chambers.

Feeno, in turn, hobbled down the hall. *Go first to the kitchen, she'd said.* Taking a backward glance to make sure Lady Idris had gone to her workshop and wasn't spying on him, he climbed the attic stairs hurriedly—on all fours—desirous to see whether Jocelyn's door and window were open. The door *was* shut, and he knocked on it. From inside he heard whispers.

"It's me," Feeno called. A yellow Jocelyn threw open the door. "You've dressed," said Feeno, as Quizzical made way for him. She then went to Jocelyn and the others and sat down on the floor with them. Feeno saw that the window was open.

"Doesn't the bronze color suit her?" asserted Brazen, referring to Quizzical's gown.

"What about my princess dress?" cried Tragic.

Feeno looked more closely at the spirit-girls, who were curled up, encircling Jocelyn. "It suits you, too," he said to Tragic.

"But isn't it lovely?" persisted Tragic.

"Each of your dresses is," said Feeno, trying to placate them all, "even the ones I can't see much of."

"Mine isn't," said Glum.

Hers was nondescript, but Feeno didn't see the need to agree with her and said nothing.

"You don't have the toad," observed Sorrowful, her eyes tearing. "Is it forever lost?"

"I didn't find it," Feeno replied, as he brushed away flies, "but I have no reason to think it's beyond hope."

"It probably will be of no consequence," said Glum.

"True," agreed Tragic. "We shouldn't count on it to keep us from a woeful end."

"I did come upon a magpie," announced Feeno. "It stole the white crystal and is flying about the house with it."

"Mother won't tolerate that," declared Jocelyn.

"But what good news!" exclaimed Brazen. "Without our mock-mother's potent bit of quartz, Jocelyn is a more equal match for her."

"I haven't seen Lady Idris so shaken," observed Feeno. "She can't rely on magic, so must resort to her bow and arrows to bring the magpie down and take back the crystal. The bird says it can find a way out, but—"

"Wait!" said Jocelyn. "Did you say the magpie speaks?"

"Its English isn't ours; it uses *would'st* and *shalt* and *thou* and *sayeth* and other odd words," answered the gnome, "but I understand it as well as I do Maag."

"I think it's most unusual for a magpie to speak in any language," said Jocelyn.

"It must be under a spell," asserted Feeno. "*Witch* it called your mother. *Inept,* too."

"The magpie said that!" hooted Brazen with delight, clapping her hands. "I like this bird."

"We must do what we can to help it escape," affirmed Feeno. "Jocelyn, keep open your door and window so the magpie can carry the crystal far from your mother."

"Where's Maag?" asked Quizzical.

"In her room asleep, I suppose," replied Feeno. "I'll wake her. She needs to know what's happening. I'll keep an eye out for Toad," he added, as he hurried out, stumbling on the threshold.

At the door to Maag's small room, which was across the hall from the kitchen, Feeno rapped. "Wake up!" he cried. "I have news that will make you glad."

"I am tofore blithe as a fowl," said a raucous voice from behind him.

The magpie! thought Feeno.

He rushed into the kitchen. It perched on the top of the cupboard, the crystal hanging from its neck.

"I was speaking to Maag," Feeno explained. "But surely your happiness won't be complete until you go home to the woods."

"That shalt make mine felicity metaphysical," said the magpie. "Yet it cannot yet be. I hath to abide hither at this abode."

"But Lady Idris has gone after her bow and arrows," warned Feeno. "You're in danger here."

"So be it," said the magpie, sounding resigned. "Doubtless maggot-pies, too, would'st not entertain me kindly. Art thou not ware I hath not the greeting of a maggot-pie? I wield a *gray English,* Iduress sayeth. Any English, howbeit . . .'Tis not what a maggot-pie doest. How would'st I fare with the flock, I sue thee?"

"You would be judged odd, I grant you," acknowledged Feeno, nodding.

"Besides, I hath traffic hither."

"Traffic?" inquired Feeno.

"Affairs," explained the magpie. "I shalt not espouse with other maggot-pies til Jocie and thou art safe."

"But . . . you don't know us."

"I hath known Jocie from her infancy and thee from the hour Iduress shot thee with an arrow."

"Have I seen you before?" asked Feeno.

"By the volume thou hath," said the magpie. "At latter supper, thou e'en gazed at me when thou poised on thy crown to hearten up our Jocie. Dost thou wanteth more instance? After, you saw me whir away unpracticed Gullible in her gilt balloon to the witch."

"Maag?" inquired Feeno incredulously.

"That is what Iduress termed me erst she turned me into a dame."

"Maag!" He would have hugged her, if he could have reached her. "Are you really a bird?"

"I feel it within mine bones," affirmed the magpie. "I hath the pith of a fowl. I was a noisome cook and heinous keeper of the abode. Yet I am an exact fowl."

Feeno tried to feel what was in his bones. "Do I seem . . ."

"As though a gnome? Thou art not fitly made, as gnomes reputedly art not. Yet hither few art as they seem. That toad, for counterpart—"

"You saw Toad?" interrupted Feeno. "Where is it?"

"I deem 'tis within the workshop of Iduress," answered the magpie. "Goldie, too, lest Iduress hath unearthed them both and placed them elsewhere. The toad be within grievous peril. More so than Goldie, I repute. Iduress seeks to rent Toad asunder for its magical bone, by which having the hag shalt summon the spirit of Jocie whensoever she wishes."

A magic bone? mused Feeno. *If it has the power to summon a spirit from Jocelyn, maybe it has the power to return it. But that would entail—*

"Wilt thou wend betimes to the workshop?" asked the magpie.

The question, interrupting Feeno's thoughts, took a moment to register. "I must go to the workshop if I am to rescue Gullible and the toad," he declared. "But how . . ." He considered the matter. "I have an idea! I'll tell Lady Idris I spied you in the kitchen. That's no lie. When she goes in pursuit, I'll steal away Toad and the golden balloon—"

"Gullible hath turned into a wench."

"Has she? Then she can run as well as Toad and me to Jocelyn's room."

"Thy stratagem is whole," said the magpie. "I am woe mine be not as downright as yours."

"How *will* you regain the language of a magpie?" asked Feeno.

"I crave thee and Jocie to salve me," replied the magpie. "I shalt first wing aloft the world for the felicity of it. Then I shalt come back hither and perch on the sill of Jocie's lodging."

"Her window will be open," Feeno assured her.

"When thou procure Goldie and the toad, thou must finger the book that lies open on Iduress's worktable," urged the magpie. "Erst Jocie hath the book, I shalt bestow upon her the shiny so she can cipher spells that shalt be to mine vantage—and haply to hers and yours."

"You make me hopeful for us all," said Feeno, as he unlatched the kitchen door to the outside. "Our future . . ."

"'Tis doubtful," said Maag, as she flew out the door.

CHAPTER 31

WEAPONRY

STANDING AT THE BALUSTRADE that overlooked the main hallway, Idris fitted an arrow into the bowstring and waited for the magpie to appear. *How did it get out of its cage?* she wondered. When she had collected the bow and quiver of arrows from a hook in her workshop, she had observed that the key was in the padlock, which lay open on the worktable. *Did Gullible have a hand in . . . No, balloons do not have hands and fingers, which they would need to insert and turn a lock. The magpie must have freed itself. But how?*

Agitated, she drew back the bowstring to the side of her mouth, noticing tightness in her shoulders and neck. *What the devil has caused that?* she wondered. Aiming at the left eye of the portrait of the father of Oldric, she let fly the arrow. Its tip struck his chin with a thud. Idris was shocked. She had never missed before. Reaching over her shoulder, which seemed increasingly rigid, she pulled from her quiver another arrow and shot it at the right eye, striking instead the middle of his forehead.

She had no need for further evidence that her aim was off and she was not herself. She rubbed her neck, which was stiffening. *The loss of the white crystal has made me tense,* she reasoned. She scolded herself for having become overly dependent on that potent bit of quartz. But the spells she had cast without it, using only the directions in her books, had come to nothing.

That had been one problem, she reminisced, that she had had to solve a dozen years ago in order to become a member of the all-male Brynmor Society of Benevolent Magicians, which was necessary as a means to advance her career. The Society did not permit the use of talismans, such as stones or inscribed rings, to perform magical feats, because they were believed to augment the powers of the magician. In short, their use was regarded as cheating. But how was she to demonstrate magical prowess without the white crystal?

Fortunately, after she had rid herself of Oldric, Elda, and Angwyn, the next meeting of the Society was not scheduled until the beginning of the academic year. That summer, she pored over the books in the library that touched upon the magical properties of crystals and happened upon a spell that made a talisman invisible. Like *Birthday Wishes,* the text was written in Gothic, making it unlikely that a contemporary magician would have read it.

She was permitted to address the membership of the Society at their autumn meeting so that she could announce the death of Oldric. Giving the members hardly a moment to digest this tragic occurrence, she stunned them by declaring that she was the protégé of Oldric and that, amazed by what he called her *magical being,* he had made a dying wish that she take his place in the Society.

"That's unheard of!" sputtered a member who had been introduced to her before the meeting as Derog. "No woman has ever been a member of the Society."

"An oversight, surely," Idris remarked sarcastically.

"Not at all," retorted Derog. "For one thing, it is well established that your gender's household duties are more important than worldly ambitions. You have a child to raise, good woman!"

Idris regarded him coldly, the look having its effect, because Derog shivered and wrapped a scarf around his neck. "I am quite capable," she said, "of both raising a child—a perfect one, in fact—and achieving prominence as a scientist and magician."

Martyn, the close friend of Oldric whom Idris had met at her wedding, intervened. "Will you please demonstrate your powers?" he asked.

"It will be a pleasure." In her hand, she held the white crystal. Although invisible, it had substance; she could feel its contour, its edges, its weight.

"We trust you will not use a talisman," said Martyn.

"I will not," Idris assured him. *Fool!* thought Idris. *He does not even question my honesty.* She looked at Derog, who was staring at her cupped hand. *But perhaps he will,* thought Idris. *I must act quickly.*

"Derog!" she shouted. He snapped his head up, and she caught his eyes and held them; she would not let them go. She snapped her fingers three times and muttered an incantation as she rubbed the crystal. He began to change.

His facial hair—the curled mustache and thick, long sideburns—seemed to crawl up his face, adding to the already billowing hair on his head. His face became rounder, his lips fuller, and his eyebrows higher. His chest puffed out, popping buttons. Derog leaped to his feet. His hips were wider and his buttocks plumper, causing his trousers to rip.

"What is happening to me?" he cried, looking himself over.

"She's turning you into a woman," observed Martyn.

"Impossible!" Derog reached between his legs and gasped.

"Missing something?" inquired Idris with a straight face.

"This must be a trick, an illusion!" he cried. "My amulet . . . Its protection of me has never failed."

Idris scanned the assembly. Everyone was gaping; they appeared dumbstruck. Someone chuckled, and then others broke into laughter.

"This is no laughing matter," fumed Derog in a high-pitched voice.

"But neither is it malicious," countered Martyn. "She's but put you in her shoes, though I imagine she'll insist you buy your own." He turned to Idris. "Couldn't you have made him more attractive?"

"I do not perform miracles," she replied.

"Change me back," demanded Derog, obviously still seeing no humor in his situation.

"I have household errands, my good woman," answered Idris. "I will return in two or three months. That should give all of you time to consider my membership in the Society. Or should we take a vote now?"

The vote was unanimous in her favor.

What a triumph! thought Idris, still standing at the balustrade, awaiting the appearance of the magpie. She readied another arrow but did not draw it back.

Her success at that meeting of the Society had been especially satisfying because it was public, which facilitated the widespread recognition she craved. It provoked her, though, that then and now she so seldom was able to do magic without her white crystal. She had magical powers within her, but she could not develop them, she reasoned, because she did not have an obliging household. She was distracted by the unruliness of Jocelyn, the language disorders and incompetence of Maag, and the unreliability of Feeno, who often hid from her when she rang for him.

Idris heard movement in the downstairs hallway and pulled back the bowstring. *Why do my hands ache?* she wondered.

Feeno appeared, stopping abruptly at the sight of the arrow pointed at him. "I'm no magpie!" he cried.

She did not lower the bow.

"I'm your servant!"

"Not for long if you insist on using contractions," Idris retorted. "I have been too lenient. As her governess, you must be a model of proper speech." She relaxed the bowstring. "Is there news of that confounded bird?"

"I found it in the kitchen," said Feeno. "It sat on top of a cupboard, and I could not reach it. If you hurry—"

"I do not *hurry,*" Idris reminded him, as she descended the staircase. "It does not befit a woman of my breeding."

She prided herself on her refinement, especially because it had come about through her own doing. Her father, Gethyn, a tenant farmer on a baronial estate, had desired a son and raised her as a boy. He had taught her from a very young age the skills of an archer and the ways to defend oneself. Once she grew into an adolescent, however, he lost interest in her and sent her to serve as a maid to the Baroness.

In the household of the Baron, she had paid close attention to the language and manners of the family, determined that one day she would escape the oppressive life of a commoner and pass herself off as a member of the nobility. A large impediment to her ambition was her rudimentary skill at reading and writing. Instruction by her mother, Ceridwyn, had been erratic, a by-product of her own studies. The primers of Idris had been not books of prayer but of herbal remedies, toxins, and occasionally (her mother tried to conceal them from her) witchcraft.

Soon after her arrival at the estate, however, Idris had a stroke of luck: unseen, she spied the Baron and the governess in an intimate embrace. When she told the governess she was privy to the relationship, the poor woman broke down in tears, saying she was being forced upon and had remained quiet about the obscene behavior of the Baron because she feared the wrath of the Baroness and the loss of employment. Feigning sympathy, Idris promised she would keep the liaison a secret if the governess would teach her to read and write (she was already good at computing). The governess gladly assented to her demand. In this way, Idris gained important skills that would enable her to bring about her own transformation into a noble lady.

She also learned to exploit her intellect and female charms to have her way in the world. And, in adherence to her father's instructions, she always carried a knife in a sheath at her waist beneath her dress, accessible through a slit. Indeed, even without the white crystal, she was not without weaponry.

"But you, Feeno," said Idris, now reaching the bottom of the staircase, "are not refined; you are of a common sort. So, with top speed, go and see that the rest of the house is closed up."

The gnome stumbled off toward the front part of the house, while Idris walked firmly (and somewhat rapidly) down the hallway toward the back, her bow and arrow ready.

She did not find the magpie in the kitchen. She checked the pantry and the room that Maag slept in, but there was no sign of the bird. *It must have flown up the servant stairs to my floor,* Idris reasoned. Averse to climbing steps that befit a maid, she hastened to the bottom of the main staircase, where she scanned above for the magpie. *It would not dare return to my chambers,* she thought. *While I was in the back part of the house, it must have circled down and found refuge in the parlor or the library, where surely Feeno will find it.*

Still . . . the magpie is more familiar with this house than anyone; it may well discover a way out, in which case the crystal will be lost forever.

An awful thought. I must not allow pessimism to undo me. She turned to the nearest mirror of the many she had added to the house (she was very fond of mirrors). This one was near the portrait of the father of Oldric. Aside from contemplating her achievements, admiring her beauty was the quickest way for Idris to escape despondency. She was not pleased, however, with what she saw. She always appeared radiant at night, but now . . . *I am wan,* she observed. *I look sickly. This pallor must be concealed without delay; I need cosmetics.*

Of these she had gained knowledge, too, in the household of the Baron, for as she matured, she realized that her outward show had a telling effect upon men, rendering them compliant. Her childhood as a tomboy who cared nothing for her appearance and hygiene gave way to an adolescence in which she flaunted her developing shapeliness. She began washing and fashioning her auburn hair. She also improved upon her facial features, stealing cosmetics from the Baroness and her older daughters. She applied them lightly so she would not be perceived as seeking to rise above her station, hence provoking the disapproval of the noble ladies.

She did, however, catch the eye of the eldest son. When she turned seventeen, he began showering her with affection, and she allowed him to seduce her. She soon realized, however, that he did not have marriage in mind, which would have made her noble. She ran away to the town of Brynmor, hoping to acquire a husband who would raise her status and secure her livelihood. She found work at the shop of an apothecary because of her knowledge of herbs and medicinal potions and her ability to read, write, and compute. There, she met Angwyn, who was not handsome but pleasant to look upon with his raven-black, tousled hair (she would see to it that it was cut shorter and combed back), dark eyes, and fair skin. Also, he displayed a generous, trusting nature she knew she could exploit to her own advantage.

And his father—what good luck!—was a professor and a magician. Idris vowed to ingratiate herself with him in order to steal the secrets of his arts and gain fame as an alchemist and sorceress. How envious her mother would be, and how awestruck her father, even frightened.

Ascending now the staircase to apply cosmetics, Idris wondered why her feet were aching. *My body is behaving strangely,* she thought. *I need my elixir.* As she rounded the top of the stairs, she felt winded and leaned against the balustrade, her bow and arrow by her side. *Must I keep watch for the magpie?* she asked herself. *No, I will leave it to Feeno. He knows not to disappoint me.*

She passed through the sitting room and bedroom and into her workshop.

"Are you feeling neglected?" she called out to Gullible. "Are you anxious to begin our game of hide and hunt? Enjoy my neglect, my simpleton. You likely will hate the full attention I give you after my daytime sleep."

Idris mixed a small measure of water with her elixir—an herb which she called *queen of the ditch* because it grew anywhere and relieved most discomforts.

Walking into her bedroom, she sat down at her dressing table and gazed at her reflection in the mirror. *I must apply paint to whiten my skin,* she observed, *rouge to highlight the sharpness of my cheeks, and cream to redden my lips.* That the lip cream contained the bodily fluids of insects ground in the lard of hogs amused her. She planned to color her hair later, completing the *unnatural* look she so adored.

CHAPTER 32

THE BRABBLE

FEENO HAD DUCKED into the parlor as Lady Idris advanced down the hallway in search of the magpie, but immediately he peeked out. *Why, the Lady is hurrying!* he thought, stifling a snicker. As soon as she turned into the kitchen, he doubled back, then scampered up the main staircase (he only fell twice) and ran into Gullible and Toad coming out of Lady Idris's bedroom.

"Thanks to Sound, we heard Mother leave her bedroom and go down the stairs," said Gullible. "We thought this gave us our best chance of safely reaching Jocelyn's room."

"Yes," agreed Feeno. "I came . . . *Why did I come?* he wondered. *To free Gullible and find Toad, I suppose. But isn't there something I've forgotten? Oh, my short-term memory is becoming as bad as my long-term one.* "Didn't Lady Idris lock you in the workshop?" he asked Gullible. "I don't have a key to—"

"Mother didn't lock me in because she wasn't concerned about me escaping," interrupted the golden spirit-girl. "Balloons can't open doors."

"So, Lady Idris still thinks you're in your balloon?"

Gullible nodded. "And she doesn't know about Toad," she added.

"There is much she doesn't know," said Feeno with a laugh, remembering the game Jocelyn, Brazen, and he had played. Reaching for the toad, he said, "We may need this fellow if we are to put the spirit-girls back into Jocelyn." But the toad scampered ahead down the upstairs hall. "Come along!" Feeno urged Gullible. "We must be quick and not lose sight of Toad."

Fortunately, the toad had the same destination in mind, for it dashed up the attic stairs, Feeno and Gullible following. The door was open, but the toad hesitated outside it, and Feeno was the first to enter Jocelyn's room.

The spirit-girls, all of whom were lounging on the floor, gestured with fingers at their lips for Feeno to keep quiet, some of them pointing at the sleeping Jocelyn in their midst. When Gullible came in, however, Bustle gave a cheer, which elicited from the others loud *shushes,* until they realized why Bustle had shouted with joy. Scrambling to their feet, they ran to Gullible, embracing her and jumping up and down.

"What's going on?" cried Jocelyn, sitting up with a jolt. "Has the tea party gotten out of hand?" She rubbed her eyes. "Did I fall asleep?"

"You did," affirmed Brazen. "You said you were feeling warm and snug, and then you dropped off to sleep. Feeno and Gullible just got back."

"We expected the worst," said Glum, addressing Gullible.

"Speak for yourself," said Bustle. "I felt sure she'd get loose."

"No, a tragic outcome was the most likely," countered Tragic.

"I imagine it can still end badly," whispered Sorrowful.

"Not without a fight!" boomed Fury.

Brazen pointed at the doorway. "There's Toad!" she exclaimed. "Where did it come from?"

"It was in Lady Idris's chambers," replied Feeno, as he fended off flies.

"Then Smolder was right," said Glum. "It *is* a spy."

"No, it hid from Mother in the ashes of the fireplace," asserted Gullible.

"And Lady Idris wants to tear it apart," added Feeno. "Maag told me the Lady believes toads have a magic bone that can summon spirits, just as she summoned each of you, but at any time."

Brazen said excitedly, "One of Toad's bones, then, might be the charm that enabled Smolder to dissolve into Jocelyn. We have only to place the toad on the girl's body for us to be drawn in."

"My idea exactly," affirmed Feeno.

"But who is it inside Jocelyn that is summoning us back?" asked Quizzical.

"Dame Kidney, I would'st deem."

"Maag!" shouted Feeno with glee.

Jocelyn and all of the spirit-girls turned toward the dormer window.

"That's not Maag," asserted Brazen. "It's a bird."

"Beseemings can belie," said the magpie. "I was a misbegotten matron, yet I am a warranted maggot-pie."

"Did I hear correctly?" Quizzical questioned the magpie. "Smolder was summoned by one of Jocelyn's kidneys?"

"Mine English, I hath been told, is of an older garb," said the magpie.

"I think," said Feeno, *"Dame Kidney* is her way of saying Mother Nature."

"Yes!" agreed Fury. "That's the witch's archenemy. Mother Nature must have a hand in this."

"How is it you speak English?" Bustle asked the magpie.

"The ground for English? Iduress doth not construe the Portuguese of Brazil."

"You speak Portuguese?" exclaimed Jocelyn.

"But a while," replied the magpie. "This English, too, I should'st gladly forswear. Mine determination be to enjoy the accent of a maggot-pie. Espy the crystal abroad mine neck? I crave to use it for such a tongue. Feelo, hath thou—"

"The book!" Feeno cried. "I was so excited about finding that Toad and Gullible were safe, I forgot the magic book. I must go back for it."

"'Tis too desperate while Iduress prowls," cautioned the magpie.

"I saw no sign of her when we left her chambers," observed Gullible.

"Lady Idris is searching the ground floor in the back of the house," said Feeno. "I must take the chance."

"And we spirits, in the meantime, will fill Jocelyn to overflowing," asserted Brazen, "unless Toad disappoints us."

The toad scampered across the floor and climbed onto Jocelyn's bed, then onto her chest. Jocelyn leaned back onto her elbows and grimaced, but Toad responded by squeezing its eyes down into the roof of its mouth, as if it were swallowing a grasshopper, then letting them pop up, which made Jocelyn laugh.

"He makes a better face than I do," said Jocelyn, still laughing.

"I want to be first," said Bustle.

"The last should be first," retorted Tragic. "I was the last released from my balloon."

"But, as the last born, doesn't Glum deserve to be first?" asked Quizzical.

"I don't want to be first," said Glum.

"Stop the brabble!" shouted the magpie.

"Brabble?" queried Quizzical.

"I think she's asking you to quit arguing," said Feeno.

"Pray, we hath no hour to bicker or dally," scolded the magpie. "Thou must be orderly."

"Good luck bringing that to pass," Feeno uttered under his breath as he hurried out, leaving the flies at the doorway.

CHAPTER 33

A BUDDING WITCH

THE COSMETICS HAVE DONE their work, Idris observed, admiring her reflection in the mirror at her dressing table. *But the elixir has not yet relieved me of my aches and pains.*

She heard Feeno sniffing at her bedroom door. "Why do you not knock?" she asked.

"I . . . I feared you might be in."

"Enter at once!" she shouted.

Her stiff neck prevented her from turning her head, so she maneuvered herself around on the cushioned stool until she faced the gnome, who was coming in with obvious reluctance. "Did you kill my bird and retrieve my crystal?" she asked.

Feeno shook his head.

"Then why are you here?"

"I . . ." He sighed. "I need one of your magic books."

"One of my books?" exclaimed Idris. "Never! But you rouse my curiosity. Why do you need a book? You do not read."

"But Jocelyn does," said Feeno.

"Gothelyn? Is she not asleep and suffering a sick spell?"

"No, she is awake and well," replied Feeno.

Her recovery is swifter than usual, thought Idris, feeling disconcerted. "Why does she want a magic book?" Idris asked. "But more importantly, why have you come to fetch it? The magpie, Feeno! That is the preeminent concern. Why have you stopped looking for it?"

"Because I have found her," said the gnome.

"Where?"

"At Jocelyn's window."

A magpie at a window signifies death, thought Idris, remembering an old tale of the wives. "Why did you not tell me at once?" she scolded. "Has it the crystal?"

Feeno nodded.

"Then I will creep into the yard and fell the magpie with an arrow."

"The shot will be difficult," said Feeno, "even for you. The magpie has come inside the dormer."

"Who opened the window?"

"I have forgotten, if I ever knew."

"If not you, who else but Gothelyn? Why has she let the bird in?"

"The magpie desires her natural voice, and to that end—"

"The bird must give Gothelyn the white crystal!" cut in Idris. *But Gothelyn does not know the spell or how to handle the crystal,* reasoned Idris, *so she will fail to give Maag what she wants. Might the magpie, then, snatch it back? Or might the child—silly youth—feel obliged to give it back?* "I must go at once to the room in which Gothelyn resides," said Idris, "and . . . Why have you paled, Feeno? You are trembling. Have you a chill?"

He shook his head.

"What, then?"

"I fear you," he said.

"Of course, you do," said Idris. "You must be used to that by now. It should not make you quake, unless . . . What wrong have you committed?"

Feeno pondered the question. "Once, when Jocelyn was six, I—"

"I do not care what you did when Gothelyn was six." Idris was silent for a moment. "I suppose I do; I want to know everything. But we will explore the matter later." She bent toward him on her stool. "There is something important you have avoided telling me. It is there on the tip of your tongue. Spit it out!"

"I . . ." He pressed his lips tightly together, contorting his face, as he struggled to stifle the truth. Idris knew the signs.

"What is amiss?" Idris pressed.

"Nothing is missing."

"I am not in the mood for wordplay," said Idris. "You showed distress over my going to the room Gothelyn inhabits. What is there, Feeno, that you do not want me to see?"

From his mouth, garbled sounds managed to squeeze out. "The girls," he finally blurted.

"What girls?"

"The truth is . . . I call them *girls,* but they are not real girls," Feeno tried to explain. "That is . . . they appear to be girls, but—"

"Gothelyn conjured them?" exclaimed Idris. "But how? She could not have had the white crystal. Has she another crystal?"

"No."

Idris felt weak. Gothelyn had pestered her about playmates, but instead of acquiescing to the refusal of her mother to allow the corrupting influence of other youths, she had gone and made some herself—without a crystal or even a magic book! Idris recalled the imaginary friend, Ceri. Was she the precedent? Idris was reeling. She had always feared the power the child might possess, given the *magical being* she herself had inherited, but Gothelyn had exceeded all expectations. Idris could not help but feel pride in her progeny. *Chip off the old block, so to speak,* she thought. *But still, a danger—possibly a big one.*

"You said *girls,*" Idris said to Feeno. "How many are there?"

"The numbers change. One vanished; others appeared. I think at present there are seven or eight."

"Seven or eight?" exclaimed Idris, aghast.

"Maybe less."

"Fewer," corrected Idris, as she labored to stand up. Her legs felt shaky. *Am I becoming weak-kneed?* she feared. *Nonsense! I need but reclaim my crystal. With it I can easily deal with the budding witch and her playmates. I will go immediately to the room I have granted Gothelyn and shoot the magpie.* Grabbing her bow and quiver of arrows, she scuffled from the room, her legs painfully stiff.

By the time Idris reached the bottom of the attic stairs, she was shivering violently. She halted, reveling in the sensation. Never had she been so cold.

This is no ordinary chill, she realized, *the sort engendered by an icy bath, a wintry night, or the north wind. This cold comes from within.* It was induced, she was certain, by the distilled dandelions, the essence of cold. She was in a state of rapture.

She swooned, collapsing onto the stairs. Rolling to her back, she luxuriated in the chilliness that filled her entire body; the cold was becoming more and more intense.

I wish time would stop, Idris thought, *and I could lie here in this state forever and ever and . . .*

CHAPTER 34

LIPS, CRIES, AND PHANTOMS

THE MAGPIE HAD BECOME weary of the brabble over which spirit-girl would enter Jocelyn first.

"Jocelyn, tell them!" demanded Brazen. "You said I'm the one you need if you are to face the witch."

"Along with Smolder," added Jocelyn.

"I'd have been next if I could have sat still," contended Bustle.

"She would have picked me," insisted Fury, "if I'd popped myself out sooner."

"Ye art acting peevish," the magpie admonished them. "Each of ye hath a place. Why be the sequence dear? Anon each of ye shalt be within Jocie."

"Not if the witch catches wind of what we're doing," said Glum, "which surely she will. Some of us could be left out."

"I'll be one of those," said Tragic, sighing.

"Should'st not Jocie pick?" suggested the magpie, "'Tis she who hath to undergo ye spirits."

"I choose Glum," said Jocelyn immediately.

"That's Smolder's influence," objected Fury. "Smolder wants a companion who is dark like her."

"Not bright and sunny like you," teased Brazen.

Glum spoke up. "But I don't want—"

"Jocelyn," whined Sorrowful, "don't you want me?"

"Or me?" cried Bustle, jumping up and down.

"Oh, I want you all," said Jocelyn, consolingly. "I don't want any of you left out."

"Could we enter Jocelyn at the same time?" suggested Quizzical.

"That might overwhelm her," cautioned Brazen. "We'd fill her with so much feeling she might burst."

They were all quiet for a while.

"Let's start with something we can all agree on," suggested Gullible.

Quizzical spoke up. "Our dresses: don't we need to remove them?"

"But my blue gown is such a lovely shade," lamented Sorrowful.

"I refuse to take off my princess dress," declared Tragic.

The magpie interceded. "E'en were it possible, a frock, drawn within the youngling, shalt constipate her."

"Oh, Jocelyn mustn't suffer," whimpered Sorrowful, slipping off her dress.

The others, too, quickly shed theirs, except for Tragic. Grimacing as if she were in pain, Tragic inched out of hers.

"What else can we agree on?" asked Gullible.

"That we should'st be square," mused the magpie. "Lottery! That is no juggle."

"Yes!" they all agreed at once.

"Those be Iduress's lips!" cried the magpie.

"Her *lips?*" queried Quizzical.

"She hath put on her paint!" answered the magpie anxiously. "Her lips hath the odor of downtrodden bugs and bacon. She be nigh, at the foot of the attic stairs."

Sound was at a loss for words. It had been enjoying the repartee of voices in Jocelyn's room, especially the *gray* English of the magpie. Sound had seized *brabble, Dame Kidney, downtrodden bugs,* and a half-dozen other collectibles, when suddenly speech and movements ceased.

Toad croaked, indicating it had a voice. Sound heard the toad shift its weight somewhere in Jocelyn's room. Sound couldn't be more precise, because it was blind.

Sound's ears were not only in the attic room; they were everywhere within the estate, which included the house, the grounds, and the farmyard. They'd heard Idris, for example, fall at the foot of the attic stairs before she, too, became still. What caught Sound's attention now was not noise but silence, especially that of Oldric, its master; the clock had stopped ticking.

As quick as a balloon's *pop,* Sound directed its attention to the sitting room, though it kept its ears open throughout the property. Sound heard a harsh *tock* followed by a quick *tick-tock,* and Elda, crying out in pain, landed on the floor of the sitting room with a thud.

"Oldric! Angwyn! Idris! Where's the baby?" Elda shouted. Sound muted the cries, thinking it might not be wise to alert Idris that Elda had reappeared. As for Angwyn, Sound hadn't heard a peep from him in ages, and Oldric was in no condition to respond.

What baby? wondered Sound.

But it had become all ears, for its original mission had been to protect Jocelyn from her mother's neglect by amplifying the baby's cries of distress, so they could be heard by Oldric and those members of the household who would comfort her.

"Maag! Feeno!" Elda called out, clambering up from the floor. She paused. "Where did you come from?" she inquired.

Sound thought she must be addressing the grandfather clock. It wished it didn't have to guess who *you* was, but people insisted on using pronouns. Sound had come to hate them (pronouns) because they (pronouns) often confused it (Sound).

"And why aren't you in the nursery?" Elda asked.

Who's you? Sound wanted to scream. Instead, it reasoned that she was now addressing the landscape painting, because it had been moved from the nursery to the sitting room.

Abruptly, Elda stomped out. In the hall, she rattled the locked door to what had been the nursery but was now Idris's workshop. (Sound loved the rattling and swallowed it.) Returning to the sitting room, Elda tapped on the bedroom door. *(A tap has nothing on a rattle,* Sound thought, ignoring it.) "Idris," Elda whispered. "Is the baby safe with you?" She tapped Idris's bedroom door more firmly.

Sound had detected some motion within the house while Elda was searching for the baby: the magpie had fluttered its wings, Jocelyn and the spirit-girls had run and slammed doors, Idris had stretched (Sound heard her joints snap) and moaned in pleasure at the bottom of the attic stairs. And Feeno . . . Where was Feeno?

No matter. Sound realized it must tell Elda where Jocelyn was, so she could protect the girl from Idris. But Sound wasn't a conversationalist: It didn't have a voice and could only repeat what it had collected. Checking its language inventory for the words "Jocelyn is in the attic," it had no luck.

Then it had an idea. Elda seemed to be looking for the baby that Jocelyn had been when Elda had disappeared. Sound had a large collection from long ago of Jocelyn's cries, including sobs, wails, and howls. It had put some of them in the pots and bowls of Elda's hand-decorated pottery. Maag, however, had hidden the pottery in the woods, which was outside Sound's range. Where else might Sound have hidden Jocelyn's cries? Had it swallowed any? Quickly it sorted through the words and noises that had been too delicious to put elsewhere.

I've found one! Sound wanted to shout. It was a heart-rending wail. Sound didn't want to give it up. But, considering its duty, it regurgitated the cry in Jocelyn's room.

"What's the baby doing in the attic?" Elda cried, as she dashed from the sitting room.

Gripping the banister with both hands, Idris pulled herself to her feet and trudged upward, her eyes on the attic steps.

Oh, for another swig of dandelions! Idris thought. *No, I must keep my balance. I have an errand, one that requires deadly aim. Only when I have killed the magpie and brought to nothing the fledgling magic of the child will I indulge myself with another sip.*

Idris heard the cry of a baby. "Is conjuring not enough?" she exclaimed, appalled. "Has Jocelyn given birth?"

"Surprise, my chilly-hearted!"

Idris jerked up her head, causing her neck to crack. She froze. There, at the top of the stairs, stood Maag in the guise of a housekeeper.

"How . . ." Idris was dumbfounded. "My crystal!" she shouted. "Where have you hidden it?"

The housekeeper did not reply to the question. Instead, she said, "By my troth, mine nymph, thou art a scurvy wench."

Idris was more confused than offended. *I must be hallucinating!* she realized. *The figure and its voice are coming from my own mind.*

"Você é uma bruxa má," said Maag.

How can I hallucinate in Portuguese? Idris wondered.

"The Port-a-Geese, my Benightedness, isn't flattersome," said the housekeeper. "I sayest you are a *bad witch."*

"I'm not!" protested Idris.

"*I am* not!" shouted Maag.

Oldric sallied forth in his former coverings (what humans called *clothes*). "You're no mother," he scolded his daughter-in-law.

"And you are no father!" retorted Idris. "Your son is dead."

"Yet 'tis afore the resurrection!" declared the housekeeper.

"You are mere phantoms!" Idris cried. "You will not stop me!" Forcing herself up the stairs, she barged through the apparitions and banged open the door to the room occupied by Gothelyn, the arrow in her bow drawn.

CHAPTER 35

CHAOS AND ASTONISHMENT

KNOWING THAT MOTHER was near Jocelyn's room, everyone had raced for cover. The spirit-girls had jammed into the closet, the magpie had high-stepped out of sight onto the roof, Toad had scurried under the bed, and Jocelyn, who'd decided someone had to be present when Mother arrived, had closed the door, then jumped into bed, pulled the bedcovers up to her chin, and pretended to be asleep. When Mother stormed in, Jocelyn jerked upright and scowled, rubbing her eyes.

"Where is the bird?" Mother demanded, the arrow of her bow pointed at the empty dormer window.

"Mother, you startled me!"

"Took your breath away, did I?" asked Mother, laughing. "Remind me later of that witticism. I want to write it in my notebook. The bird, Gothelyn. Where is it?"

"What bird?" asked Jocelyn.

"Oh, have you a flock of them?" jeered Mother. "You know full well the one I want—the magpie that wears my crystal around its neck." Turning, she pointed the arrow at Jocelyn. "Maag!" Mother called out. "I doubt you have gone far, not until you have the tongue of a magpie. Show yourself, or I will put an arrow through the heart of the child."

"Thou would'st martyr thy daughter?" cried the magpie in disbelief, as she peeked around the corner of the window into the room. "What fashion of dame art thou?"

"One who knows how to get her way," said Mother. "Come further inside so we can negotiate a trade—my crystal for your voice."

"Why should'st I credence thee?" asked Maag.

"Because you have no choice," replied Mother. "Be quick! I do not have a good grip on the bowstring."

As the magpie hesitantly stepped into the dormer, Mother swung the bow and arrow in her direction.

"Mother, don't!" shouted Jocelyn.

At that moment, Feeno charged into the room, his head lowered. Mother, apparently seeing him from the corner of her eye, managed to step aside so that the butt he intended was only a glancing blow. Mother stumbled, however, and loosened the arrow into the wall, as Feeno fell on his face.

Having regained her balance, Mother screamed at Feeno, "How dare you!"

"Thou, Iduress, hath undone thy murderous vantage," remarked the magpie as she regarded the arrow in the wall. "Naught one of us hath to partake the ghost. Vouchsafe us to bear truce."

Mother reached over her shoulder for another arrow, but she fumbled it, dropping it to the floor.

"Thy grip be unfirm," observed the magpie.

"Think so?" scoffed Mother. "Watch how I handle this." From inside her dressing gown, she withdrew a knife.

Having scrambled to his feet, Feeno, in turn, pulled a knife from his pocket—the kitchen knife for paring vegetables.

"You challenge me?" exclaimed Idris, laughing. "And with a thing so small?"

The spirit-girls spilled out of the closet.

"What do I behold?" cried Mother. "Here is your flock, Gothelyn. Why, you made them in your own image. Where is the baby?"

"I'm the youngest," said Bustle.

Mother eyed her. "You are not a baby," she observed.

"I've matured," explained Bustle.

Mother brandished her knife. "Stand away!" she warned the spirit-girls, who had begun to circle her. "I have not approved of you; it is certain I will not."

"And it is as certain we won't approve of you," retorted Brazen.

"Won't" whined Mother. "Gothelyn, I see that you have not taught them well. Have you told these miscreants you are entirely devoted to me?"

Jocelyn shook her head vigorously. "That's not how I feel," she said.

"That is! That is!" shouted Mother. "The words are distinct. Stop firing apostrophes at me!"

"I can't very well speak properly while inside myself I seethe," retorted Jocelyn.

"Smoldering, are you? I remember those years. You were sullen. Menacing. But you outgrew that behavior; I insisted upon it. It appears, however, these creations of yours have been a bad influence. Put them away!"

"They're not toys, Mother."

"Then what are they? Their colors . . . You, the bronze girl. Tell me your name."

"I'm Brazen."

"Brazen?" exclaimed Mother. "I once called Gothelyn that. How rude she was then."

"Impudent, too, bless her," said Feeno.

"And bold," added Brazen. "I'm proud to say, Mock-Mother, I vexed you more than any of the others."

"Fare not kindle those others," warned the magpie. "Iduress could not rein the moods of Bustle or Fury. All of the spirits maddened her."

"Spirits?" questioned Mother. "Of Gothelyn? But they are contained within . . ." She searched the ceiling and glanced around the room. "Where are the balloons?"

"We've shed them," said Sorrowful with tears in her eyes. "I rather miss mine."

"Don't be sentimental," chided Fury. "They're deservedly popped."

"Popped?" repeated Mother. She scanned the floor. Spotting remains of the balloons, she picked up some and fingered them.

"We are the outcome of your magic," said Glum.

"Why didn't you know that?" Quizzical asked Mother.

"Because she's not perfect," said Brazen.

"Not so!" cried Mother, waving her knife at them. "It is you girls who are at fault. According to the spell in *Birthday Wishes,* you are supposed to be particles of color, signifying moods; instead, you have bodies. But once I slash them, the colors will be scattered to the corners of the world, as I predicted."

"Their bodies art not solid," said the magpie.

"Maag and I have touched these spirit-girls," offered Feeno. "They're a force, like the wind."

"Their bodies art ethereal," agreed the magpie. "Can thou sunder a breath, a cloud, the firmament? How so, a spirit?"

"We'll blow you to the next world!" asserted Fury.

"The devil you will," retorted Mother, advancing on the spirit-girls.

Jocelyn stepped in front of her. "Don't hurt them!" she cried.

"Stand away!" yelled Mother.

"I won't!" retorted Jocelyn. "You'll have to kill me first."

There was a standoff, Mother and Jocelyn looking the other in the eye. Mother seemed puzzled, Jocelyn determined.

There was a barely audible whisper.

"What?" called Mother, cupping an ear. "Speak up!"

"HUSH!" The voice filled the room.

"Where are you?" demanded Mother as she circled in place, unable to locate the intruder.

"Achoo! Achoo! Achoo! Achoo! Achoo!"

"Those are my sneezes!" exclaimed Feeno, sounding proud to have been singled out.

"Yours?" objected Mother. "But you did not sneeze."

"I did a few hours ago."

"Are you daft?" shouted Mother.

Suddenly the air was rent with thuds, clunks, and thumps, then moans, squeals, and screeches. Mother clapped her hands over her ears and staggered from the force of the din. Jocelyn, Feeno, and the spirit-girls, too, covered their ears, the magpie burying her head under a wing. But Sound increased the volume, so it did no good. Jangles, clangs, creaks, and rattles joined in. It was an uproar. Glasses clinked, dishes clattered, balloons popped, water splashed, hands clapped. A bedlam of noise. Discordant. Jarring.

Then, as suddenly as it had begun, the confusion of sounds ceased. Mother and Jocelyn unclasped their ears, as did Feeno and the spirit-girls. The magpie raised her head. There wasn't the slightest sound. To Jocelyn, the silence was as disturbing as the noise; she'd never imagined that silence could be so loud.

Mother, however, breathed a sigh of relief. "What on earth was that?" she exclaimed.

"Sound," explained Feeno.

"Of course it was *sound*. It would have wakened the dead."

Suddenly a woman rushed in. "Where's the baby?" she cried.

"I'm the baby," said Bustle.

"Gullible, too," added Jocelyn, wondering who this woman was. "They're a mix of toddler and—"

"This Elda is not real!" shouted Idris. "The real one walks in the woods. But . . . how can you see this Elda? She is a figment of *my* imagination, not *yours.*"

"Grandmother?" exclaimed Jocelyn.

"I will tolerate no more hallucinations!" yelled Mother, slashing at Grandmother with her knife.

"Mother, you've cut her sleeve," cried Jocelyn. "And there's blood!"

"Hallucinate these!" Grandmother shouted, reaching into her pockets and tossing leaves and fragments of wood over Mother.

"How dare you litter me with foul nature!" shrieked Mother, brushing her hair and clothes with her hands. "My face! My neck! My hands!" she screamed. "They burn! Are you striking me with live coals?"

"Charms to send you from this house," answered Grandmother.

Jocelyn saw blisters rising on Mother's skin.

Toad scampered out from beneath the bed, up Mother's dressing gown, and croaked in her ear, "RrrrrrrrrrrrrrrrrrRUP!"

Mother jerked her head back in horror. "Husband?" she cried. She tried to swat him off, but Toad scrambled to her back, clinging there, just beyond the reach of her rigid arms.

Out of nowhere came an ear-piercing screech, and the hullabaloo commenced anew. Hoots, taps, raps, rat-a-tat-tats. Snorts and squawks. Sheep bleating. Wolves howling. A thwack. A peal of laughter. Thunder rumbling. The tick-tock of the grandfather clock. Pandemonium.

Mother dropped her hands from her ears. "Why is it so hot?" she yelled above the clamor.

"It's not!" returned Jocelyn, but she could hardly hear herself shout.

"I'm burning up!" yowled Mother. "Are my clothes on fire?" She threw off her dressing gown (Toad along with it) and yanked her shift off over her head. Naked, she rushed toward the window, apparently seeking relief in the cooler, outside air. The magpie retreated, fluttering its wings and hopping backwards, then spun and shot into the sky, as Mother squeezed into the dormer.

"Mother!" cried Jocelyn, racing to the window. "Outdoors isn't safe, haven't you always said?"

"I'm aflame," shrieked Mother, as she burst through the open window.

Jocelyn lunged into the dormer after her, but Feeno and several of the spirit-girls grabbed her legs and held her tight. Mother had dropped onto the steep roof and spun around. Jocelyn watched in horror as her mother clawed the roof to keep from sliding. At the edge, she reached toward her daughter, her face showing utter astonishment.

And then Mother fell. The noises abruptly ceased. The silence was eerie and unnatural. Soon, it was broken by what sounded like shattering glass.

Jocelyn watched the magpie circle down toward Mother, then looked away, not wishing to see her mother's broken body. After a short while, Maag flew to the roof near where Jocelyn extended from the window. "Iduress is breathless," the magpie reported. "Expired."

"Poor Mother," lamented Jocelyn.

"She certainly was that," retorted Brazen, her voice crackling.

"Fault her later, Brazen," scolded Jocelyn, turning her head slightly to the rear. "She was, after all, our mother. We can feel sorry that was so, but we can also feel sorry she's dead, because now there's no chance to make things better between us."

"That's so sad," lamented Sorrowful, choking.

"Save your tears," grumbled Fury, her voice like the sound of faraway thunder.

Jocelyn began pushing herself back through the dormer, as Maag squawked, "Aag? Maag? Chack! Yak! Queg! Queg!"

"My, you sound like a magpie!" Jocelyn congratulated her. "Perhaps we won't need the magic book and crystal after all."

"Isn't it . . . curious," noted Quizzical, her speech faltering, "that even with Smolder inside her . . . Jocelyn is sad that Mother is dead?"

Why do all the spirit-girls sound as if they are losing their voices? wondered Jocelyn, as she stepped down backwards to the floor. "I'm not Smolder," she answered Quizzical's question. "At times, I am like her, but I always have traces of other moods that may appear full-blown at any moment." Turning around, Jocelyn gasped. The spirit-girls were shimmering in the candlelight and losing their shapes. “Where are you going?” she cried, panic-stricken that they were leaving her.

“Trust that it is somewhere near your heart,” said Gullible.

“Rather overly optimistic, aren’t you?” sneered Tragic. “I’d say we’re being undone.”

“Decomposed,” agreed Glum, sighing. “Rotting.”

“Not so,” objected Bustle, her voice low and feeble. “Have you forgotten the physical form we took inside Jocelyn, then the balloons? We’re returning to our original state. Don’t you feel the excitement and the energy of it?”

“Take heart, everyone,” murmured Brazen.

The spirit-girls now hovered in the air, each bunch of colored particles keeping to itself. Jocelyn saw with astonishment that Feeno had burst through his clothes and taken on the aspect of a reddish-brown deer with antlers, his tail, unfortunately, too short to defend against the flies that descended upon his hindquarters. Toad was . . . *Oh, my! It’s come out of its skin and grown large,* observed Jocelyn, *forming into a . . . Yes, there can be no doubt: Toad has turned into a man.*

“I didn’t expect to introduce myself to you in this fashion,” he said, grabbing a blanket to cover his nakedness. “But here I am . . . in the flesh.”

Jocelyn asked, “And you are?”

“Your father.”

The clusters of particles, which had been dancing in the air, coalesced into a mix of colors, then swirled into Jocelyn—every last one. *This is too much!* she thought before everything went dark.

CHAPTER 36

MIXED FEELINGS

"HER HEARTBEAT IS NORMAL, as is her breathing," said a man. Jocelyn didn't recognize his voice.

"She shows good color," said a woman.

She sounds like Grandmother, thought Jocelyn.

Then a man she'd heard before asserted, "She was overwhelmed by the feelings that flooded her, but she'll be stronger for them; I expect Kettle will be with us before long."

"Father?" inquired Jocelyn, her eyelids fluttering.

"By your side," he said, "and better suited now for a daughter's gaze."

Her eyes fully open, she saw that, indeed, he was wearing a shirt and trousers. Another man, older, was crouched on her other side. She lay on the floor of her room. Above her, Grandmother hovered.

"This is your grandfather," Grandmother said, indicating the older man.

"Father . . . Grandmother . . . Grandfather." Jocelyn studied each in turn. "Where have you been all my life?"

They hemmed and hawed.

"That will take some explaining," Father finally said.

Jocelyn raised herself onto her elbows and gazed at the younger man. "You say you're my father, but how can I trust you're not really a toad?"

"Good question," he said, nodding. "I was a toad for so many years, I might as well be one. It was your mother's magic, though, that made me a toad. I'm a man—most assuredly."

"At the least," said Grandfather, "we must credit Idris with a sense of humor."

"Oldric!" scolded Grandmother. "Must you start again with your nonsense? Angwyn is not contemptible."

"And neither are toads," declared Father. "You have only to be in their skin to realize that. Or gaze into their eyes."

"Why are you blushing?" asked Grandmother.

Father reddened more. "It's hard to explain," he said.

"As for where Elda and I were," said Grandfather, "it was just as Idris said. I've been 'round the corner, and your grandmother has been wandering the woods."

"I still don't understand," said Grandmother, shaking her head, "though I see the proof before me. Jocelyn has grown from a baby to a . . ."

"I'm thirteen years old," Jocelyn announced proudly. "Today is my birthday."

"Congratulations!" exclaimed Grandmother, beaming. "The day will be yours. But thirteen? How is it possible (when it seemed but part of a morning) that I walked for nearly thirteen years? Shouldn't I feel weary?"

"You haven't aged," observed Grandfather.

Grandmother looked him up and down. "You have," she said.

"You think I don't know it? I registered every second. As a long-case clock—"

"You were the grandfather clock?" interrupted Jocelyn.

"Aptly named, that *grandfather clock,"* said Father, laughing. "I doubt you found it amusing."

"It showed some wit," admitted Grandfather. "But a keeper of hours and the fractions therein? A humorless, tedious pastime."

"But an important one, Grandfather," asserted Jocelyn. "You kept me on time."

"Of that I'm proud. I so enjoyed the pats you gave me."

"They made you hum," said Jocelyn, smiling.

"When I leaned against you in the sitting room," the son said to his father, "did you feel the warmth?"

"It made me whirr," acknowledged Grandfather.

"That's the closest we've been since I was a boy," said Father. "Of course, I thought you were a clock."

"And I thought you were a toad," said Grandfather.

"The warmth doesn't lie," said Grandmother softly.

"I envied that toad," said Grandfather. "Its mobility and independence, the variety of its experiences."

"A toad has its shortcomings," said Father.

"Ah, but it doesn't have the back-and-forth of a pendulum and the tick-tock reminding me constantly that time was passing and I was wasting it. If not for the diversions—my stopping time when Idris was in mid-stride, Sound exercising my brain with tidbits, Maag tickling me with a duster, Feeno oiling my gears—"

"Where are Maag and Feeno?" cried Jocelyn, sitting up and peering around the room.

"Maag flew away," said Father.

"She wouldn't have," declared Jocelyn. "Not without saying good-bye."

"She may have said good-bye," responded Father. "Aag! Yak! and other calls I hadn't the breeding to interpret. She had a wild look in her eyes, as if we were not creatures she wished to linger with."

Jocelyn pushed herself to her feet. Swaying, she took her father's arm, until she steadied herself, then walked gingerly to the dormer.

"Not too far out!" cautioned Grandmother.

Is Grandmother afraid I'll fall? wondered Jocelyn. *I won't; I'm not a child. Or does she fear I'll collapse at the sight of Mother? She need not worry. I won't look; I have no wish to see Mother's shattered body.*

Jocelyn scanned the sky but could see nothing of the magpie. Tears filled her eyes. *How I will miss you, my good mother!* she lamented. *Who will brush my hair and bathe me and sneak me sweets and tell me to pick up after myself and to wash my hands before meals and to keep my feet off the dining table? No one, not Grandmother or Father or Grandfather, can take the place of you, because they will never talk or be funny like you.*

"Where is the crystal?" she heard Grandfather ask.

"The bird kept it," replied Father. "Likely she's hidden it among her collection of sparkly things, as magpies are apt to do."

"Just as well," said Grandfather. "The chances of misfortune are too great, especially if it's in the wrong hands."

"Is Feeno . . . a deer?" Jocelyn asked, as she stepped down onto the floor from the dormer.

"He's taken on his true physical nature," affirmed Father, "as have Maag and I."

"How did it happen?" asked Jocelyn.

"Idris died," explained Grandfather. "When my encasement collapsed around me and I emerged from the wreckage, I realized she was dead. When the magician dies, her spells are broken. I knew that all the time but had no way to convey it or bring it to pass."

"Idris didn't have to die for me to overcome her magic and escape Angwyn's painting," said Grandmother. "In his glorious woods, a wise woman told me to look for something familiar, but out of place."

"A woman besides yourself?" questioned Angwyn. "In my landscape?"

"You'd be surprised what is beneath your oils," said Grandmother. "I kept my eyes wide open, leery of even a blink, until I came upon my family's silver spoon lying on the trail. I retrieved it, then noticed, not twenty paces off the path, as if hanging in thin air, a painting of our sitting room, though it had but a single chair and a long-case clock in Oldric's style. Before I had a chance to examine the room more closely, a powerful wind picked me up and blew me into it." She rubbed her rump. "I'll be sore for a while."

"Sorry about that," apologized Grandfather. "Your return caught me by surprise. I tried, but I didn't have time to break your fall."

"How could you have done that?" asked Grandmother.

"By stopping time," said Grandfather. "Oh, I'll explain later. I'm sure we've all had experiences that will take some time telling."

"Is Feeno . . . Is the deer still in the house?" asked Jocelyn.

Grandfather shook his head. "I heard clacks and clicks in the upstairs hall," he said. "When the deer came to the entry to the sitting room, it froze in fear, poor thing, then rushed on down the main staircase. I followed it to the front door, where it butted against it. The deer was frantic and barked at me. But I whistled, and it backed off enough so I could throw open the door. Once outside, it bounded off, favoring its rear left leg, but that didn't deter it as it raced across the grounds and disappeared into the woods."

I've lost Feeno, too, Jocelyn reflected. *I'm happy for him, but . . . what am I to do without my playmate, nanny, and best friend?* Her first memory of him was his carrying her, and his feet slipping out from under him, and his bouncing down the stairs on his backside, holding her in the air. Though he must have suffered from it, he'd always laughed when he told her she'd giggled and shouted, "Again! Again!"

Maag's gone, Feeno, Mother—everyone I grew up with, she realized. *I can't help feeling sad for Mother. Why couldn't there have been a happy ending for her as well as for the rest of us? But if there was, what would have become of Father, Grandfather, Grandmother, Maag, and Feeno, not to mention me?*

"Mother had to die, didn't she?" asked Jocelyn.

The adults looked at one another.

"I think it is well she did," Father replied.

"How did she die?" asked Jocelyn. "She said she was burning up. The morning wasn't hot. Was it Grandmother's charms that killed her? Or was it the fall?"

"The charms were meant to drive her away and protect us from her," said Grandmother. "Perhaps one of us should . . . should see to Idris."

"I already have," said Angwyn. "After I put on some of your old clothes, Father, I went outside and examined the spot where Idris had struck the ground. There was no fire or smoke. She'd died from the fall, shattering into tiny bits of ice. The pieces were colored—brown, red, yellow, black, pink, white. I'd have said the composition was lovely if I hadn't known what it consisted of. What's left of her after she melts into the grass, I'll bury."

They were all silent for a while.

"Part of me is sad she's dead," said Jocelyn at last, "but part of me is glad. Is that awful of me?"

"Not in the least," said Grandmother.

"I have mixed feelings, too, Joycelyn," said Angwyn, encircling his daughter's shoulders with his arm.

"I haven't," mumbled Grandfather.

"Oldric!" chided Grandmother, though she couldn't conceal the smile behind her hand. "We need to raise the spirits here, especially Jocelyn's. We have a birthday to celebrate."

"I've never had a birthday party," said Jocelyn, a surge of excitement causing her to jump up and down. "I've often imagined one. May we have hard candies, cakes, and other sweets?"

"Of course," affirmed Angwyn. "And we can play games and sing and dance. But first we need to go downstairs to the dining room and eat the good breakfast that's being prepared for us."

"The breakfast is making itself?" wondered Grandmother. "Oldric, is this your trick? Haven't we had enough of magic? Who knows what mischief—"

"It's not his doing," interrupted Father. "We've acquired a cook. While I was outside, Lyel—"

"Our longtime servant?" inquired Grandfather.

"The same. He walked up to me from the farmyard, somewhat dazed, along with Alun and Fianna. Idris had transformed our former servants into sheep. Lyel was nearly butchered, he told me, until Idris thought better of it, worrying that a servant likely would prove poor fare for a Lady."

"I'll have no lamb for breakfast," joked Grandfather.

"I ate this morning just before my walk," said Grandmother. "Wait! That was thirteen years ago. Why haven't I an appetite?"

"We're all a bit confused," said Angwyn.

He and Jocelyn followed Grandfather and Grandmother as they left the room. At the top of the attic stairs, Angwyn took Jocelyn's arm.

"I need some steadying myself," he said. "How are you feeling?"

"Tired, Father. Along with everything else, I didn't get much sleep last night. But my spirits are good."

EPILOGUE

THE GRIM REAPER scratched his ear with his scythe. *These itches are intolerable,* he thought. *I really need a bath.*

"I did not call for you," said Idris.

"The call is mine to make," retorted Reaper. "I've come to collect you. I just left Fynbar, who died in his sleep. A much better way to give up the ghost than pitching yourself off a roof."

"I slipped," protested Idris.

"Don't whine," said Reaper.

"I do not *whine*. It was not my choice to die. Bring me back to life at once!"

"Be realistic, Idris. Just look at yourself." He indicated with a gray, bony finger her scattered remains. "Even if I had the authority, I couldn't fit those dissections together. Besides, they're melting."

"That is not my body," declared Idris, as she looked around, apparently for hers.

"It is," insisted the Reaper. "The colors are those of the organs, bones, sinews, fluids, and whatnot of a human body. Moods, too. Who else could it be?"

"But . . . it is ice," said Idris.

"It is," affirmed Reaper. "You first came to my attention today when you were indulging in distilled dandelions, what you called *the essence of cold.*"

"I wanted to be as coldblooded as I could," explained Idris.

"Aye, your concoction was masterful," Reaper complimented her. "But it turned you to ice. The fall killed you, Idris, but you would have died in any case. You were freezing to death."

"That cannot be," objected Idris. "I felt as if I were burning up. Was it from the reaction of my skin to the bits of nature that Elda soiled me with?"

"They likely contributed," replied Reaper. "But many who have frozen to death in snow and darkness have reported to me that shortly before losing consciousness, they had a sensation of extreme heat. Paradoxical, isn't it?"

"I insist you stop using contractions."

"That's not for you to say," said Reaper.

"You are more outspoken than I remember from your visits," observed Idris.

"That's because I'm not grinding my teeth to keep silent."

Idris thought for a moment. "May I remain here as a spirit?" she asked.

"You wish to haunt this house?" questioned Reaper, aghast.

"It is the site of my life's . . . the chief work of my life," she explained. "Gothelyn was nearing perfection. Perhaps I can still be of some influence on her."

"Yours is a rare request," said Reaper, "and one I seldom grant, even when the person to be haunted is a menace. That is not the case here. I will not allow you to possess Jocelyn. Besides, the charms against evil spirits that Elda collected in the woods—what you called *bits of nature*—wouldn't allow you to stay near."

"Evil? Surely, I am not—"

"I mustn't dither," interrupted Reaper. "I have other obligations. Come along, Idris."

"Where are you taking me?" she asked.

"You'll see. It's not far."

ACKNOWLEDGMENTS

SPECIAL THANKS to my daughter, Bronwyn, and my son, Thomas—my inspirations. Many thanks to Rosalyn Art and Sharon Weld, with whom I had long talks about writing this book, and who wouldn't let me quit. I am forever grateful to my friends, Bob and Olivia Waterman, and to my wife, Linda Hughes, who read numerous drafts of this story and kept coming back for more.

Many thanks to Deborah Steinberg, my developmental editor, for recognizing that humor was foremost in this dark, satiric tale. Thanks, also, to my publisher, Susan Shankin, and copyeditor, Brenda Lange, at Precocity Press for their kindness and brilliance. Thanks to Tim Kummerow for his evocative design of the book cover and to Darcy Hughes at Dream Book Marketing for developing a distinctive marketing plan.

My appreciation also goes out to two writing groups for their thoughtful critiques. One was led by the late Judith Serin (special thanks to Janet Giannini), the other was drawn from the Bay Area Writing Project, including Marty Williams, David Braden, Charlie Stephens, Meredith Pike-Baky, Carla Williams-Namboodiri, Page Hersey, Grace Morizawa, D.M. Kloker, and the late Mark Ali.

I also wish to thank Rebecca Ballotta and Britta Jensen for their valuable insights.

Special thanks to Lenzie Williams, my tai chi teacher, and Heidi Kasa, my short story marketer, for their contributions to my well-being.

I'm grateful also to Emmett, Cleo, Luca, and Nico (my grandchildren) for the joy they have given me, and to my daughter-in-law, Bianca Omena Maximiano, for her help with the Portuguese language of Brazil.

This book is in memory of my wonderful brother, Bob Hughes.

ABOUT THE AUTHOR

JIM HUGHES is a writer and former teacher whose work is shaped by his years in a multicultural elementary school, where he was honored with a district Teacher of the Year award. He later wrote the "Home Room" column for *Essential Teacher,* an international quarterly published by TESOL (Teachers of English to Speakers of Other Languages), in which he shared narrative reflections on classroom life.

He has contributed to four books, one published by TESOL about teaching English as a second language, the other three by McGraw-Hill.

Years ago, he published a short story in *Readers & Writers* and received an honorable mention in a *Crosscurrents* short story contest. Recently, his story "Can of Corn" appeared in the *Folio Literary Journal* (2026). And, he co-authored a novel, *God Wife,* based on the real-life story of Mani Nepali, an orphan who grew up in Nepal.

He holds a PhD from the University of California, Berkeley. For his dissertation, a third of which was on Shakespeare's *The Tempest,* he won the best political science dissertation award in the western United States.

He now teaches tai chi, plays with his grandchildren, and writes fiction. He lives with his wife, Linda, in Berkeley, California.

www.ingramcontent.com/pod-product-compliance
Lightning Source LLC
LaVergne TN
LVHW091136080826
845145LV00008B/2175

* 9 7 8 1 9 7 2 5 6 1 0 6 5 *